Dark Don't Catch Me

VIN PACKER

Adams Media

New York   London   Toronto   Sydney   New Delhi

Adams Media
An Imprint of Simon & Schuster, Inc.
57 Littlefield Street
Avon, Massachusetts 02322

For information about special discounts for bulk purchases, please
contact Simon & Schuster Special Sales at 1-866-506-1949 or business@
simonandschuster.com.

Manufactured in the United States of America

Library of Congress Cataloging-in-Publication Data has been applied for.

ISBN 978-1-4405-5811-5
ISBN 978-1-4405-3958-2 (ebook)

This work has been previously published in print format by Fawcett
Publications, Greenwich, CT.

A DARING LOVE AFFAIR THAT AROUSED THE VIOLENCE OF A SMALL SOUTHERN TOWN

Dixon Pirkle first saw her at a committee meeting at the county courthouse. Her beauty hypnotized him. He couldn't keep his eyes off her. She was colored but her face was almost white. Barbara James returned his stare in the same way. The fact that he was white and she was black could not stop them.

He looked at her lying in his arms and saw the contrast of their colors forming stripes in the moonlight. "We got to get out of this town —we got to get out of Paradise, Barbara," he whispered. "We could go somewhere nobody'd know. You're white enough. Who'd ever know?"

She turned to him. "The only two that really matter, Dix. Us. We'd know."

In the long run, would violence and murder convince him?

1

*Soft long-looking white hands give him gum. Good legs,
sweet voice asks solicitously how are you. And smell the
perfume! Like lilacs? Like jasmine? Naw, hell, Russian
Leather, man! Arpege! Chanel! Something big! Know your
brands! Big men order by brands, like Al saying, "Gimme
Vat 69 and soda!" Not just scotch and soda. That's nowhere.
You ever gonna be a big man? Aw, yeah. . . .*

"*Are you comfortable?*"

"*Would you like more gum?*"

"*Is this your first flight?*"

Ummm, living! How did you get so big so quick?

*Millard Post grins and wishes to weeping Jesus H. every-
one he knows; and all the creeps he used to know (little pukes
he could do rings around these days); and sweet money men
he was going to know (were going to know him); dames and
broads and millionaires, could see him right now. Man, they'd
flip!*

"*Yes to all three," says Millard Post.*

And thank you, baby, all dressed in blue. . . .

*He leans back in the deep soft seat after fumbling to fasten
the belt. Careful not to brush the arm of the lady seated beside you there, man, but naw, there ain't going to be no trouble at all! He tries very hard to keep the smile from playing
on his lips. Simper like someone gone soft in the head just for
this? You screw; this is nothing! If there were only someone
to see you though, fellow—someone you know from the
Panthers, 121st Street, or North Trades High.*

To say, "That's not Millard Post, is it?"

*On the ramp coming out to the plane he had not been
able to resist turning around as he got to the silver slide-*

steps and waving up at the observation platform where there were people gathered.

—So long, suckers!

—Bye, bye, Baby-O!

—Man, I'm cuttin' out now in a sweet, sweet style!

One other time he'd done something big and there was no one to witness it. That was the day Dandruff Laquales, War Counselor for the Diamonds, rival gang to the Panthers (lousy spic! Always beating on Negroes half his height and weight!), cornered him in a vacant lot up on 127th. Even though Laquales was six inches taller; two years older, and twice as tough—with a switch-blade in the deal, Millard had won out over him, using only his fists and his knee. But no one had seen him do it. That soured it some.

This is different. Bigger! Traveling on a goddam DC-6 like some kind of smart money man in Endsville!

So nobody waves good-by . . . Who needs it?

Millard shrugs, a fifteen-year old Negro, lighter than most, and taller than other boys his age. Better build too. Sharp. Knows the score. Speaks the jargon. Walks cool with the cool. He never punked out yet; not on anything; not on anyone; no deal ever made him chicken.

Before this morning he had never been quite so much on his own. He had some misgivings—Keep your place, Millard, his father had warned, from the moment you leave this house, you're going south of Harlem. I said, south—but what the hell was going to happen, f'Chrissake.

He knew he was the only Negro on the plane. The few Negroes he had seen at the terminal, and later inside the airlines building, were hauling baggage. (All right; so what?) Still, nothing was any different than it is up in Harlem; except it's better. Really better.

At the ticket counter the man had called him "sir."

Coming aboard the plane, the same hostess who had given him the gum and smiled at him, had greeted him warmly (could melt asphalt with that voice!) "Good morning. How are you today?"

Millard settles comfortably. This is a trip he's going on; not a goddam war he's going to.

He reaches into the pocket of his blue serge suit for the letter.

6

His hands shake some; gotta admit he's scared to fly—a little.

Unfolding the letter he reads Bryan Post's scrawled words with the same remote twinge of disgust which he felt the first time he ever read it. A feeling striped with some vague shame at the fact Bryan Post and he are blood relations.

His father handed him the letter two days ago.

"It's from your uncle," he said. "I can't go. I can't see how I can go."

With considerable difficulty, Millard had made out the writing:

Dere Henry Post I want tell you Hus sic an going pass befor you kno it an would be teribul if you dont come here befor she pass soon as can so come quick lov yur bruthur Bryan Post

"Goddam!" Millard had said. "He can hardly write English!"

"You hang around your Cousin Al and learn words like that. And you'll get a swat for saying them!"

"I'm hip Al writes better than this, man!"

"Dad's what you call me!"

"Dad, then. But I never saw writing like this before."

"There's a whole lot you never saw, boy."

"Is his lid flipped?"

"Thank your stars, Millard, you're getting an education. That's all!"

"No punctuation even—not a lousy comma even!"

"Millard, listen to me . . . I want you to go."

"Me go!"

"It's your grandmother dying, boy."

"Man, I don't even know her, Dad!"

"It's my mother going to pass away and one of us is going!"

"I got school . . . Education, you know?"

"I can't take off from my job, boy—your sister can't take off from hers. But you can get excused from school."

"Naw, naw."

"You'll fly down so as not to waste time. You can come back by Greyhound Bus. We'll use the money I've been saving for the Hide-a-Bed. Couch is good enough to sleep on another year."

7

"What about the backache you say it gives you?"

"Backache's better than a soul-ache, Millard. Hussie Post was a good mother to me, good as your own mother to you before she passed."

"Naw, Dad, I don't want to."

"It's out of the realm of what you want now, boy. You're going!"

Then slowly the reluctance Millard had transformed itself into a heady kind of enthusiasm. He had never been farther from Harlem than Rockaway Beach. Most of the members of the Panthers hadn't either, and when he announced his news of the journey to the gang, it was met with a certain awe on their part.

"You going to fly all the way down, Mil?"

"Man, Mil, you're going to travel!"

"You're cuttin' classes, huh, Mil? Crazy!"

His sister Pearl had actually ironed his handkerchiefs, instead of just folding them over once they came out of the Laundromat; and she'd bought shoe polish and done his loafers. See his face in the shine!

"What you taking your Panther jacket for, huh?" she had said, watching him pack; hanging around while he was packing as though he were going to China. "Don't you know it'll be too hot for a leather jacket in Georgia?"

"I'm taking what I'm taking," he had said importantly.

"Millard? On your way down when you get stopovers in all these cities? You going to drop us a card from them?"

"If I get the time, Pearl-O. I'll see about it."

Even the lecture he had received from his father had not completely destroyed his enthusiasm. His father was a great lecturer anyway; about nothing. What he told Millard about the Southern white people's feelings toward Negroes, had startled Millard some—but more because of the fact his father really believed that crap about practically every Southern white man having a sheet with holes cut in it, hanging in his closet for that happy day a colored person got out of line.

"Man, a lot's changed, since you were down there," Millard had said. "We learned all about it in school . . . Besides, I hold my own with the spics, don't I? Spics push us around plenty and I can hold my own. I'm hip, Dad!"

8

Pearl had said. "That's right, Pa. It's not so bad any more. It's not good, but it's not so bad."

Henry Post had straightened himself to his full five feet and bellowed: "You forget school when you go down there! You forget what you learned, and carry on the way I say you should! You 'sir' everyone! Everyone! And don't be looking white folks in the eye, Millard! Them white folks aren't like spics one whit! You crawl to them if you got to! Hear?"

"Sure," Millard had said. "Sure, Dad."

He had winked at Pearl across the room; they'd grinned together.

Sure, sure . . . All right it is going to be different down there. Millard jams the letter back in his suit pocket. His father is given to exaggeration a good deal of the time, he decides. Like when Millard joined the Panthers. His father raised hell because he said all gang boys used dope. Millard grins to himself recalling it. Not a hop-head in the bunch; that's how bad the Panthers are hooked.

Millard thinks: besides—believe all the old man's bed-tales about Georgia, being on this plane would make me a living creep.

Besides—not worrying about the white people. Worrying more about the colored. Bryan Post—Uncle Bryan—and Aunt Bissy. And Cousin Marilyn; Cousin Claude. And Cousin Major . . . Major—what kind of name is that for somebody?

If the bunch of them can't write a letter between them better than the one sent off—weeping Jesus!

"It's probably just true of the older folks." Pearl had discussed the matter with him. "Because back in the days when they were going to school things were all different. Maybe they didn't even go to school at all, our aunt and uncle . . . But you know, Mil, now every kid goes. You wait, I bet our cousin will be just as sharp as you are." She'd laughed and poked her finger in his ribs. "Least as sharp as you think you are."

Behind Millard the door of the DC-6 swings shut; engines start their roaring. Big deal! Living! Millard grips the sides of his seat. Goddam, it is no picnic at that!"

"Your first time?"

She's a soft-spoken, middle-aged woman sitting beside him. "Yes, ma'am."

9

Calmly she knits a pair of argyle socks.

"Once we get up you'll feel better."

"What I'm worried about right now, ma'am, is if we get up."

She laughs; she's nice. "Oh, don't worry, son. We'll get up."

"You traveled a lot, huh?"

"I make this run about once a week. Just to Washington."

Then they are taxiing out far into the field, and over the loudspeaker the hostess with the soft white long-looking hands is using her candy tones to tell everyone not to smoke, to fasten belts, to expect luncheon in flight.

The plane takes the air. Millard feels like he's flying it himself. Leaning forward, he watches the land recede under him.

—So long, suckers!

Gee-ha, lookit it get smaller! Look like sticks down there.

"Man!" slips out.

The lady looks at him; nodding. "There now, like it?"

"Yes, ma'am! Yes, sir. We just—took off. Crazy!"

"Maybe you'd like to sit here by the window so you can see better." She stops knitting. Smiles at him. "I'll be happy to change seats with you. I make this run all the time."

Millard doesn't look her in the eyes, but he asks, "You sure?"

"Sure," she says, getting her belt loose.

2

THIS is Paradise.

"Listen to them niggers laughin'!"

White faces across the street watch black faces.

"Yeah, niggers always got a joke."

"What you s'pose make them laugh all the time?"

It's in the state of Georgia, right in the middle, where much of the land surrounding it is skeleton-poor, worn out and abandoned to gullies, broomstraw and scrub oaks.

Black faces laugh up a storm:

". . . so after Saint Peter say, 'Look here, nigger, you can't get into heaven if you're walkin'. A body wants to get into heaven's got to ride into heaven!'—well, after that, this nigger strolls around heaven on the outside figuring how he gonna get in. Then he see a white man walkin' toward heaven, an he tell the white man, 'can't nobody get into heaven walkin', boss.' An he say to the white man, 'Mister, whyn't you ride me in, huh? That way we both get in . . . So the white man ride the nigger up to them pearly gates. An Saint Peter say, 'White man, you walkin' or riding?' White man say, 'Ridin'!' . . . An Saint Peter say, 'Good! Park your horse outside and come on in!' "

It's a country seat in the gut of the red hill region, a little town where 906 people live; the warm and wary kind of little town where 896 of them know the other ten are going to a barbecue tonight out on Linoleum Hill, where Thad Hooper's place is.

"What's the matter with you, nigger! You heard every joke there is twice?"

"Don't say nigger to me. The name is Major."

"That make me a nigger and you a Major, huh?"

"What's the matter with you, Jack? How you ever going to expect white folks to stop calling us niggers if we call ourselves that?"

"Boy, you expect to get white folks out of the habit, then you can stand worms on their tails."

"Still, Jack, don't call me nigger."

"I'll call you Major Post who don't know his pee smells, nigger!"

Two of the Negroes laugh; not Major Post, though.

Tink Twiddy says, "How come you don't like the joke Jack told, Major? By goose eggs your big mouth going to break if it smile?"

"Tell the joke to the white crackers standing across the street and they'll think it's funny."

"Well, it is funny. I liked to die laughing when Jack told it!"

"You crow-bellies going to die that way anyhow!"

"Trouble with you Major Post is since you quit Linoleum

11

Hill and went to work at that she-yankee's you got hot pants for white quail!"

There goes Major Post; walks right away from them.

Linoleum Hill got its name from some of the colored in Paradise who couldn't say Magnolia Hill. An hour or so ago out in front of the county courthouse, loafing around on the well-whittled bench, Doc Sell, the county coroner; Colonel Pirkle, the editor of the *Paradise Herald,* and some other sitters there ribbed Thad Hooper about it when he passed by.

"Hey, Thad?" Doc Sell said. "You know I'da never thought it of you?"

"Yeah? Thought what wouldn't you have?" Hooper paused on his way to his car.

"That you was a goddam coon-coddler?"

"Aw, get!" Hooper guffawed. "You're drunk as a skunk at a moonshine still!"

"Well, boy, didn't black apes name your hill, huh?"

Hooper himself had led the laughter, his huge square hands hanging on to his large and solid hips; his long firm legs giving a little at the knees, as his wide and strong shoulders shook, and he tossed back his head, a broad grin cracking his wide and handsome countenance.

"Gee-on, y'old coot!" he'd called back, continuing to his car; then, waving, "See you all tonight, hey!"

In Paradise they say the reason Thad Hooper is so good-natured the whole time is because of her. And that's the same reason he's richer-acting than the real rich from the cities like Atlanta and Savannah and Macon—because of her; and why he's more informed than most in Paradise (outside of Hollis Jordan, who nobody *can* understand anyway) and why he's big-looking without being fat; and why he's so well-liked by everyone from the Reverend Joh Greene, in whose church he serves as elder, to old black Hussie Post, who doesn't like anyone, and whose family sharecrops on Hooper land. In a sentence, it's why he's Thad Hooper—because of her . . . In Paradise they say it's a psychological fact that a man with a wife like her has got luck's kiss to fire him on to doing anything he takes a notion to do, better than anyone else can.

"Yeah, and Thad knows it too," one of the bench-sitters said after Hooper had left and they were all discussing him and her. "He knows it, cause even now after two kids he's

12

still always got his hands on her somewhere—on some part of her only he's got the right to touch!"

"So what?" Storey Bailey, Thad Hooper's best friend, put in. "What's that prove?"

"Proves," the sitter said, "he's sort of letting everybody know she's his property. It's like another man having an Indian-head nickel he's got to touch for luck."

Storey said, "Hell, you kidding? Hell!"

A second sitter spoke up, "I noticed that about Thad too. Oh, he don't do it obvious, mind, but I seen him do it. Out at the Friday dances, I seen him holding her so that his right arm kind of dangles down her back around her fanny—or even down here on Main Street when she's standing talking to someone with him. I seen him with his arm around her waist and one of his fingers sorta snaking up around her boobies. I seen him do it too."

Storey Bailey's face got red. "Aw, hell!" He acted disgusted.

"Well, what's the difference anyhow." Doc Sell shrugged. "Man's got a right to feel up his own wife!"

"But I'm telling you if Thad does do it, he don't even *know* he's doing it!" Bailey said.

The sitter sighed; spat. "She sure is beautiful, Vivian Hooper."

"All I'd have to do to tell a corpse," Sell said, "would be to stand Vivie over it. If it didn't move then, that'd be a dead man, all right."

Colonel Pirkle mopped his brow with his shirt sleeve. "Yep! She's like irrigation to these drought-swollen parts."

"Half-past twelve. I got to get me back to my mill." Storey Bailey turned away abruptly.

"Don't go away mad," the coroner shouted at his back; then chuckling to the others said, "I think ole Storey's got a thing for Vivie Hooper."

"Maybe so, Doc," the sitter said, "but Kate Bailey sure ain't gonna let him do a dong-damn thing about it!"

It is hot in Paradise this Tuesday noon; hot and still humid from yesterday's brief shower—a warm, sticky drizzle that did little more than stir the dust on the redclay-caked roads. It is far too hot to quarrel, Bill Ficklin decides as he parks in the circle before the courthouse.

13

"All right," he tells his wife, cutting the engine, "I'll ask the boys if they've seen Major. But—" he starts to add; then decides against it. He pushes down the door handle to get out.

She says, "But *what?*"

"But I think you're making too much of the matter."

"Fick, I tell you it's in little ways like this we've got to be firm with him. Now you know I think the world and all of Major, but—"

Bill Ficklin answers, "All right. Okay," slams the door shut, and crosses to the square.

Ficklin is superintendent of schools in Paradise; a chunky, happy-faced fellow who favors tweeds, smokes a pipe, and looks a young forty-five. Before he came back to his home town, he taught civics at the University up in Athens, and the first time he ever saw the girl who became his wife, she was wearing bobby socks, leaning seductively against his desk, and asking him questions about the next day's assignment. She stood out from all of his other students, not only because she was a Northerner, but because she was more flamboyant; less unsure of herself, and almost patronizing toward Ficklin, at those times when she would corner him before or after class, or encounter him on campus. There was always a streak of bright color about her; a fire-colored scarf, an angora sweater of deep azure, or a brilliant kelly-green stripe down a quiet gray dress; something arresting in her attire that seemed to parallel the wild streak of independence in her personality.

She would meet him on the library steps quite by accident, knowing him no better than any of his other students; and stopping, smiling up at him with her large shining green eyes, she would say something like: "Why, hello, Professor Ficklin! Isn't it a gorgeous day. But you look a little tired, hmmm? I think you ought to just relax a little more."

Coming from any other co-ed, Bill Ficklin would have simply ignored the remark and the searching look. He was one of the youngest members of the faculty; and he was a bachelor, so he was accustomed to the whims and fancies of many of the girls he taught; accustomed and somewhat heavily resigned—but Marianne Powell affected him vaguely, though from the very beginning he was not certain why that was.

"It's quite simple," a colleague remarked one evening in the faculty lounge, after he had been chiding Bill about his "tender tête-à-têtes" with a student—and Bill Ficklin had admitted his fascination with Marianne—"she's pretty. She's gay. And you're falling in love with her."

Ficklin's marriage to Marianne at the year's end created a mild scandal in university circles. There was seventeen years' difference in their ages; and while Bill Ficklin was a rather conscientious, serious, but by no means timid or puritanical, man—she was a quite frivolous, capricious nineteen years old.

Whenever they had a disagreement, such as the one this morning about Major Post, Bill Ficklin always thought as he thinks now: nine years have sobered her considerably beyond the point he had expected when he had first married her. At twenty-eight she is still pretty and young and gay; yet more and more an irritating rigidity is cropping into her personality, coupled with a vague restlessness. It still irks Ficklin to recall her last summer's suggestion (which he had rejected with an unprecedented burst of temper) that they take separate vacations, even though she had insisted, after his rage was spent, that she had only been thinking of him.

This noon he had come home for lunch and found her near to angry tears because young Major Post, after emptying trash, had not replaced the cans in the cellar. She had demanded that while Bill Ficklin drove her to the band rehearsal at the Methodist Church, they stop off in town and try to find Major and make him return and finish his chore. Often, in between the Negro's morning job at the Ficklins and his afternoon job up at the Hooper's, he ate his lunch down under the trees across the street from the county courthouse. The small area there where the local Negroes were prone to gather was known in Paradise as "Black Patch"; but when Ficklin glanced over there as he was parking his car, he saw no sign of Major Post.

"Get out anyway," his wife said, "and ask Doc Sell. He's right there, Fick." She had pointed out the coroner on the bench. "He knows Major."

So Ficklin is doing as she directed now—reluctantly, and somewhat puzzled at her determination in such a small matter; but it is too hot to argue.

In Paradise, people like Bill Ficklin; but they say he's got a weakness that could make him unpopular: when the Supreme Court ruling ordered desegregation in the public schools, Ficklin called it progress. Of course he didn't start any campaign to enforce the law—he isn't a radical—but he

15

did speak out in favor of putting the Negroes on an equal footing with the whites, and that alone was enough to make a lot of folks in the town wary of him. Doc Sell, for one, became not only wary of him, but disgusted with him; and even now, as he watches Ficklin approach, he feels a twinge of fury. He thinks: Fick married himself a goddam Yankee and turned himself into one of these nigger-lovers; and smiling, touching a finger to his brow in a salute, he says: "Hi, boy!"

"Hi, Doc. Colonel. Hi."

"Who you rooting for in the series, boy?" Colonel asks.

"Dodgers, I guess. Feel sorry for them. Nice to see them win one."

"Yep!" Sell muses, "you're partial to the underdog. But I thought you'd be for the *Yankees,* boy."

Ficklin is oblivious to the masked insinuation. "You seen Major Post around?" he asks.

"I saw him a while back. Wasn't an hour ago, was it, Colonel? Wasn't he over there in Black Patch laughing up a storm with them other niggers?"

"Yes," says Colonel, "but I guess he went on."

"You going to Hoopers' tonight, Colonel?" Ficklin lights a cigarette before turning back to his car.

"I wouldn't miss one of Thad's barbecues."

"Well, I'll see you there then. Ada coming?"

As he pauses to suck in some drags on his cigarette, the horn of his automobile honks.

"Wife's in a hurry, eh?" Sell smiles. "All them Yankees rush."

"Yes, Ada'll be along," Colonel nods.

"Well, got to get my spouse over to the band rehearsal!" Ficklin waves and starts back to the car.

Watching him go, Doc Sell says, "Ain't it just like Fick to hire the uppitiest nigger around to work for him!"

"Hmmm?" Colonel murmurs abstractly, thinking. They all know about Ada. Funny I never realized until right now that they all know about her.

For the most part in Paradise people lead a quiet kind of routine existence that keeps them over-all content. But like people anywhere they sometimes get a hankering for some excitement. A barbecue, like the one the Hoopers are throwing tonight, is one way of satisfying the yen; and there are

16

others with other ways. Maybe the colored get together out at Moccasin Gap and "whup it up" on stumpwater; or maybe some of the poor white "lintheads" that work the mill in nearby Galverton pay a call on Miss Mary Jane Frances Alexander's establishment, where even if the humping isn't as wild as Macon tail, it's cheaper and easier to get at. Individuals, like Hollis Jordan, might work it off by strolling through Awful Dark Woods and belting out a lot of high-sounding poetry for the oaks and black gums to bounce off their trunks; or some, like black Bryan Post, might ease it out of the system by somersaulting clear down Main Street on a bellyful of homebrew beer, while folks standing around gawk and giggle and guffaw.

There are ways and ways to provide Paradise with this excitement it sometimes craves; and one of the best and most popular ways is to get the band out and playing. When fireworks don't faze folks much any more and county fairs begin to wear off, the Paradise Bigger Band brings almost everyone back into the fold of 906 citizens of the city; proud and pleased as punch with life in Paradise. Folks say even if the only piece the P.B.B. could play was "Marching Through Georgia," there'd be a crowd on hand glad to hear it.

Over at the Methodist Church where Kate Bailey is waiting to rehearse the band, the atmosphere is tense. The members of the P.B.B., all women, sit cradling their saxophones, trumpets and clarinets; nervously smoothing their hands along the gaudy silkiness of their bright gold satin band blouses; while Kate Bailey stands in that stick-straight way she does when anything upsets her, with her small hands folded together in front of her, and her tiny round eyes peering furtively at the Reverend Joh Greene's wife, trying to stop her from continuing.

". . . and at the crossroads, as I was saying," Guessie Greene, who has just arrived, goes on, depositing a bunch of autumn leaves on one of the folding chairs, and beginning to unbutton her blue angora sweater, "Hollis Jordan himself was ahead of me in his car, heading out for the woods, no doubt, and——"

More intensely, Kate fixes her eyes on Guessie's face, trying to warn Guessie, trying to tell Guessie who is there, who just materialized at the band rehearsal unannounced——but

17

Guessie does not see the visitor and continues too rapidly and haphazardly to get the message:

". . . when the train came along, you know what he did? He just sat there in his car with his hand on the horn, blowing that horn the whole time it took for the train to go by, blowing it like a crazy man, as though his blowing was going to affect that train any. I had to laugh to myself to see him sitting there mad as anything blowing that horn!"

"All right, everybody, all right," Kate starts screeching frantically. "Even though Marianne's late, we'll start right now. Get set! 'Loch Lomond' first! Get set!"

"I swear sometimes I think that man is missing upstairs," Guessie adds. "Hoo, I do! I liked to die laughing when I saw that crazy old Hollis Jordan—" and then she stops, because while she was saying this, she was seeing for the first time, that Ada Pirkle is sitting there in the chair by the wall, sitting and listening; and Guessie's words just trail off like air seeping slowly out of a rubber tire; and there is this awful moment of sudden, sick silence.

Then Bigger Band members rattle their sheets of music, shift in their seats, shuffle their shoes on the cement floor, while Kate Bailey begins tapping her feet and shaking her fingers, singing in that squirrel-high squeaky voice of hers:

By yon bon-nie banks and by yon bon-nie braes,
Where the sun shines bright on Loch Lo—

Until everyone in the basement puts their instrument in position, trying desperately to deprive the moment of any significance by immersing it in the clamorous noise of the Paradise Bigger Band.

And typical awful, Ada Pirkle thinks; I live only for Dix.

18

3

WALKING AWAY from Jack Rowan and the others down on Main, Major Post sees Dix Pirkle being stopped at the corner by the Reverend Joh Greene. Passing the pair, Major hears Joh Greene say, "Hey, now, Dix, that was a right smart editorial you wrote for your father about Senator Henderson. You know you're right, Dix, the Senator may be old, but he's still a good man."

"Thank you, sir. Glad you liked it."

Joh Greene chuckles and rubs his hands together.

"You know, Dix, I'd like to have a little chat with you, if you can spare the time. We could walk over to the vestry if you got the time to spare. Got a radio over there we can hear the game on. What do you say, Dix? Can I see you on it?"

"Well, sir—" Dix interrupts his conversation with the Reverend as Major passes them.

Dix says, "Hi, Major."

"Dix."

"Who you rooting for, Major?"

"I'm not following it, Dix."

"You're the only one that isn't, Major," Dix calls after him.

Dix Pirkle is all right, Major thinks, but always goes out of his way. Why? Like his father, some; following in his father's footsteps; working for the *Herald;* chairing committees to raise funds for a new Negro school—the progressive type of Southerner, too progressive to say nigger; not progressive enough to say Negro; so say Nigra. He's all right, though, as all right as a white can get and live in Georgia too. Had his share of troubles besides; losing his wife like that to cancer—and still so young, only nineteen or so; the both of

them married right out of High and then she died, leaving
him a son under two years . . . God, and everybody in Paradise knows Dix Pirkle's mother is a mess.

Major forgets Dix and turns up Church Street, remembering again Jack Rowan's joke. He's still mad at it; mad at
Jack for telling it; mad at himself for stopping long enough
to listen to it. *Park your horse outside and come in.* Yeah,
nigger, you never will get to heaven; even if a white man
tries to ride you in. That's funny, sure enough, like all Jack's
jokes are; Jack's and nine out of ten of the Negroes' in Paradise; always got to feed their bellies with crow in that insidious way; make it a joke they're nothing but "niggers;" take
all the traits the white folks say they got—hear *them* tell it
all Negro men sleep under tents for thinking about white tail—
and make it a joke, and tell it and haw-w, gaw-dog, laugh!

Major sinks his long hands into his khaki-colored cotton
trousers, kicks a stone off the sidewalk on Church Street as he
heads off in the direction of Brockton Road, the good part of
"The Toe," colored town. He is a strong-looking, six-foot
Negro; sixteen, with a straight, sure gait, and dark, alert,
solemn eyes. He has an hour to kill before he's due at Hooper's
to help Hussie with the barbecue, and he kills such saving
hours with Betty James when he can; when she's off on a
break from the department store on Main, closed this afternoon because of the World Series.

All along Church, radios and TV sets blare; and down on
Main the loudspeaker at the County Courthouse is carrying
the game, so the bench-sitters don't have to move a muscle
to know the score. Even over at the mill in Galveston, where
Major's dad, Bryan, works as a "doffer," pushing carts of
bobbins around and dodging the lint, the game is being piped
into the loom and spinning rooms.

The early October sun shines on the pavement, before the
pavement ends and the dust and dirt of the red clay of
Georgia begins as Major comes into Brockton Place; at the
head of The Toe in Paradise. Here there are the rows of non-
descript houses huddling near one another, less like the shacks
in the tip, where Major himself lives; but still carrying the
stigma of the colored in their backyards, for save for a few,
the outhouses look and reek the same anywhere, and only a
few know plumbing. Not even the James house knows it: Betty

20

calls it James Manor; "Well, welcome to James Manor, Mr. Post," she always says; and Betty's father is a doctor.

"The point isn't to leave Paradise, Major," he tells Major when they talk about how Major wants to get the money somehow, God knows *how!* to go off to college and learn to be a doctor himself; then get free from toting for white folks; working sun-up to sundown from one job to the next, even doing sharecropping out at Hooper's when he couldn't get out of it; "The point is, Major, to leave, learn, and then return. Our people here can't spare your kind."

And the whites can't spare you either, doctor of medicine or not, Major had thought when the doctor had first said it to him; thought that, and remembered an afternoon nine years back when he and Betty stood on the James porch and heard the short, square-shouldered, heavy-set plantation manager from over in Manteo tell the doctor: "Mr. Robertson's got to have extra hands right off. Got a truck waiting on Main to haul you over there."

The doctor saying: "I'm a doctor. I have my work at the clinic to do."

The answer barked: "That's what the trouble's all about, *Doctor!*" Fury registered in the cracker's voice, snapping *doctor* snidely. "You boys all go up North and leave the crops to die while you study books to teach you how to come back and sass-ass the land that gave you your breath; and sass-ass the white man that shared everything but his wife with you. Maybe you're holding out for that, *Doctor!*"

And the doctor said tiredly: "Sick folks are at the clinic right now waiting for—"

"Sick niggers sick of doing honest day's work. Sick? Plantation's sick too, *Doctor!* Sick because sick niggers don't want to pick. Very, very sick! And you're a doctor, *Doctor*, so c'mon and quit assing around!"

"All right. Yes . . ." Sighing the ghost sigh of the slave, sighing, "Well, all right," and starting down the steps.

"And bring them two sassy-assed doctor's coons over there!"

"The boy isn't mine. Please, sir—the girl is only sev—"

"Bring them, Doctor Black Buck!"

Then Major had his first cotton-picking lesson; in late summer when he was seven; over in Manteo, gotten to by a truck jammed black like sardines. Stoop before the plant, pull from the bolls, slap in the sack, and sing defiance:

21

Old massa say, "Pick Dat Cotton!" (yell it like a
   cracker would)
"Can't pick cotton, massa," (whine it like a nigger
   should)
Cotton seed am rotten! Ha! Ha! Ha! (yiii, giggle!)

But just *sing* it. If you ain't singing keep yo big mouf
shet.

*'S okay to sing frig this pickin if you pickin as yo
   singin!*
Sho, it am!
*'S okay to sing frig the massa if yo singin as yo
   pickin!*
Sho, it am!
*Frig the cotton; frig the massa; can sing it if yo
   pickin!*
But you can't sing frig the massa's wife
Not even if yo pickin!
Not even if yo pickin!
Not even if she friggin yo while yo pickin!

"Leave, learn and return . . . Where'd it ever get you, Doc?"
Major had asked him.

"I got two pretty daughters I raised right. Right and well.
Now you *know* that. And I got my work over at the clinic,
and I got——"

Plenty of nothin; nothin's plenty for me, Major had finished
it in his thoughts.

Two pretty daughters. "One as near white as pidgeon
droppings," Tink Twiddy said once about Betty's big sister,
Barbara. "Now how you spose that happen? Musta been one
nigger wasn't in the ole woodpile, by goose eyes!"

And Major had told Tink hotly, "She was Doc's by his first
wife that died."

"Oh yeah! By goose eyes I nebber nebber knowed ole Doc
James had him white tail before black."

"Haven't you ever heard of a light-skinned Negro; haven't
you ever heard of anything but white tail, black tail! Don't
you ever stop thinking of——"

And then Major Post had turned away from Tink Twiddy,
disgusted with himself for bothering to justify anything about

22

Doc James before the likes of Tink Twiddy—and the Tinks, all of them, in Paradise, Georgia, with their perpetual palaver hinting at interracial sexual doings. Major hated the way just everything seemed to get turned into talk like that; everything from a simple conversation about the Jameses to an epithet chalked on an outhouse wall, to a joke told on a street corner.

Major's own family carried on that way; all of them; all except his grandmother, Hussie; and sometimes Major wondered why in hell it was; because as a kid, before he'd grown to hate that talk, he'd gone right along with the rest of them; singing things like:

> Here come the white boss wife
> Hot to change her luck
> Knows there's nothin better
> Than a nigger for a —

Before he'd grown to hate that talk; before he'd even known the significance of the talk; when he was no higher than a field weed and still sat in the tin tub with his older sister to bathe, not even sure what the difference was if there was any, he'd learned to sing rhymes like that, tell jokes like that and giggle at them, side by side with learning not to look white folks in the eye; to call them *mister* and expect to be called "boy" by them your whole life long because in their minds Negroes never became men, no matter years.

Why in hell was it, he wondered; where in hell did that talk belong; why? Once he asked Betty's father.

Who said, "Well, Major, well, I know. Now how can I explain?"

"What I don't see, Doc, is why Negroes say it. Who wants white women?"

"Well, Major, well—look at it this way. Since the Negro got to this country, Southern men have been worrying about protecting Southern white womanhood, see. You know how they say, 'Well, if we let the rule get broken; next thing we know one of them Nigras is marrying our sister.' "

"I don't see what that's got to do with it! Why do Negroes have to joke about it, as though the white man was right about that being the only thing a Negro wants; about that be-

23

ing so when it's not so! Who wants a pale old white woman, Doc? Why do Negroes talk that way the whole time?"

"Well, Major, look at it this way. The white man's so sure that's what the Negro wants he's made to so the Negro's got to laugh at that whim; better than let it subdue his mind and soul. Major, the Negro learned a long time ago the reason for all the customs and laws; the segregation—all that, Major, was set up and kept going here just so the Negro doesn't marry the white man's sister, whom he probably wouldn't want to marry in the first place, whom she probably wouldn't want to marry either. White menfolks, Major, don't have a whole lot of self-confidence, or else they got a closet full of neurotic sisters. Anyway——"

"What's that got to do with how the Negroes talk, Doc?"

"Now, I'm getting to that, Major . . . You see the white man succeeds in keeping us in cotton fields, in movie balconies, and on Jim Crow cars—for the most part, he succeeds there. But in the realm of sex, Major, sometimes he doesn't succeed—or sometimes we like to imagine he doesn't—and that's the most sacred realm of all to the white man. So when Negroes say their jokes about Rastus getting caught with the white boss's wife, that's sort of their way of saying to themselves: We're just as good as the whites; this proves it. We're better because we're better between the sheets."

"I hate that talk!"

"Well, Major, I know, but there's little enough to laugh at down here. Little enough. And our people are poor and ignorant. Lord help them; and the whites will keep them that way if they can."

Remembering that conversation as Major turns down Brockton road, Major recalls Mrs. Ficklin watching him all morning, sitting out on her side porch fanning herself and watching him; then near noontime when he was hauling the ashcans back up from the burner her asking him:

"You ever been up North, Major?" She was leaning against the porch post, smiling, the sunlight showing through her sheer summer dress, to the slip, to the panties. "Have you, Major?"

"No, ma'am."

"Never have, huh? Act like you have sometimes."

"I've finished all my work, ma'am. May I go, please?"

24

"Would you like a cool drink first?"

"No, ma'am, thank you, I don't need a cool drink."

He recalls, cursing his own guts as he does, what he thought while she was saying it:

Thought: What do you want from me? What, huh?

Thought: Here comes the white boss wife——

Then, rushing down the long gravel driveway, thought: God damn it, Major Post, you're like all the rest. Think there's no such thing as a white woman offering a colored boy a cool drink of water without spreading her legs for you after! Think like a goddam crow-bellied know-nothing instead of knowing. Instead of knowing that all that Mrs. Ficklin wanted was to be nice; and you start with your sullen tone; your cheap and tacky "ain't no Klu gonna get me for giving you some jog-jog, so git away from me" tone; just because she tried to be nice. Mrs. Ficklin is a Northerner, now you know that, Negro. Up North they do that. Down here she tries and you're not ready to be emancipated yet; you got to think you're dirty, filthy crow-belly thoughts that make you imagine your pants house a gold nugget, and your head houses fat-back!

"What're you scowling at, Mr. Post?"

Major didn't even see Betty sitting on the front porch as he came up the dirt path to the James house.

"Scowling at scowls, I guess. Hi!"

"Hi! Want to go for a walk?"

"Huh, sure, if that's what you want."

He grins at her; grabs her hand; a short thin girl, pretty, with a shape ripening to a young woman's; a springy kind of gay walk and laughing sixteen-year-old sweet eyes; with a smile cotton-white and wide.

"How long you got off?"

"I'm due at Hooper's in an hour."

"I got the day."

"Ummm-hum, I know. I got to do the barbecue. Dad's taking the pickup to Manteo; meeting my cousin-from-up-North's train."

They cut through the sandhills out into the fields, off toward the black pine, where beyond them in the distance trucks and wagons, piled high with newly picked cotton, head out on Route 109 to line up at the gin over in Galverton.

"You mean he's still coming? With Hus back up and well?"

"We tried to stop him," Major starts; embarrassed to tell again what Betty already knows, that Major's dad can't keep a nickel out of a bootlegger's palm, "but somewhere between the Western Union Office and our place, my dad lost the money, then forgot he even had a reason for having it." Major laughs, not meaning it, always embarrassed before Betty, unable not to compare their two families.

She wears a red and white flower-splotched dress; matches the color the sun makes the hills—scarlet; they both wave at Jack Rowan's kid brother, Will, heading off for picking at the Sell farm. It's "in season" now; colored schools close at one to let the kids out for the fields; colored cabinets stock up on liniment for the black backaches the fields promise.

"Won't he be mad when he gets here?" she says.

Major shrugs. "What can you do?"

"I bet he'll be furious, Major!"

"I'm just glad Hus didn't pass. That's all."

"Oh, gee, sure. Me too."

"Got your father to thank. Like always."

"You got that tone in your voice today, Major?"

"Yeah? What tone's that?" Major knows; Grouch County again; God, when would he get out of that county and back to living! The thing at Ficklins still bothered him; all she wanted to do was be nice; and he had to "crow" himself; damn his black skin!

"Please somebody be in a pleasant mood today," Betty says. "Please, somebody."

"Why, honey? Is somebody else moaning the blues like me?"

She stops in the field they walk in; turns and looks up at him; her dark eyes serious now, no laughter there nor any hint of it. "Major?"

"What's the matter, Betty?"

"Major, promise me you won't tell something."

"No. No, I won't."

"You know why I said we should take a walk instead of sitting on the porch."

"Why?"

"Daddy's having it out with Barbara. He came home from the clinic for an hour just to catch her when she came from teaching."

"Yeah? About what?"

26

"Major, promise!" Her eyes plead, her wide lips quiver some, and the clean soft honey-look of her skin with the red of her dress and the red of the hills in the sun. "Please!"

"I do. I do."

"Well—" she pulls a weed from the field, looking down and away from Major's eyes—"well, last night Barbara said she was going for a walk with Neal Bond. It was late when she left and Daddy said how come so late, and she said Neal just got off from the filling station, so Daddy said have a good time and didn't think anything more about it. Then he got a call out to Myerson's. Mrs. Myerson had triplets, Major."

"No kidding! That little thing!"

"Yeah. And anyway he was there till late because Mrs. Myerson had a long labor, and Daddy came home near midnight down the track-crossing road near Awful Dark Woods, and he was driving along and then he saw her. He saw her walking there."

"Who—Barbara?"

"Yes . . . Barbara . . . He stopped the car and picked her up, and he was mad because it was so late, and with her having to go through the cracker section to get home from the woods, he was mad and wanted to know what Neal Bond had on his mind making her walk by herself. She said Neal and she had a terrible fight, and she wanted the air, and wasn't even aware which way she was going, and she guessed she'd gone too far. Daddy said gol-durn right she had."

"She's been sort of funny-acting ever since her boy friend got killed in Korea, huh? What was his name, anyhow."

"Who—Howie? I don't know she has. How you mean?"

Major doesn't know. Just seems odd Barbara James never got herself married, was all. Maybe too sick studying grief. Prettiest Negro girl around marrying age: almost bright; almost light; almost white, yah-ha!

Major says, "How old's Barbara?"

"Twenty-six. Ten years on me."

"Just seems odd she never got herself married, is all."

"Says she's not in love. I don't know."

"Must be she never got over him. Howie."

"I can't remember him hardly at all. I was only around twelve when he was courting her and all. I just know one day she got the letter he was dead and had hysterics. He went

North to college too, I remember that. Studying to be a teacher."

"Must be she never got over Howie."

Betty shrugs, bites her lips, worries a slow second, then continues, "Well I *do* know I never saw Daddy so mad as he was last night; and then today, pained, he was. Full of pain at it."

"Guess I don't blame him. Still she's a grown lady it seems."

"Still, Major—wait. I got to finish. When they got home there was Neal sitting out front waiting and wanting to know why he hadn't seen Barbara in weeks."

"Huh?"

"Yeah! And Barbara she just walked right on in and went to bed. Crying."

Major sucks in his breath, whistles it out. "What'd it all mean."

"You know what Daddy thinks, Major?"

"Hmm?"

"Well, you know whose place is up near Dark Woods."

"Huh! Naw, that doesn't mean that Barbara was—"

"And listen more, Major. I heard Daddy tell Mom after I was in bed, that minutes before he happened on Barbara there in the woods, he'd seen Hollis Jordan out strolling; because he remembered he'd thought at the time that Hollis Jordan sure was a peculiar duck out exercising his bones past midnight."

"Aw, naw!"

"Yes, and back there just now I heard Daddy say: 'You hear me well, Barb, I got my suspicions and you got your excuses. I don't know who you were with or what you were with; but hear this, Barb, I'd sooner on my eyes rather have you messing with the lowest white lint-dodger than have you messing with Hollis Jordan!"

"Lord, he said that. Lord, he sure hates Hollis Jordan. I didn't know!" Major says; thinking even the Jameses have to look out for it; even Barbara James with all her college is susceptible, is going to disappoint the doctor yet, and get white hands on her; *let* them too; *want* them even, maybe. God that would kill the doctor if it's sure. But why Hollis Jordan he hates? Why not any white? Why better have a cracker than Hollis Jordan; that was funny, sure enough.

Sure, because Hollis Jordan is crazy and that's a fact.

Still, choosing between a cracker and a crackpot, Doc chose the cracker; now why in hell? Why not just say no goddam white hand is going to feel you; no matter where you ache and how; why not?

"How would Barbara know Hollis Jordan anyway?" Major says; no one else does. "I didn't even know she knew him."

"Me neither."

"Then how does she?"

"That's what Daddy's aiming to find out!"

Wind waving the field weeds feels cool; good.

Suddenly Betty says, "Major, let's run!"

She starts off ahead of him. Laughing? Uh-uh. Just going fast. Hollis Jordan? Whew!

"Hey gal, wait on me!"

4

Twenty minutes out of Newark Airport candy-tone gives this to Millard:

MENU

SHRIMP COCKTAIL   SAUCE ROUGE
CRISP SALTINES
BONED BREAST OF CHICKEN
CANDIED SWEET POTATOES   GARDEN FRESH PEAS
COTTAGE CHEESE SALAD WITH FRESH FRUIT SECTIONS
MAYONNAISE DRESSING
DINNER ROLL   CREAMERY BUTTER
CHERRY TART WITH WHIPPED TOPPING
COFFEE   TEA   MILK

"Man!"

"Sounds good, doesn't it," the lady beside him says.

"Boy, feed you like a king!"

"Umm-humm. Yes, they do. Good flight. Here, put your pillow on your lap."

"Hmm?"

"Your pillow. To put the tray on when she brings it."

"Yeah? All right. Boy!"

"It'll make it easier for you," the lady says, and smiles.

5

GOD IS LOVE.

The sign says it on the basement wall of the Methodist Church; while Doc Sell's wife takes the tuba solo in "Loch Lomond."

> *. . . Where in deep purple hue the Highland Hills we view*
> *And the moon coming out—*

"What *about* Ada Pirkle?" sometimes those in Paradise ask.

"All I know of it," someone is sure to answer, "is that she was the talk of the whole county back in thirty-six or -seven, back when she was going to Athens to the university. She was different then, all right. Prettiest girl in these parts next to Vivie Hooper, who was Vivie Claridge then, you know. Course she wasn't so saucy then, neither as she is now."

"Was Colonel courting her then?"

"Nope, not yet, he wasn't. Neither was Hollis Jordan, and that's the funny thing about it. Course she knew Hollis. Lord, she *knew* him, but no one would ever thought there was anything between the two. Hollis was ten years older, after all, and an atheist. Known atheist."

"Caught at it, were they?"

"Naw, gaw, that's the funny thing about it. They weren't caught at *it*. Thad Hooper, you see, and Ada's old man—since passed—they were out for coons that afternoon. Up in Awful Dark Woods. Ada, she was down from Athens on one of those college weekends, and along came Thad and her old man and find her there with Hollis Jordan. Up in the clearing near the Judas Trees."

"What doing?"

"That's the funny thing about it, too. The way the story got back, Ada was just standing there in a state of nature, and Hollis Jordan was fully clothed, down on his knees before her."

"No more to it than that?"

"Hell, that was pretty darn near enough for anyone! Ada's old man, he says, 'Ada, put your things on back and come along.' By this time, course, she's crying, and Hollis Jordan just standing there telling her not to. Hooper took a swing at him then, Hooper being no more than a boy beside Hollis Jordan, and Hollis Jordan let him. Stood and let him; saying nothing. The way the story got back Ada didn't put no more on than her dress—carried all her undergear. And then not saying anything more, she plum went along with her old man and Hooper."

"No more to it than that?"

"Nope. That's the funny thing about it."

"*. . . and the moon coming out in the gloaming. Oh, you'll take the high road . . .*"

while the whole Paradise Bigger Band comes in then. The tuba solo ends, and only Ada Pirkle makes no noise in the basement of the Methodist Church. . . .

"Come on, Ada," he said. "Look at all that scalybark on the ground. You look pretty, Ada. College did something for you."

"I thought a lot about you, Hollis."

"Sometimes when I'd miss you I'd come out here to the clearing and recite all those poems we read out here together. I'd pretend you were right here beside me."

31

"But you didn't write me."

"I did too."

"Oh, *finally!* Finally, you did."

"I've got my problems, I guess. My share."

"What are they, I wonder."

"Look out for that branch, Ada. That's a mean one."

"I see it. Hollis?"

"Huh?"

"You still an atheist?"

"I never was, Ada. A man that doesn't call God by his first name isn't necessarily an atheist. I've got a faith."

"But you don't *believe* in God."

"In other things. Related things."

"Like?"

"Like the land. Like those spiderwebs over there on the hedgerows, and the morning glories down behind my place, growing on the bean poles. Like your breasts too."

"Hollis, please."

"Aw, Gawd, Ada, what's the matter with saying that?"

"It's dirty."

"You think that?"

"Well, it's like you're always bringing up things like that in the middle of something you're saying about something else altogether. I don't know."

"I'm not going to worry the subject, Ada."

"I don't know how to explain it."

"Look at the chinquapins over there!"

"It's not that it makes me mad or anything, Hollis. It just makes me feel—tacky."

"Okay, Ada."

"Don't you see what I mean?"

"Umm-hum."

"Particularly when we haven't ever—"

"Ever what?"

She stopped the same time he did; stood and looked up at him, him down at her. A long time, it seemed, before his arms pulled her into his body, and bending for her mouth his own worked on hers, slowly, finding hers in every way; for a while and more. The first kiss they'd ever taken from one another. And she could actually feel it, through all of her, not like the other times when she necked around with the boys from High, or the Pike House she was dating in up in Athens;

not like that at all. Which was the reason she had to laugh—to stop it.

He let go of her and said solemnly, *"The broken little laugh that spoils a kiss* . . . Well, then, c'mon, Ada. We'll be at the clearing soon and we can talk. I want to hear all about what you've been learning." Disappointed, hurt.

"Where's it from, Hollis?" And she was sorry, and the feeling through all of her was physical, too still, and what could she say?

> *The broken little laugh that spoils a kiss,*
> *The ache of purple pulses, and the bliss*
> *Of blinded eyelids that expand again*
> *Love draws them open with those lips of his—*

"Oh, I know. Shelly."

"No. No," he said. "You haven't been keeping up with things up there in Athens. It's Swinburne."

"Oh, gee, sure." What could she say?

Ada Pirkle was Ada Adams when he came to Paradise to settle. She was twelve and he was twenty-two. Before everyone found out he had inherited wealth they speculated as to what a young fellow like him was going to do with the Veer place he bought, when Bill Veer went into lumber and moved to Macon. As it turned out he grew pumpkins, apples, scuppernongs, zinnias, dahlias, and chrysanthemums; none of them for sale. Not a patch of cotton, nor a row of corn heads.

He came, they heard not from him, but from the postmaster who judged by his mail, somewhere from over in Criss County, Georgia, and near as anyone could figure he had no living kin. Why he ever picked Paradise, no one knew.

"As a rule," Pop Maurer, the postmaster used to say, "you can judge a man by his mail, but this one only gets three kinds: bank mail, mail from some book store in Atlanta, and seed catalogs. Never says thank ya or good morning."

In Paradise they say about some. "Well, he's a colorful character anyway." About black Bryan Post, who hardly ever is completely sober, they say it—not out of any crazy admiration for a souse, but out of a helpless appreciation for the wild and fantastic performances black Bryan can't keep from giving when the gin's full to the top in him. They say it about "Can't" Twiddy too, because he's so bad clear through and never was any other way, that the evil in him is first monotonous, then laughable in its awful extreme. And they feel almost sentimental about Can't, because he's theirs, and he's never let them down by acting any other way than the way he's promised his whole seventeen years. About senseless Lennie Waite, they say it, not in a mean way because he's off his tick, but in a gentle, chiding way, because he's been around forever telling them the things God whispers to him at three o'clock every third Tuesday, and saving olive pits. . . .

"Well, he's a colorful character anyway," they say, not with acceptance; still not with resignation, either, nor tolerance, but more with some insidiously tender sentiment, that has some sly peppering of possessiveness over it.

Hollis Jordan is one of those about whom they say this. His solitary figure looming in the shadows of some spent field, gilded by a harvest moon, is as indigenous to Paradise now as is the weather- and time-whipped county courthouse in the town's square. His reticence is as familiar as Doc Sell's garrulousness. The story of that day in Awful Dark Woods with Ada is a part of the folklore of Paradise.

How Ada came to know him, Ada only knows. The Adamses were his nearest neighbors; that everyone knows—still his nearest neighbors could be his farthest, so conspicuously did he keep his distance. Mostly he worked his land, and stayed out of town, except to get supplies.

Reverend Joh Greene, who had more conversations with Hollis than anyone else in Paradise, said, "Hollis Jordan talks about the land like it was a woman."

"Did he read you any poetry?" someone asked him.

"I read *him* poetry," Joh answered. "When you try to sell a man something, you talk in his own tongue."

"Maybe you'd be better off telling him as how them pumpkins he's growing look like the behinds of every bad woman you ever saved from sinning again."

"Naw," Joh laughed. "Hollis Jordan isn't buying any faith."

The winter Ada Adams was sixteen was the first time she ever spoke with Hollis Jordan. Hoschton High was making plans to present "Strange Interlude" for the Drama Club's spring production, and Ada had a craving to play the part of Nina Leeds. After school that afternoon she had walked out toward Dark Woods with a copy of the play under her arm.

If she could get off to herself where no one could hear her, she had an idea she could become Nina Leeds incarnate. She walked deep into the woods until she came to the clearing near the Judas Trees—two years from the time that that clearing became notorious—and began reading Nina's lines. She was a long time reading them aloud; feeling them deeply the more time she was there, and when Hollis Jordan came upon her, she was in the center of the clearing, her voice raised to the old noble oaks; the light blue wool dress clinging to her in the breeze, with her long red hair tangling around her shoulders, and her blue eyes shining with excitement as she began act six:

> *I wonder if there's a draft in the baby's room . . .*
> *Maybe I'd better close the window? Oh, I guess it's all*
> *right . . . he needs lots of fresh air . . . little Gordon . . .*
> *he does remind me of Gordon . . . sometimes in his eye—*

Then she became aware of Hollis Jordan standing there looking at her.

"Oh, gee—no!"

"It's all right. You were doing fine."

"Oh! I could die!"

"Strange Interlude?"

"Yes. Gee, how'd you know?"

"I know it."

"I guess you think I'm crazy."

"I don't think that at all."

"It's a part for school . . . I thought I could do it better out here where nobody'd hear me . . . I never thought . . . it's so embarrassing!"

"Don't be embarrassed. I read a lot aloud out here."

"I *know*. But I'm doing it for school."

"I'm not. So I should be the one to be embarrassed."

"I didn't mean anything like that."

"Look—"

"I guess you think I'm crazy."

"No. No. Look, maybe I could make it up to you for being a Peeping Tom."

"Oh, you couldn't help coming along. It just embarrassed me."

"Is there a part I can read?"

"I—don't know. I guess there is."

35

"All right, then. Let's get down to work. Okay?"

"Well, gee. Gee—sure!"

He was twenty-six then, a great, tall fellow, with a long lean look like a climbing weed, a rugged farmer's face, stained red from the sun and wind, beautiful white teeth that showed when his wide curving lips spread in a mild grin, and a broad and bony masculine nose. What Ada remembered most about him that day was his hands and his voice. He held the book for them with his hands. Ada had never known a man to have such huge hands, their fingers long and square; the flesh of them clean and tanned and solid. And his voice, when he read the role of Marsden, was clear, deep and powerful, giving meaning to those words Ada never knew existed. He stood beside her in his blue wool shirt, his worn black corduroy trousers tucked into his high boots, the thick mop of wild black hair cropping out from under his red cap, and they read for hours.

When they had finished they were tired, and it was late, after sunset. Together they walked slowly back toward town, with the slate-gray sky above them pressing on the dun fields in which coffee-colored stalks of last year's cotton stood around shabbily.

Neither said very much to the other. But Ada was glad, strangely glad he was with her. The blue supper smoke from the chimneys off in the distance seemed somehow divorced from those moments, and she found herself listening to the sound of the acorns crunch underfoot.

They came to his house first, a small brown frame one hidden by the huge boxtrees surrounding it.

"Well," he said, pausing before the wrought-iron gate, "it has been a strange interlude."

She said, "Thank you very much."

"Good-by," he told her, looking squarely at her. She murmured something, gazing away from him; then turning, went on. A curious light hid in her lowered eyes.

When she got home, her father said: "That Hollis Jordan you was talking to, Ada?"

"Just walking a piece with him. Not saying much."

"He's crazy!" her father said.

"Sure is!" she said.

That night Ada took the red autograph book she'd been saving for the Christmas Club Frolic, and turned it into a dairy.

"Why do I care so much about what people say all the time?" was all she wrote on the first mint-shaded page. . . .

After that there were other times; more times than most knew or cared about. Ada's father was a widower who worked hard at farming, and made no bones about visiting Mary Jane Frances Alexander's establishment for relaxation. He saved his money religiously, and worried about sending Ada up to Athens to college when she finished at High; and when Ada told him sometimes she had had conversation with Hollis Jordan, he listened and grunted and likened it in his mind to the way her mother used to take in any stray hound that bayed within a mile of their place, and gab at it like it was human.

"What's he talk about?" he'd asked her once.

"Oh, nothing."

"They say he's educated."

"Some," playing it down.

"He's crazy!"

"Not so much."

"Even a little's too much."

"I know it," Ada would say. "He reads poetry aloud."

Sometimes, just so she could talk about him, she made fun of him, because that was the only way anyone talked about Hollis Jordan in Paradise. She had a hunger to say his name; to tell things he said to her—not everything, though; and then she felt a certain sorry grief when her girl friends would laugh at what she told them, even though the way she told them was amusing and meant to be a joke.

"You mean he made you get down and feel the earth?" they'd scream uproariously.

"That's the truth." Ada would giggle, with her heart aching. "He said, 'Ada, feel it! Feel this land with your fingers! Smell it and taste it! Roll in it and it'll make you clean and true!" I said, 'Roll in it, Hollis Jordan? *Roll* in it!"

" 'N what'd he say then, Ada?"

"Oh, I don't know," she'd answer them; suddenly tired of the game she was playing against herself. "I guess he read some of his crazy old poetry."

He read poetry almost all the time to her, and she to him, reading poems he had selected for her, as though their first meeting when they had read together was to establish the pattern of their future meetings. While she saw him more times than anyone but he or she knew, there was no regularity to

37

those intervals; and they were spaced weeks and often months apart. She would walk purposely to the woods to find him, and at times she would find him; other times, merely sit there in the clearing alone, wondering about him, and wondering what was happening to her because of him.

Never once until the day of their humiliation did Hollis Jordan speak to her of any feeling he might have had other than a friendly one. What she never got used to about Hollis when they were together was the way he would tell her things about herself, which a man to Ada's mind didn't tell a girl unless there was something between them. The third time they were ever together, out in back of his place, when she was watching him mend a fence worn in with the wind, he stopped what he was doing suddenly and said, "You have fine legs. Are you going to college?"

She never knew how to answer him when he said things like that. She even loathed him some, imagining the dirty pictures in his mind. Yet at night sometimes for no reason she would wake up restless and warm; take off her flannel nightgown, and stand naked before the open window in the cold breeze and wish she had a reason to cry. . . .

Hollis and she grew on one another like intertwining vines of ivy along some old, cold wall, without either of them really knowing it. They began to finish sentences for each other, and to laugh too much too easily together. They learned to walk in silence, and to hand one another leaves, or stones, or pine cones, for no reason. Yet when it came time for them to be separated, she told him.

"Well, I'll be going up to Athens next week."

"I'll miss you, Ada."

"Athens isn't so far."

"Still, you'll be meeting new people. You'll have to hit the books too."

"Where'd you go to college, Hollis? Did you?"

"Nope. Athens, Georgia, huh?"

"Yes. Dear old Athens."

"Uh-huh. Well, you come home brilliant, hear?"

"I hear, Hollis."

It was two weeks and twenty letters after she went to the University when she received her first communication from Hollis. The lines scrawled on the postcard were familiar ones:

I wonder if there's a draft in the baby's room . . . Maybe I'd better close the window?

And I'll be in Scotland before you,
But me and my true love will never meet again . . .

The Paradise Bigger Band hammers at the piece ambitiously, with Kate Bailey tapping out the rhythm. Doc Sell's wife holds her lips from the tuba to allow Guessie to take her notes on the drum; all of them are in accord, and Ada remembers:

"I didn't mean to laugh back there, Hollis, when you kissed me."

"I know you didn't."

"I wish I knew how to be more honest with myself."

"We all have trouble in that department."

"Hollis, I used to laugh about you to people. I used to tell things we did together like it was a joke, like I didn't even care about any of it, like you were some kind of character."

"I guess I am."

"No, don't say that. Don't laugh, Hollis. Do you know something?" She was eager now, suddenly buoyant, possessed of some new feeling of liberation, and the physical too, still. "In Athens, when I'd be out on some silly, tacky beer party, sitting on some boy's blanket on the ground while he was trying to paw me, I used to think what you always said about dirt, about how good it felt in your hands, and how it smelled and tasted. And I'd get this idea, Hollis, that I had to get away from there and go someplace by myself. And I'd miss you so, Hollis. I know we never talk like this—you and I—but Hollis, I'd miss you!"

"All right," he said, putting his arm around her. "All right, Ada."

He touched his mouth again to hers, and she leaned deeply into him then, her own mouth warm and alive, no longer passive against his. Her eyes were half shut watching him, and her breath came and went in little quick gasps, drinking his. For a long time he kissed her, until her hair was all shaken down, touching his cheeks and shaking around his face, while the man in him grew; and unbuttoning her; then buttoning her up again, whispering some vague, nearly incoherent something about not wanting to do that to her; but she put his fingers back on the buttons and begged him with that gesture.

When his own hands fumbled clumsily with the clothing he undid, hers hurried the undressing, until he felt the warm bare arms around his neck. He held her in his lap, embracing her nakedness with a trembling strength. And then, before the time of their love, he was compelled to lift her from his lap, to kneel there in the clearing before those young unpendulous breasts, the lithe body clad in its garment of nudity. He knelt, clinging to those ripe white knees in that instant before he would bend them in the act of love—

When, "Ada!" they both heard. "Ada Adams!"

And as any two ever caught near climax by an outsider, they felt immediately ridiculous, rude, and laughingly unattractive.

"Ada! Put your things back on and come along!"

"No more to it than that?"
"Nope. That's the funny thing about it."
"But that didn't make Ada the way she is now, you think?"
"The whole story ain't been told, for my cotton!"
"Imagine the bastard getting her to do a regular old strip-tease up in Awful Dark Woods!"
"Aw, sheet anyway! He's crazy! Didn't even fight in the war!"

"Very, very good!" Kate Bailey says at the end of "Loch Lomond." "Now we'll try 'Turkey In The Straw'!"

Marianne Ficklin hollers over to Ada Pirkle, "Ada, honey? How come you don't take up an instrument? Do you good, honey!"

" 'Turkey In The Straw,' " Kate Bailey says. "Page Six. Ready?"

6

VIVIE HOOPER turns the volume down on the small portable, and leans forward in the rocker to see who is driving up to the pumps outside. Then she gets up: twenty-eight, not too tall, but straight-standing, and quiet and graceful looking, as though her own awareness of her beauty has made her feel some sense of responsibility which must make her express to others an aura of inviolate dignity and stunning, kindly poise.

Her magnificent pitch-black hair spills to her shoulders, the gleaming soft-white-skinned perfectness of them, hidden by the simple black dress with its round Peter Pan collar. The dress is not designed to highlight her voluptuous figure—Thad ordered it for her from Atlanta; a surprise—but almost as if in protest the breasts and hips of her push through the cotton fabric proudly to show themselves. She is long-legged for a girl her height, her ankles curving thinly and exquisitely above the black ballet slippers. Her face is radiant, even now when its expression is solemn; the long black lashes of her deep blue eyes are lowered; the wide lips curving generously, lightly painted rose color; her skin is flawless, like burnished ivory. She has, for someone so vitally beautiful, some sweet and incredible shyness to her make-up; striped with a paradoxical air of calm composure. Her voice is husky, low; its tone, gentle.

Walking to the door and opening it, she calls out, "Hi, Storey! What brings you around this time of afternoon?"

He cuts his motor and grins at her, wiggling over and getting out on the right side of the new light-blue Ford. "Thought you'd be up at the house fixing for the barbecue, Vivs."

"Hus is doing all the fixing. You know Hus. She hates meddling."

He stands under the stark black-lettered sign which reads:

41

Hooper's Place—Gas and Pop, with the smaller sign attached: *Scuppernongs For Sale—50¢ gallon—20¢ for all you can eat!*

And he thinks as always with wonder upon the fact he, Storey Bailey, made more of himself than Thad Hooper; he, Storey Bailey, head superintendent at the Galverton Mill, with his farm growing a good crop in corn and cotton too, came out the better. For he never would have thought it as a boy— younger than Thad by eight years, beholden to Thad Hooper. He was so very beholden that the night with Vivs, even before Thad and she were officially engaged, had made him vomit afterwards, and swear no other lapse in loyalty to Thad—because even though it was not official between Vivs and Thad, who better but Storey Bailey knew his idol's intentions toward her. And he had forced it out of his mind, rooted it out, married Kate (a really good woman) and paradoxically done better than Thad. He was almost ashamed because he had.

"Hey, girl, how come you're minding the station? Ole Thad got you working now, huh! Whew, hot!" He mops his brow with a large square white handkerchief. The roundness of his face, the ruddiness of it and the tilt to his near-pug nose, coupled with the towhead, gives his countenance a boyish look. His lean, gangling frame, slightly awkward and disconnected in its gait, lends him still more youth; and Kate, older-looking but in fact two years his junior, says always at church supper socials: "Pass the salt to my son, please," and people in Paradise laugh good-naturedly with her at the remark.

"Today's the anniversary," Vivie says. "He's taken little Thad and Emily up to the grave."

"Oh, yes? I saw him earlier out in front of the courthouse. The anniversary today, hmmm? And still having the barbecue?"

"Thad says it's right we should; says she would have wanted it that way, for him to be surrounded by his friends—our friends."

"Hard to tell, isn't it, how she'd feel about it?"

"I guess he grew her up right along with him in his mind, Storey."

"I guess Thad did . . . I hardly remember her; just that they were twins and it nearly killed him when she died."

"Yes. They were twins . . . I don't remember her either."

"Seems like we were all but babies when she was living anyway."

"Come on in and rest. Have some pop. How's Kate?"

Storey follows her into the filling station, a mile down from the Hoopers' house, with the land in between their land; but poor top-soil land, less fertile than Storey's own, with only a cotton crop, and none other to speak of save for the scuppernongs.

He says as they go: "She's down rehearsing the band."

"Oh, of course. Tuesday."

"Umm-humm. Every Tuesday."

"You want orange or grape?"

"Grape'll be good."

"She certainly likes working with the band, doesn't she, Storey?"

"I don't know that she likes it. It's hard, don't let anyone kid you about that, Vivs, but you know it's real worthwhile. I guess everybody in Paradise is crazy about the band."

"Sure, I know it's hard work."

"Kate's a good woman," Storey says. He looks solemnly at Vivian Hooper, swigs his grape soda, and sets it down on the wooden table. He says in a surprisingly sober tone: "Yes, we married ourselves to good people, Vivs. We married ourselves to fine people."

Vivian Hooper hears little or none of the explanation which follows for having the afternoon off from the mill at Galverton. Her mind harps on that statement, on its insinuation—imagined?—and again as countless times before with Storey, times when his eyes turn away from her own, having come up her body too suddenly to see it fully; yet just that furtively that she imagines he is thinking back in time to that night; *she* remembers it all again too.

Eleven years ago:

"Vivs? Thad says he's got to stay on and close up the exhibit for his dad. Says that I might as well run you on home."

At the county fair, the summer Vivian was just seventeen, Storey nineteen, and Thad twenty-seven, the oldest bachelor in Paradise—outside of Hollis Jordan, who was crazy and never would marry a girl in her right mind. It was at that county fair that Thad Hooper's father had set up an educational exhibit based on producing sorghum molasses the old-fashioned way, with an old-time sorghum mill complete with a mule crushing the sorghum cane, and the syrup cooking over

43

the wood fire. And during this the old man had caught the virus, and Thad had taken over most of the duties. . . .

"Why, thank you, Storey," Vivie had said, "but I don't know that I feel like going *home.*"

"We could walk around some and look at the exhibits."

"Oh, I've seen them all . . . I don't know . . . Since Thad got tied up here, we just haven't been anyplace at all but here."

"Well, you want to drive around or something?"

"Why, thank you, Storey. I guess that might be fun."

She had always genuinely liked Storey Bailey. They were nearer in age than Thad and she were, and sometimes when she was first going out with Thad, she wondered if she weren't more pleased over the fact that she was dating Storey's idol more than at the fact that she was dating the most eligible bachelor in Paradise. She used to like to tease Storey some.

"I was out with Thad Hooper last night, Storey. He mentioned your name several times."

"He *did!* Well, what'd he say?"

"I don't know that I rightly remember. Something, though."

"Well, good or bad?"

"I don't remember, Storey. I just remember he mentioned your name several times. He certainly is nice."

"He's a swell guy, all right—Thad Hooper is. I guess I think he's just about one of the nicest guys around here."

"I guess you think a lot of him, all right."

"Don't you, Vivs?"

"Oh, he's all right, Storey."

"All right? You ought to be proud! He's going to be mighty big some day. You'll see!"

"Yes sir, he mentioned your name several times."

She liked Storey Bailey in a different way from the way she liked Thad. In Paradise, Thad was the county promise; got along with everyone, was considered bright and aggressive and good. He was a serious sort, made serious, some said, when his twin sister died; and he was more mature, harder—Vivian Hooper always thought—to talk to, maybe because of his age. But Storey was the kind of boy she'd sit with with her hair done up in curlers, and laugh and talk with him without even thinking about it. And Storey was shy in some ways in which Thad Hooper was more reserved than shy. Thad Hooper had principles; while Storey just seemed to have pent-up emotions that he was scared to let loose. . . .

44

How they ever got out to Mike Fairchild's place that night, both Storey and Vivie remember in separate ways. Storey has long since put it out of his mind; but if it were recalled to him, he would remember that Vivs made the remark in the car.

"Storey, you know what I hear? I hear out at Mike Fairchild's you can buy moonshine and soda, and sit right there and drink it."

And Vivian Hooper remembers it as Storey saying:

"Did you ever have any moonshine before? Oh, I suppose Thad's introduced you to that long ago."

And herself answering, "Naw, gaw, Storey—you don't know Thad well. He wouldn't touch it. Since his sister's death he's vowed . . . I guess he's right, isn't he?"

"Oh, a little won't hurt anyone, Vivs."

No matter how each one remembers it, the fact stays they went to Mike's and drank glass after glass; until they were giggling up a storm; and Storey, as Vivie remembers it; and Vivie, as Storey remembers it—

Said: "We better go out in the car and sit in the fresh air a bit, and get ourselves back to normal before we drive on into town."

As they both remember it they just got to kissing each other out in the car, lightly at first, laughing about it; and then after a while she was telling Storey: "No farther than that, Storey! I never let anyone do this. Gaw, Storey!"

Then, as Storey remembers it, Storey broke away before they had gone all the way; and as Vivie remembers it Vivie pushed Storey away when she heard a zipper unzip. But as they both remember it, they stopped; said seriously to one another that what had happened was awful and neither one's fault; and Storey said he would step inside Mike's for just a minute, and she should fix herself there in the car; and he would be back, in a minute and drive her on home the way he should have, the way he'd promised Thad to begin with. . . .

Inside Mike's, Storey went into the men's room; leaning dizzily against the sink there, shaken and sorry as he thought about Thad, but wildly excited at the thought of the girl waiting out in the car; he stood remembering her gasps and moans of joy as his hands explored her. He remembered her body moving in that strange rhythm of passion he had never recognized in any other woman but the one in Mary Jane Frances Alexander's establishment, where he and some of the other

45

seniors had gone the night of graduation from Hoschton High; and he had felt himself torn terribly between a loyalty to Thad and an immense and tender emotion toward Vivs, who had given him the gift of her response. He stood pondering this new plight for a long time, unable to find any solution, but staying there in fear and some uncertain glory. Just as he was leaving the men's room, Vivs got out of the car, worried at his absence, to come into Mike's and get him.

Storey was sober by then; sober and unnerved; and when he passed by Mike and Mike said, "How about it, Bailey? Want a shot for the road?" Storey summoned up some false tone of bravado and laughingly shouted, "Hell, I can get *two* fingers in!"

And that was what Vivie heard when she opened Mike's door. She heard it and was horrified to think she knew what Storey Bailey was referring to. She slammed shut the door with a ringing bang and ran crying to the car.

"Two fingers it is!" Mike said, pushing the glass toward Storey.

And Storey, staring toward the door where a second before he had seen Viv, murmured, "Now, what the dickens?" drank his corn down in a gulp and took after her.

"You're filthy!" she said the instant he entered the car, giving him no explanation for her wrath. "You're rotten clear through, Storey Bailey!"

Storey could find no reason for her to turn on him in that way, save for the fact during the interval they were separated she had thought over what had happened and regretted it and then decided to blame it on him.

He said: "It's not me that's filthy or rotten! Oh, Christ, didn't I see you squirming like some bitch all hot, didn't I!" He was furious with her for turning the incident that had thrilled him into something evil.

"Rotten, filthy, rotten!" she had wept.

And Storey, seething now: "All I feel sorry for is Thad, who doesn't know you got a whore's body. All I care is to get you home and out of my car!"

So that neither ever understood the other or what had happened between them; but they rode each hating the other for what each one imagined the other had made of the affair.

And Storey, on the way back down Route 109, stopped, got

out and vomited, while she cried the whole time, neither one saying any more.

Whenever they met after that time—each avoiding that first meeting until ultimately it was inevitable in the smallness of Paradise—there was a noticeable strain upon them in the beginning, a too-conscious effort at civility, which though alleviated in time, nevertheless cropped up again at certain intervals through the years. Though Thad, who never knew, still said, "Storey's my best friend . . . Funny that he married Kate . . . Not that Kate isn't one wonderful woman, but she's so serene for Storey."

And Vivian Hooper knows that only that night—parked outside Mike's with Storey—did she ever feel passion—not before or since. And she resents Storey for it, and for the fact that when she had gone in Mike's after him, before she had heard his remark, she had wanted to say, "Storey, I don't want to marry Thad. Gaw, Storey—I'm not sorry for what happened just then. It was something beautiful, and I could be me. I could be *me!*"

"You look beautiful even tending a filling station, Vivs," breaks through the wall of memory.
"Why thank you, Storey." He has forgotten, she thinks to herself; he doesn't think about it as I do. "Why thank you."
"Yeah, you do."
Softly in the background the radio plays:

> *Cold corn bread and fatback*
> *Oh, scat on back to me*
> *You see*
> *You see*
> *I got to have my cold corn bread*
> *And fatback - scat back*

Even if Thad didn't make out better, Storey thinks as he looks across at her, he deserves Viv; Viv needs him too. Joh Greene often said: "Men and women got the devil in them, got the apple embedded right in them; and some fight the apple and some let the apple grow bigger and bigger until it's bigger than them. And every man and woman knows what they're doing about their own apples; and nobody has to tell them

47

that. And I say, you man—letting the apple grow, you man—find you a woman who'll fight that apple in you like she fights her own apple; and you woman with that apple in you growing —find you a man who'll fight that apple in you like he fights his own; for the weak hold the strong up and the strong gets stronger with the weak leaning on them. And that way only shall we all know God, and we got to know God. We're nice folks—we got to know Him, for God likes good folks."

And Storey remembers once Doc Sell said after church service, "Hell, Storey, it's gaw-awful plain whose apple's growing and whose apple ain't in your family; but what I never could figure out is whose apple's growing and whose ain't in the reverend's house!"

"What you sitting there grinning at, Storey?"

"Huh? Oh, something Doc Sell said one time, Viv."

"Bill Ficklin told me the other day Doc's the only one opposed to building the new colored school."

"Oh, well, you know Doc well's I do, Vivs. He don't think the nigger's got any business going to school in the first place."

"Fick's real hot under the collar about that school, isn't he?"

"Yeah, he is. I think being married to a Northerner's got something to do with it. Course I like Marianne."

"She's got Major Post working for her now, you know. The other day Thad asked him why he wasn't picking any this year and he said he had a job over to the Ficklins."

Vivian thinks to herself that she is sorry Major is not up on the hill as much as he was before the Ficklins hired him. Major and she always got along—he wasn't at all like Post niggers. Where'd he learn all he did—from Doc James? Ever since Doc James moved over from Criss County, the first colored doctor in Paradise, he stuck out like a sore thumb before the other niggers; widowed and with that near-white daughter. Then he married himself to some nigger lawyer's girl from Macon, brought her back and him and his family never held down niggers' jobs; never talked much nor acted either like niggers. She remembers Thad saying, "I saw a nigger on Main today wearing a necktie. What next!"

"No."

"Yes, I did. And this'll rock you. He's a doctor."

"No.!"

"Yes, he is . . . Well, Vivie, I don't know. Maybe it's a good thing. Maybe it's high time Paradise had a nigger doctor. I

48

think maybe it's a good thing. Niggers get sick like anyone else, and white doctors shouldn't have to handle them. Syphilis and all."

Storey finishes the grape pop, sets it on the table, stretches, and yawns. "Well, I know this much anyway. If we don't get the niggers a new school, we gonna have them in white schools 'fore we know it. Supreme Court made that ruling about desegregation, and 'less we got something to fight back with, we gonna have to abide by it!"

"Thad says we never will. Says we'll just change the white schools into private schools."

"Yeah, but we still got to give the niggers better 'n what they got now or we can't *do* that. We get someone like Tom Sellers in this year—and get rid of Senator Fred Henderson—things will be getting done around Georgia."

"That's what Thad says. Practically everybody's seen Sellers; shaken his hand and all."

"That's right. Thad's right."

"Yeah, Thad is . . . I guess always."

"You know how I feel about Thad," Storey says. He looks at Vivian Hooper furtively as she collects the empty pop bottles; looks at the black cotton dress, knowing the voluptuous world of flesh the cotton conceals. It's right she's married to Thad, he thinks; good that she is. Thinks, I ought to run down to Church Street and see if Kate's finished. He wonders why Thad let himself take on so much weight. He's nearly fat now, and Viv stays the same, never seems to change.

"Yes sir, I think the world and all of Thad," Storey says, pulling himself to his feet.

"I know you do," she tells him, thinking Storey has no right to drive out here and look me over like he does, like he doesn't know I know he does; and then go on back to Kate. Like back from hell and the devil himself. Is that how he thinks of it?

Thad always says: "Some men, I suppose, think just because you're built so well, you're one of these physical kinds of women. It's a narrow-minded conception. I know if Thel had lived she would of had to deal with that problem herself. She was well developed even at fifteen, you know, Vivie . . . I remember she was. Would have been beautiful . . . Everyone would have thought she was one of those physical kinds . . . She was *good*, though, I can tell you . . . Not like that at all."

"You tell Thad I was by, hear, Vivs?"

49

"I'll tell him, Storey. See you tonight."

"Colonel coming?"

"Umm-humm. Him *and* Ada, I expect."

"Ada too?"

"Well, that's what Colonel said."

"You give Thad hell for me, letting a pretty girl like you tend the station, hear?" Storey laughs, hanging on to his hips—the same way Thad does, she thinks. How he mimics Thad— "I'll be looking forward to tonight, Vivs."

"Sure enough, Storey."

"Well, bye!"

"Bye, bye!"

"See you tonight. You tell Thad I was by looking for him."

"All right, Storey. So long."

Then she turns the volume back up on the radio; oblivious to the hillbilly music that blares out of it; and sitting, rocking, she again remembers: *"Oh, Christ, didn't I see you squirming like some bitch all hot, didn't I?"*

And: *". . . just because you're built so well, you're one of these physical kinds of women. It's a narrow-minded—"*

And: *"We married ourselves to good people, Vivs."*

Then worries: Hope Hus thinks of the okra for the stew; Hus always forgets the okra.

7

"This is Washington, D.C.," the voice of the hostess says. "We will depart immediately upon taking aboard the new passengers. Those remaining on the flight, please keep their seats."

The woman beside Millard Post shoves her knitting into her bag, and sighs. "That was a nice smooth landing."

"You're getting off here, huh?"

"That's right. Well, it's been fun talking with you."

"Same here, ma'am."

"How far do you go before you change planes?"

"I think to Charlotte."

"Well—have a nice trip, Millard."

"Same here, ma'am."

"Bye."

"So long," says Millard.

He leans forward and looks out the window of the plane at the Washington airport. There is a clock inside and he can just make out the time through the glass window. Two o'clock. At North Trades High the cafeteria would be emptying; the Panthers would be heading with their trays back from the table on the left, which was their special spot. Some of them would cut this afternoon and head off to the poolroom to hear the Series play-off. A lot of them were for the Dodgers because of Willie Mays, but Millard had his dollar on the Yankees, because they could play better ball sitting on their hands. There'd be a lot of excitement at the poolroom. What the hell!

Millard sees the woman who had been sitting beside him go through Gate 7 up the stairs, out of sight. For the first time this afternoon, he realizes a slight pang of loneliness. He *reaches forward in the pocket of the seat in front of him for the cellophane-wrapped folder with the words:* "Your Souvenir of This Trip" *printed upon it in black letters. Rifling through it he takes out the stickers, looks at them, imagines how they'll look stuck to his cardboard suitcase, and places them carefully on the inside of his suit pocket. Then he searches through his trousers for a pencil to write on the postcards.*

Passengers start pouring down the aisle, and Millard cannot concentrate on the message to his friend, Toe-In Funk, chief of the Panthers. So far he has written only Toe-In's address and the words: "Hey, Square, how's it hanging?" . . .

He leans back and looks up at the people going by him. Soon everyone seems to be seated but one gross man carrying a briefcase and a gray fedora. Millard hears the door of the plane slam shut. The man stands looking around him, then at the empty seat beside Millard. He frowns, throws his fedora up in the rack; then slumps his heavy body down into the seat, sighing, and fastening his belt, not looking at Millard.

The smoking sign blinks on; as the plane's engines roar.

"Hello, sir," *the hostess says to the fat man.* "Have you eaten?"

"No, I haven't."

Millard notices how tense his voice sounds, sees his fingers drum the leather arm rest.

"I'll serve you as soon as we're aloft, sir," *the hostess says.*

The man does not answer, grunts, and still frowns.

As the plane taxies out on the field, Millard thinks of the way he had felt at Newark that morning and compares his own nervousness then with the man's actions now. He pities the guy; weeping Jesus, poor sucker.

Millard says, "Is this your first flight?"

The man does not answer; perhaps does not hear Millard above the engine's noise.

Louder, leaning closer to the man, Millard says, "Once we get up you'll feel better."

Then the man glares at Millard, his eyes narrowed.

"No kidding," *Millard tries again.* "As soon as we get up you'll feel better . . . I know how you feel . . . I felt the same way myself."

Millard hears him cuss as he looks away.

Weeping Jesus, the goddam bastard's got the shit scared outa him!

Millard smiles to himself and feels good; flying in a goddam DC-6 is Endsville. Who's scared, f'Chrissake. Not Millard Post.

But the man beside him looks like he'll bust a gut over something.

8

REVEREND Joh Greene says, "Dixer, you're a fine boy, Dix. You got a good head on those shoulders."

In the background the ball game goes on; Yankees and Dodgers tied. Dix Pirkle crosses his legs, lifts the glass of beer and sips it, wondering what the Reverend's building up to; thinking, no it's impossible. Not that, not yet. Eventually, though, he supposes. Like *she* said: "We won't be able to keep it a secret, Dix. You know that."

Christ, the sweetness of it, the great big sweetness of it; and the thought that when they do find out—those in Paradise—what will they make then of the gentleness and sweetness between him and her now?

Dix sinks his lanky body further into the worn leather arm-chair in the vestry. He thinks, He can't know about it—not so soon.

Dix is husky; with thick black hair and blue eyes; a slender nineteen-year-old who looks too young to have a son over one —when he had started to mention Dickie to her last night, she'd said, "No, Dix, that part of your life I can't share, like so many other parts. No, Dix."—who acts too mature for his age. "Bright kid," Colonel's folks in Paradise say. "Writes editorials just like he'd gone off to college the way he should have."

"Yes sir, Dixer, you take after your father."

53

Dix nods. "I hope so, sir," knowing the intonation in his voice makes it definite between the Reverend and him how he feels about his mother. Christ, how did Colonel take it! How did anyone in the house; how did he, Dix?

With horror he remembers coming home from the paper a month or so back to see his mother, hysterical, sitting on the floor clutching Dickie in her lap. The infant had fallen from the bed while her back was turned, and Ada, sobbing, hunched over the baby clumsily trying to soothe away its fright. Dix, examining the child, carefully, feeling the delicate infant's bones, remembers feeling at that moment a terrible resentment of the past which had killed Dickie's mother with cancer and left Dix's own mother alive.

"I wanted only to help, Dix!" Ada Pirkle had sobbed hysterically. "Just help! Dix, you've got to let me help!"

Joh Greene leans forward, stretching his hands out across the desk blotters; his fingers rubbing page edges of *Time*. "Dix, we get mixed up sometimes. All mixed up."

"I know."

"It's our apples, Dix. Our apples. The devil knows how to make them grow bigger than we realize before it's too late."

"Yes, sir."

"Dix, I want to ask you something. Dix, do you know how big your own apple is?"

"Reverend, sir—I don't exactly know what you're trying to say to me."

"How long's Suzie been dead, Dix?" Reverend Joh Greene asks.

"Be two years, soon."

"She was a good wife too, I don't have to tell you that. When Colonel first came to ask my advice about you marrying so young, I remember I told him, 'Dix might wait, but maybe his apple won't . . . I'm in favor of getting that apple under control, Colonel.' You remember, Dix, you were a wild kid."

"Yeah. Yes, sir."

"And then the Lord took Suzie home, may her soul rest."

"Reverend," Dix Pirkle says, a strain of impatience in his tone. "What are you trying to say? That I should remarry?"

Reverend Joh Greene gets to his feet. He snaps the radio off, walks around his desk to Dix Pirkle's chair, and stands with one hand sunk into his black trousers, one hand on Dix Pirkle's shoulder.

"Dix," he says softly, "I know you miss Suzie. I'm a man of God, but I'm a man too. I know a man needs a woman, a good woman, Dix. Maybe I *am* saying you should remarry." He pauses, his face thoughtful. And Dix sits feeling relief flood through him, glad it wasn't what he feared, glad for only a moment before Joh Greene speaks again. "But I'm here to tell you, Dix Pirkle, once you start up with a colored girl, no white girl's ever going to satisfy you again."

A sudden heavy silence hangs over the room as the blood rushes upward in Dix Pirkle's, filling his face with red warmth; his knuckles tighten to white as he makes his hands fists. He sits there, aware now that the ball game has been turned off, and aware of the loud-sounding tick of the vestry clock and the reverend's hand on his shoulder.

He says finally: "How—how did you know, sir?"

"That's something I can't say, Dix."

"Does—Dad know?"

"No, Dixer, he does not. I figured you and me could talk about this without anyone knowing."

"Someone must."

"No one that cares to tell your dad, Dix, or anyone else. God's work is done in mysterious ways. You'd be amazed, I think, to know who came on God's mission to me to give me this information."

"Not the doctor!" Dix exclaims. Lord, he shouldn't have let her walk home; why *had* he?

She'd insisted: "Sometimes I think I know Paradise better than you do, Dix, though I've lived here less time. You can't drive me home I want to walk anyway, Dix. I want to walk in this night."

"No. No. Son, what does it matter who knows? What matters is to end it! To end it, son. To end it before it's too late." Joh Greene steps away from Dix; leans back against his desk.

"Reverend, listen," Dix protests; remembering the shame —not anger or resentment or even reproachfulness—he had seen in her eyes the day she had taken him through the colored school; the shame there, as though she were apologizing for something white folks did; or for what she was—for being colored. And the way she had said last night: "I wish I could help being black; wish we all could; so we wouldn't have to live

55

with an I-can't-help-it philosophy. It's no good, Dix . . ." And
he remembers her tears dropping on his shirt last night: "No,
Dix, I'm *not* crying. Why should I? What's there to cry over?"
Dix Pirkle says, "Reverend Greene, listen, she's a fine girl.
There's nothing about the devil in her, Reverend."

"Did I say she wasn't a fine girl, Dix?"

"No, sir. I just want you to know that I respect Barbara."

"Is your way of respecting her shown by lying on the ground
of Dark Woods with her, Dix?"

Christ, how did he know all that!

"Dix," Reverend Greene says, "in order to respect anyone
you have to first respect yourself. Can you respect yourself
after lying on the ground with a nigger girl?"

Dix jumps to his feet, his young eyes ablaze. "Christ, what
the hell kind of minister are you! Call a human being a nigger!
Christ, what the hell kind of Christianity is that!"

"I was making a point, Dix, that's all. I was trying in my own
way to make a point. A man that turns a colored girl, a decent,
intelligent, fine colored girl into the object of his lust, turns that
lovely girl, whose color is not his, into a *nigger,* in the eyes of
all the world. Do you see what I mean, Dix?"

Dix whirls around and faces Joh Greene. "I don't want
Barbara just for that! Is that what you think!"

"*Just* for that?"

"I wouldn't even care if that wasn't—I wouldn't care if—"
Dix stumbles over his words, sighs, shakes his head. "You don't
understand, Reverend. I think of Barbara James the same way
I'd think of—well, Suzie . . ."

"God help you for making that comparison, Dix. God forgive you for it."

"Reverend, listen to me. Back six months ago, when I got
on the committee for the new Negro school—I met Barbara
then. Reverend, she's—good and decent and—"

"Did I ever say she wasn't, Dix?"

"Well, what are you saying? Are you saying that she's a
devil? That she's dirt, or something less than that! Are you
trying to tell me my mother's white; or that the white girls in
this town, the stupid, dull—"

Joh Greene puts his palm up. "Stop right there, Dix."

"Well, what are you trying to tell me that I don't know! That
I was with her last night! That you don't approve! That nobody

56

in Paradise would approve! That she's Negro and I'm white!"

"Simply this," Joh Greene says. "You're taking a Nigraw woman and making her into a nigger, Dix. And you're making yourself into a sick, nigger-chasing white man. I know what happens to white men that hanker after dark skin. I know from experience as a minister in Christ, from seeing it happen, from remembering the way it happened time and time again to such white men; sick men! Their strength was all sapped out of them, Dix. White men and dark women aren't made to know one another in a carnal way, or they'd be the same color. They aren't made to, and the white man isn't up to the dark woman: even though he may think he is, he isn't. And he gets sick from it, from lusting for it, and he gets the disease of it and he lusts for it and loses his strength to it; and he can't look on his own color any more, because after a dark woman no white woman can satisfy a man. No good white woman—good in her heart and mind as in her body—would be expected to satisfy a man in the way of the dark race; and so it's a poison, Dix. I'm here to say that I see the poison being injected into your veins, and I know the antidote, and I—as well as any man—want to help my brother, want to say I know the antidote for the poison you've taken into your body, and the antidote's name is never again see her; and its name is to kill the apple before it kills you; and its name is hallowed be the memory of Suzie; and its name is Dickie my son, save me from spoiling our name; and its name is Barbara James, Nigraw woman, fine and good—*not* nigger! and its name is pray for us sinners. And I call it Christ Jesus!"

Dix Pirkle stands stunned, angry, silent. For a slow moment the Reverend Joh Greene's eyes needle him. He turns his head from the minister, looks down at the worn oriental carpet; numbed—not with fear or regret or humiliation, but with furious resentment. No good white woman would be expected to satisfy a man in the way of the dark race. With the aura of impotence that overcomes him so he can find no words to answer Joh Greene, and fumbling futilely for them, he knows the stubborn imperviousness of the minister's mind.

Dix Pirkle stands silent.

Slowly Joh Greene walks back behind his desk, pulling a large white handkerchief from his pocket and mopping his brow carefully. Then, shoving the handkerchief back into his

57

trousers, straightening his shoulders, his face more placid now, the reverend says very softly: "That's all, Dix. That's all I wanted to say to you."

With a quick flip of his wrist, he snaps the radio back on.

Then, grinning suddenly, he says, "We got to see how them Yankees are making out, ah? Hey, Dixer, get to work on that beer!"

9

ON HIS WAY back from the grave, in the small rear-view mirror of the car, Thad Hooper can see the top of his daughter's head, as she bobs about—the hair neatly parted in the middle and braided at the sides. The pigtails frame her face in an austere plainness that to Thad's mind greatly enhances her looks. Like Vivie, she is raven-haired; but most of her features are similar to those which run in his family, almost identical to his twin sister's, in fact; but her character and temperament are those of Vivie's. Beneath the Hooper features, it seems, even at the age of five, lay her mother's faint restlessness, with its need for gentle bridling, her vivaciousness, and that intriguing ability to charm everyone.

Jumping up and down, singing gaily to herself, and hanging her small hands out the window, Emily Hooper is in sharp contrast to little Thad, age nine, seated complacently beside his father in the front seat. Thad glances at his son, and smiles to himself. To his way of thinking he has everything to make him happy. He loves Vivie and his children dearly—Emily, particularly, gives him most joy, increasingly so as she grows older, so reminiscent of Thel at that age—and Paradise is his home and has always been his home; it's where his friends are —Storey and the others—and his roots.

58

Catching Emily's eye in the mirror, Thad makes a face at her.

The child ignores this. "She is gone but will not be forgotten," she says in her sing-song tone, "until the stairs grow old."

"The stars, big girl, the stars," Thad says.

"Can't stairs grow old, Daddy?"

"Yes, they can. But you remember how it was written on your Aunt Thelma's grave. Stars!"

"I don't like Aunt Thelma. She's dead."

"Now, that's no way to talk at all, big girl. I'm surprised at you!"

"She's dead, though."

"Yes, she is dead," Thad Hooper says.

"Why is she?"

"Only the Lord knows that answer, big girl."

"Lennie Waite talks to the Lord every third Tuesday at three o'clock."

Thad chuckles. "Yes, he does," he says.

"And he has boxes and boxes and boxes of olive pits and some day me and Marilyn Monroe Post are going to steal them away from him."

"Now, now, big girl. You remember what I told you. Little nigger girls can think of lots of mischief to get into, but you're a little white girl."

"Marilyn Post pulls her bloomers down and lets little Thad see her, D.._dy."

Thad flinches noticeably; frowns at the road ahead of him; hears his son say, "Shut up, you bitch!"

"All right!" Thad Hooper snaps angrily. "All right!" He instantly pulls the car over to the side of the road; cuts the motor and swings his shoulders around in the front seat of the car, facing his son, who won't look at him, but looks instead at his hands.

"What did you call your sister, Thaddus?" he barks.

"A bitch!" the boy says belligerently. "Cause that's what she is!"

"Little Thad looks at Marilyn Monroe Post's private," Emily whines, "and he touches——"

"Emily, be still, big girl!"

"Well, he does."

"I do not, you bitch!"

59

"Thaddus!" Hooper's big, square hand reaches out and cracks the boy's head. The boy's hand reaches up and touches the spot, and then drops. He turns his face toward the window, away from his father. Tears sting his eyes.

"I didn't want to hit you, Thaddus, but you're getting too big for your britches."

The girl is silent now in the back seat; watching with fascination.

"You don't know what it means to have a sister, do you?"

"Yes, Dad," the boy says meekly.

"If God took our little girl away from us, how do you think we'd feel, Thaddus."

"Bad," the boy says. "But she's always telling lies . . ."

"I'm not interested in lies now, Thaddus. I'm interested in how you feel about your sister. Do you remember what was written on your Aunt Thelma's grave?"

"Yes, sir."

"Say it, Thaddus."

The boy murmurs: "She is gone but will not be forgotten, until the stars grow old and the sun grows cold and the leaves of the Judgment Book unfold."

"That's all I have left to remember my sister by," Hooper says. "Just that inscription and that piece of gray stone."

"Yes, Dad."

"But you have a real live sister, don't you, Thaddus?"

"Yes, Dad." A tear escapes down his cheek; he brushes it away with his hand.

"Little Thad's bawling," Emily says.

"Quiet, Emily!"

"She's always telling everything I do like that," the boy says.

"Never mind that, Thaddus. You're pretty lucky to have a sister, do you know that? A pretty little sister you can love. You know that?"

"Yes, Dad."

"All right. All right. Then what do you say to her?"

"I'm sorry," the boy says.

"Don't say it to me, Thaddus . . . Say it to your sister."

"I'm sorry, Emily."

The girl looks at him through serious eyes. "Don't cry, little Thad," she says.

Thad Hooper smiles. "Now, that's better. That's more like

brother and sister," he says, turning the key in the ignition and starting the motor. "Now that's a whole lot better."

"But he does," Emily Hooper insists, "and he puts sticks up her!"

The Hooper house, a mile down from the gas station they run, is set off from the road, and surrounded by elms and pines. To the left of it cotton whitewashes rows of fields; and to the right the rise of Linoleum Hill begins. The air that late afternoon in October is cooling, but still not enough for topcoats. A good evening for the barbecue, Hooper thinks, as he swings his Chevrolet up the gravel drive, noticing Marilyn Monroe Post as he passes her, standing barefoot near the edge of the drive dressed in one of Emily's old ginghams, and chewing her dip stick, staring at the passengers in the car. Emily waves and giggles; while little Thad pretends not to see her. And once Thad parks the car in the open under a black-gum, his daughter leaps out and runs down to greet her playmate.

When little Thad starts to ease his slim, short figure out of the door, his father says: "Just a second, son."

"What?" the boys says, with a look of surprising innocence fixed on his face which he always manages when he knows he's in trouble.

"Is what your sister says true?"

"No, it's a dirty lie."

"Now, boy—you watch your tone and language!"

"I don't even care about Marilyn Monroe Post!"

"You don't have to care about a nigger girl to fool around with her, Thaddus. Now I want to know is it true?"

"No."

"All right. All right, Thaddus, but you listen to what I tell you. I was a boy like you once too, you know; and I know the little nigger girls are naughty, and I know little boys like yourself are just as naughty, and I want to tell you something about that. It's not nice for your sister to see you being naughty with a nigger girl, you hear? It's very bad for little Emily, Thaddus. Now, you're a lot older than your sister, big fellow. Now, you got to look out for her. Little girls aren't supposed to know about naughty things, you hear me?"

"Yes, Dad."

"Little white girls got no business ever in their life seeing naughty things. You hear me?"

61

"Yes, Dad. I'm not naughty either."

"Well if you're pulling nigger girls' bloomers down you ain't going to win the Bible in Sunday School!"

"I didn't pull them down."

"Whatever you did. She pulled them down or you pulled them down. However it was, Thaddus—you're a little man, big fellow, and you got to see that your sister is protected! You hear?"

"Yes, Dad."

"Because sisters just don't grow on trees."

"Claus Post has got two sisters and one in the oven; says he knows it's a sister cause it don't kick Bissy's belly none."

Thad Hooper shakes his head. "Boy, I don't know," he says, "seems to me when I was your age I didn't know boo about bellies *or* ovens."

"Claus Post says Bissy ate a watermelon seed and it's going to change into a sister."

Thad Hooper hoots. "That's right, huh? Okay, son!" Then, more serious, he says: "But you remember what I said. I don't want you behaving around your sister in any naughty ways, or talking naughty either. Don't you go talking about ovens and watermelon seeds in front of your sister. Hear?"

"Yes, Dad." The boy shrugs. "I always spit my seeds right out!"

"C'mon now, into the house. We got to see what your mother's been up to!"

Clamping his big arm around his son's shoulders, Thad Hooper starts toward the two-story red brick house. As he nears the side door he sees Major Post come out, carrying the big black kettle Hussie will cook the stew in at the barbecue.

"Hi, boy!" Hoopers calls.

Major barely speaks.

"Who won the ball game, Major?" little Thad asks.

Major mumbles something unintelligible, and keeps on going, his shoulders sagging with the weight of the heavy iron kettle. Hooper removes his arm from his son, and pushes his gray fedora back on his head, spits, and stands spread-legged with arms akimbo.

Then he shouts to Major Post's back: "Just a damn minute, boy!"

"Sir?" Still holding the kettle, Major turns sideways in his path.

"Put that thing down while I talk to you, boy."

Bending, Major drops it.

"Little Thad asked you a question, Major."

"I said I didn't know."

"We didn't hear you, boy. You didn't speak up."

"Thing's heavy," Major says. "Hard to talk and tote too."

"Well, Major, then you should have put it down. You *know* that. You've changed, haven't you, Major?"

"How do you mean, sir?" Major has an angry tone to his voice.

"You have. Don't have a civil word for anyone any more, boy. Don't think you're a picker any more——"

"I work for Mrs. Ficklin, Mr. Hooper. Now, I told you I did."

"I think working for a Northerner's made you uppity, Major."

Major Post looks away from Hooper. "No, sir, working for a Northerner hasn't, no sir. *That* hasn't!"

Little Thad stands quietly beside his father in that interlude of heavy silence between Hooper and Major.

"Is there something on your mind, Major? Something you want to get off your chest?"

"I don't know what good it'd do," Major Post says, and adds, "sir."

"Now, that's unfair, Major, and you know it! Haven't I always got along with your folks? With Hus too, don't forget. With Hus too. And there aren't many in Paradise can say that."

"Yes, sir. You always get along."

"Well, *don't* I?" Hooper's temper is beginning to rise; god-dam sassy-assed nigger; acting like he's one of them high-collared, fly-weight dudes of the East; standing there begging to be whipped when he knows Jesus well he won't be——not by Thad Hooper. That's not Thad Hooper's way with his niggers; never was. Goddam sassy-assed nigger just testing his dander!

"You do, sir. You always get along. I don't have to study that point any!"

Hooper stares at the Negro; the Negro lowers his glance. Hooper stands there staring at him for a minute; not saying anything. Little Thad stands as still as the Negro and Hooper, and the only noise they can hear is the background noise Hus makes in the kitchen, banging pots and shuffling silverware and singing: *"Well, you seen how they done my Lord; never said a mumbalin word; they pierced him—"*

Then Hooper barks: "Nigger! Nigger, pick up that goddam kettle and tote it to where it's going!"

Major bends to pick it up.

"What do you say, nigger?"

"I say, sir. Yes, sir," Major Post answers.

Then he grabs the iron kettle by its handles, picks it up, and trudges out in the direction of Linoleum Hill.

As the two Hoopers start into the house, little Thad says: "Hus is singing 'Never said a mumbalin word.' Must be she's mad at something. Always sings that when she's mad at something."

Upstairs in their bedroom, Vivian Hooper is lying on the bed in her bra and pants, nearly asleep, when Thad opens the door.

"I wish you wouldn't *do* that, Vivian," he says as he shuts it behind him.

"Hmm, darling. Do what?" She stretches luxuriously, and props herself up, leaning on her elbows, her black hair spilling down her back. "What, honey?"

"Sleep half naked. Door unlocked and all."

"Psss—Thad! No one here but Hus."

"And Major."

"Aw, Major. You know better than that."

"I don't know what I know about that uppity nigger. I just met him in the yard and got a taste of it."

"That reminds me, darling, I've got something to tell you. Did Em and little T stay out to play?"

Thad Hooper tosses a light green silk robe at his wife. "Put this on, will you!"

"All *right,* Thad. Thanks for handing it to me."

"The kids could walk in here just as well," he says. He undoes his tie, and jerks it from his shirt collar; then peels off the jacket of his navy blue suit.

"So how would *that* hurt any? Law!"

"You don't think kids are aware of things like that, hmm?" Thad answers, as she gets up slowly and slips the robe around her. "Well, you're damn wrong, Vivian! Kids *are* aware. Brothers and sisters and all—they're aware. Now, don't tell me. You're an only child. So don't tell me. Why, I was aware of things my folks didn't even think I was aware of when I was no bigger than little Thad. And he's aware too. Don't you try to tell me otherwise!"

Vivian Hooper ties the belt around her robe as her husband sits on the bed to remove his shoes. She says, "Oh, I know that. And that's what I want to speak with you about, Thad."

"I remember how Thel used to look at me when we were taking our baths together as babies. She used to look right there at me."

"All kids do that, honey."

"Well, they shouldn't! How do you know! You're an only child. How do you know what kind of ideas it gets them."

"Thad, I want to talk to you about Hus."

"Well, d'you hear what I said? About wearing something when you lie around here. Hmmm?" He reaches out, his face unsmiling, his eyes traveling leisurely along his wife's figure; he touches her belt.

Vivian Hooper smiles at him. His finger stays locked around the belt.

"I hear," she says.

"You shouldn't be all uncovered," he says more quietly. "You never know." His finger slips away from the belt and loosens it. His hand rests inside the robe on the elastic of her panties. "I worry about you, Vivie."

"Aw, Thad. You don't have to."

"I think I do."

With his hand still there she moves in closer to him, feeling his fingers touch the flesh of her stomach—fingers that are cold, but fingers that warm her, long, large ones that rest there on her flesh. She moves in further, so that his hand slips down; she looks at his eyes. "All right," she says. "If you say so."

"I suppose I ought to get dressed now," he says. "No one's coming in suits, are they?"

"No, it's informal. You don't have to yet, though, Thad."

"Well, what's this all about?" he says, as she presses his hand with her own.

"I missed you."

"I've had a bad day," he says. He pulls his hand up and out; rubs it with his other hand. "A lot of bad memories."

"I'm sorry," she says. She moves a little away from him, disappointed, knowing now he will talk of Thel. She pulls her belt around her robe again. "It just seems so long ago," she remarks almost to herself.

65

It seems *what*, Vivian?"

"Nothing, darling."

"No. What'd you say?"

"I just said it seems so long ago—Thel's death."

"I see," he says; miffed; suddenly busy with his shoes.

"Oh, I didn't mean anything by that, Thad. It's just that she's been dead twenty-four years. I just meant that it seems a long time ago."

"So I don't have a right to remember her on the anniversary of her death, is that it?"

"Oh, Thad, honey——" She goes over to him, starts to touch him.

"Keep your hands away!" he says. "Never mind!"

She stands away from him; watching him as he takes his shoes off and shoves them under the bed. "I'm sorry."

"Then change the subject."

"Yes," she says. "I have to, anyway." Walking across the room, pausing at the dressing table and picking up her hairbrush to stroke her hair as she talks, she says, "Thad, Hus is very, very angry."

"Is that something unusual?"

"I think she's quite justified this time, Thad."

"Oh?" He looks up at her, regretting his slight fit of temper then as he sees his lovely wife performing the familiar ritual of hairbrushing which has never ceased to interest him, and fascinate him because of her grace and beauty as she bends slightly and lets the raven softness of the hair hang shining. "How come, Vivie, honey?"

"Little Thad injured Marilyn Monroe Post, Thad," his wife tells him. "This morning, down near the fields on his way to school. He and the Sell boy took a stick and——"

"Oh, that's it, ah? I know about it."

"You *know* about it?"

"Yeah. It's pretty bad too. Emily saw him. Brought it up in the car when we were on our way back. I gave him a good talking to. I told him off, don't you fear."

"I wonder if he even knew what he was doing. He's so young, Thad."

"Naw, honey, he's just that age when he starts getting curious about nigger girls. Nine or ten's when they start. I just don't want him doing any of that stuff around Emily."

Vivian Hooper sets the brush down and walks over near

the bed. She leans on the back of the cushion-covered rocker. "Honey, I hope you made more than that clear to him. He *hurt* Marilyn. She had to go to Doc James."

Thad smiles. "G'wan, I just saw her out in the yard, sucking on her dip stick."

"That may be, Thad, but Hussie says she was bleeding. She was bleeding so bad Bissy didn't pick, but stayed home with her."

"Bissy's lazy, honey. She'd make her own self bleed to get out of picking."

Stepping out of his trousers, going to hang them up, Thad gives his wife's cheek a pinch. "Now, don't you go worrying about little Thad doing a nigger in. Hell, Vivie, all white kids play house a bit with the nigger gals. And the nigger gals love it. Don't you worry none!"

"Not six-year-old nigger gals, Thad. Marilyn Monroe is only a year older than Emily."

"She's a nigger, Vivie. Heck, they're born with their motors running. Now, you know that!"

"But he *hurt* her, Thad. Sticks! What if he did that to a white girl. Or, gaw, Thad, what if someone did that to our little girl!"

Thad Hooper grabs his khaki pants from the bureau drawer and shakes them out. "White boys don't do that to white girls, now, and you know it well as I. It's instinct to get a nigger girl on the ground. Pure instinct. They grow out of it, and you know it. It's a stage they pass through. Then little nigger girls just ask for it."

Vivian sighs. "That's just fine! Just ignore it? So long as Emily doesn't have to see it, just ignore it! Well, Thad, I don't think little Thad even knows what he's doing; nigger girl or white child; and he *does* have a sister, Thad, whom he's around plenty. The same as he's around Marilyn Monroe Post!"

About to step into the khakis, Thad stops. He holds them in his hand and stares at his wife; with big, round, shocked eyes. "What the heck in Jesus are you saying, Vivian?" He walks over to her. "What the heck in Jesus!"

"Just that he ought to be told it's wrong to do that to any girl. Thad, he's a baby yet. He's only nine!"

"No, I mean before that."

"About Emily and him? Well, Thad, they share the same room, and—"

"Is that what you think?" he says in a voice he makes in-credulous.

"Is what what I think? That he's getting curious? Yes!"

"And is what you think that he'd ever—*ever*—do anything to his little sister?"

"Well, Thad, you said yourself a few minutes ago that kids notice a lot more than folks think about members of the family. You said—"

"You know something, Vivie?" Thad Hooper leans against the blue-flowered wallpaper and folds his arms across his chest; stands in his shorts; his white shirt; and his garters holding up his socks. "I think I'm going to allow you to join the Bigger Band. Play an instrument."

She says, puzzled, "But I always wanted to. Why now?"

"Before, remember, Vivian, I said I thought blowing horns made womens' busts get too blowy-looking. Too top-heavy. Well, blowing horns *do* do that, but I've got half a mind to let you anyway. Vivian, you know I think you're dwelling on your-self too much, thinking too much, or being around by yourself. I come home and find you lying naked on the bed and all."

"I wasn't naked!"

"And then you get that funny way you get sometimes."

"What way?" Vivian Hooper's face takes a red color.

"You know what way. Sort of squirmy and wiggly, like you couldn't wait. Like love didn't have anything to do with it."

"Thad, *please!* I don't know what you're angry at, but please!"

"You know full well! I come home and find you naked on the bed and then I find out you're feeling that funny way, and you get that injured air when I don't indulge your way, and you *know* I just got back from Thelma's grave. You *know* that. But that doesn't stop you feeling funny, not even *that*. Like an animal!"

"Thad!"

"Yeah, Thad! But that didn't stop you. What'd you think I'd be wanting to do on the anniversary of my twin's death, hah? Did you think *that?* Was that why you had to get so nasty and make the remark about how she's been dead too long to be mourned any more? Did that feeling make you say that?"

"I didn't say that."

"No? I thought you did . . . And then the next thing you said is very interesting too, Mrs. Hooper. The next thing you

68

went about suggesting was that little Thad was going to be doing dirty things to little Emily!"

"Oh, gaw, Thad! That's not true!" Vivian Hooper shoves the rocker hard; walks away from it, so that it stays rocking in the center of the floor, while Thad remains leaning against the wall, watching her.

"As if to profane *any* brother and sister relationship there is, huh?" he says.

"I'm not going to stay here and listen to this, Thad."

"I'm all through saying my piece, Vivian. You better think about it. Maybe a French horn's what you need right about this point."

Vivian Hooper starts for the door. "I'm going down and see how Hussie's coming with the stew," she says.

Thad Hooper reaches out and catches her arm; jerks her back.

"You're not going out of this room in that Cellophane-thin bed gown!" he says. "You're going to get yourself dressed before you go running around!"

She looks at his hand, wrapped around her wrist. She says quietly; crisply: "All right, Thad, let go of me so I can dress."

He does and then goes to the rocker; stops its motion and sits down in it, starting its rocking again. He watches her.

Undoing the robe, Vivian Hooper hangs it in the closet. She reaches into a bureau drawer, takes from it a white satin garter belt, and slips it around her waist, tucking the elastic garters through her pants. She slips stockings over her feet and up her slim, long legs, fastening them to the garters, smoothing the seams. Then she pulls a white nylon slip over her head; and afterward, reaches for a cherry-colored cotton dress, which buttons in a row of infinitesimal pearls all the way down the front. Fixing herself in this, she slips her feet out of her white mules, and into heels.

He says nothing, but rocks in the chair, its slight squeak loud in the quiet room. Pausing to check her reflection in the full-length mirror and to touch her lips with a red stick and to powder her face, she runs a comb through her hair before she turns to leave the room, feigning complete ignorance of his presence there.

As her hand touches the knob, Thad Hooper says: "Vivian?"

"What?" She does not look at him.

"Turn around," he says.

69

She turns and looks at him coldly.

"Come here, Vivian," he says. His lips tip in the barest grin.

"There's a lot more to do than quarrel, Thad."

"Come here!"

"Thad, I don't like the way you talk to me."

"Are you coming over here?" he says.

"No, I am not."

He says, "Oh, yes you are," and getting up he takes three long steps to her, jerks her arm, and brings her back to the center of the room.

"Thad—"

"What'd you put your clothes on for?"

"You said to, didn't you?"

"Now I say *not* to."

"Thad, listen—"

"*You* listen," he says. "You listen to me! You get yourself undressed!"

While down in the kitchen, Hus sings:

> "*God knows they pierced him in the side*
> *He never said a mumbalin' word,*
> *Not a word, not a word . . .*"

And Major Post out on the hill kicks the kettle, cusses, grabs his toe, grimacing.

"You took your bloomers down," Emily tells Marilyn Monroe Post.

"I knows that," the child answers. "Doc James gave me a dip stick. You ain't got any!"

While the pickers come from the fields.

"Hey, Claus Post, wait!" Little Thad calls to his playmate, running toward him, grinning, "Claus, wait for me!"

Claus Post turns; begins to smile gladly, then remembers and says, "I can't play with you no more, little Thad. Hus don't want me to no more."

"Huh?"

"No more, cause what you done to my sister."

"Huh?" Little Thad pauses halfway to his buddy; looks at him, stunned. "Huh?"

"No I cain't. I got to go home."

70

"What?"

"I cain't and that's the law, cause Hus say you dirty naughty boy!"

"You listen to me," little Thad starts. "You listen to me. You. You. You *nigger!*" little Thad shouts, and stands there shouting it. "Pick up that goddam frame of yours and tote it where it's going."

Claus Post begins to run.

"Nigger!" little Thad raves. "Bitch! Bitch! You ovenbelly bitch!"

Up the road, Bryan Post, heading for the pickup he's got to fetch his kin from up North in; the pickup he's going to borrow up at Hooper's house.

While in their room Thad seeks the adjacent flesh, and she yields to him in a sigh that is his name.

10

Millard stares out the plane window of the immense expanse of white sky, and then shifts restlessly in his seat, bored and tired of sitting still silently.

Beside him the large man reads a copy of True, *turning the pages noisily; sighing from time to time in an impatient sound; and trying to catch the eye of the hostess by wagging his finger toward the cockpit, near where she stands. Finally he reaches across Millard and punches a bell with his thumb—three quick jabs.*

"Does that call her?" Millard asks.

The man ignores the question, and resumes reading.

Shrugging his shoulders, Millard pretends to whistle some melody softly and glances down at the postcard he is attempitng to write to Toe-In, and lifts his pencil. Under how's it hanging, *Millard prints:* The poor bastard riding next to me has the shit scared out of him. Crazy! Man, Crazy!

"I'm sorry, sir," the hostess says apologetically, candy-toned and smiling at the man. "I'm going to bring your lunch right away."

"Look," he drawls, "aren't there any other seats in the back of this plane?"

"I'm sorry, sir. We're filled to capacity."

"This is really something, I'll tell you!" he says. "This really is!"

"I'm sorry, sir."

She smiles again and goes back down the aisle, and Millard glances at the man. His face is all red; poor sucker, Millard thinks. Then, seeing the pillow squeezed in the pocket of the seat in front of him, Millard grabs it.

"Here," he says, pushing it at the man.

The man looks startled. "What the hell is this!" he bellows indignantly.

"For your lap," Millard answers. "To put your tray on when it comes." He smiles at the man. "It'll make it easier for you."

For a moment the man stares at Millard; his eyes derogatory. Millard looks back at him, puzzled.

Then in a swift and violent movement of his big body, the man sweeps the pillow to the floor and kicks it over in front of Millard's feet. And in some fast and hotly trapped flash of thinking, Millard's mind says, You big fat sloppy jew-kike; you goddam yid, you—you—before words stop coming to his brain. The hands that offered the man the pillow slide under Millard, and he sits on them numbly, turning his head toward a sky that is suddenly unbelievably all white.

11

LATE that afternoon, driving back from the site of one of the captured stills, Colonel Pirkle half-consciously composes the lead he intends to use in his write-up of the bootleg crackdown for the *Herald:* This morning the country jail yard in Paradise looked as if the sheriff had gone into the used car and taxi business. . . .

It did too. There were six taxicabs, two trucks, and five private cars lined up in the yard. Chuckling a little as he remembers the scene, Colonel nonetheless stays staunch in his belief that there has been altogether too much laxity on the part of the courts in the moonshine drive. Despite the fact that the law did manage to confiscate and impound the machines transporting the "shine," and to arrest fifteen men and one woman involved in selling, transporting and possessing it, Colonel, as well as everyone in Paradise, knows that before the ink is dry on the bonds posted the defendants will be back in business. That is one reason he had driven out to see the still; to check first-hand on how effectively the agent had destroyed it, and to confirm his conviction that the agents had done a thorough job, and that it was not they who were responsible for the perpetual recurrence of bootlegging in the county, but some of Paradise's own law-enforcing citizens. That really made Colonel angry.

Colonel is a medium-sized, solid-looking man in his early forties; a man who keeps Horace Greeley's quotation about the function of a newspaper Scotch-taped to his desk blotter:

THE BEST USE OF A JOURNAL IS TO PRINT THE LARGEST
PRACTICAL AMOUNT OF IMPORTANT TRUTH—TRUTH WHICH
TENDS TO MAKE MANKIND WISER, AND THUS HAPPIER—

Beside this there is a picture of Dix and Suzie taken outside the Methodist Church right after Joh had married them; a photograph of Ada taken the very afternoon she had surprised him by coming down from Athens and announcing she'd marry him if they'd elope immediately.

Resting on top of the blotter is one of Dickie's baby shoes, which Colonel had sent off to Atlanta to have dipped in bronze and made into an ashtray. . . .

Colonel drives slowly in the dusk, drinking in the sights and smells of the country surrounding Paradise, seeing not the drab and dreary look of the landscape as a whole, with its red dusty roads and unpainted shacks, from which television antennaes protrude, its gray houses with overgrown lawns where broken rockers rest to be rained on, and its worn-out barren poor look. Colonel sees singular things that spell home to him, and the approach of late fall—dying goldenrod, and sycamore leaves dancing in the dust a car makes, hay stacked in fields, cotton in fields and beside it the pickers who stay late still bent over the crops, and on the road now and then a truck filled with the cotton going to be ginned. At the crossroads he sees Hooper's place, and turning off into town, he sees the colored school up on the hill.

Whenever he sees that school, he becomes irritated with young Dix for Dix's support of Senator Henderson. Colonel and Dix don't disagree on very many issues, but on this one they do. What surprises Colonel about it is that Dix has been back and forth to the colored school a few dozen times—even written up an interview with the James girl for the *Herald;* and made any number of speeches at the P.T.A. and Masons about the loathsome conditions.

"It's going to stay that way as long as we got a fellow like Fred Henderson in," Colonel had argued with Dix. "Now Fred's a nice fellow, mind—I don't have a thing against him. But he's too busy worrying about the international situation. He's putting fires out in houses across the street and *his own* house is on fire, Dix. You know the Nigraw school's a filth pot!"

Dix said, "Sellers won't do it any faster, Dad. The Negro school is up to us locally."

"There's where you're wrong, Dix," Coloned had insisted. "Now you know damn well there's no one more in favor of states rights than Governor Tom Sellers. He speaks right out

74

against segregation too! Fred don't do that! No siree, Dix. Sellers will get things done in our state. He knows goddam well that if we don't get to providing equal rights around here, we're gonna have those Nigraws going to school right alongside the whites. And, Dix, that just ain't fair to the Nigraws. It'd give 'em all inferiority complexes, and stir up a whole whale of trouble. Now you know that!"

The colored school is a two-room shack set on the hill; heated in the cool months by two black potbellied stoves. Twenty-two years ago, in a flush of public enthusiasm, it was painted bright red, but since that time the weather has eaten away at the paint and on into the wood. Five years ago a citizens emergency committee headed by Bill Ficklin erected a new outhouse for the girls, because theirs had been swept away in a wind storm and they were using the same one as the boys.

"I don't see what the hell difference it makes," Doc Sell had argued at the town meeting when the proposal came up. "Them niggers ain't shy about doing it in front of each other. They ain't like us."

Joh Greene had cinched the proposal by saying, "But we got to provide them with the chance to be like us. If they can't, they can't, but we got to give them equal chance. So I say put the outhouse in. If it's never used, no one can say it's because it isn't there to be used!"

In his editorial supporting the outhouse proposal, Colonel had written: "It's a step in the right direction, and there are still bigger steps to be taken. The colored school in Paradise stands up there on that neglected hill like a naked beggar-hag!" That's why the school is called the Naked Hag.

"Well, anyhow," Doc Sell had laughed when he read it, "can't say that's a hag without a pot to pee in."

Driving down East Street with its rows of comfortable frame houses, with their lawns and dying flower beds looking bleak after the summer's bloom, Colonel parks in front of his own two-story yellow frame house. As he goes up the sidewalk he notes with some irritation that the lights are on in every room; and remembers Ada's insistence last month, "I don't know how the electric bill grew to that size, Pirk. Must be the meter's off kilter!"

Opening the door, tossing his cap on the straight-back chair in the hallway, Colonel calls, "Dix?"

He listens for an answer. Then he calls, "Ada?"

Walking back through the hallway and into the kitchen he sees Cindy, the maid, holding Dickie on her lap as she spoons strained spinach into his mouth.

"Hello, Cindy," he says, walking over, removing his handkerchief from his pocket and bending to rub off a drool of the liquid from the baby's chin. "Hi yah, Dickie-bird. Hey, boo! You're drooling!"

"Ain't gonna do no good whiping it off, Mr. Pirkle, sir. He just gonna drool more."

Cindy is a tall, skinny Negro in her twenties, a pretty, lazy-looking girl with a beanpole shape and an almost too placid disposition. Often her complacency irritates Colonel, as it does now when she answers his question: "Cindy, where's Mrs. Pirkle?"

"I guess she's upstairs."

"What do you mean, you guess, Cindy? Is she or isn't she?"

"Was the last time I looked, Mr. Colonel."

"Did she tell you to feed Dickie?"

"I reckon I don't have to be told no more," Cindy answers, heaving a long sigh.

"Dix isn't home?"

"No, sir, Mr. Colonel. He ain't come in all afternoon."

"Well, what are all the lights doing on?" Colonel snaps impatiently.

"I guess they was left on, Mr. Colonel."

"Well, I guess they'd better be left off, Cindy! I'm not a millionaire who can afford to be paying thirty-dollar light bills every month."

"Yes sir."

"When there's no one in the room, the lights should be out."

"Yes sir, Mr. Colonel."

"I'll see you at bath time, Dickie-bird," Colonel says to the baby. "I'll bathe him tonight, Cindy."

He leaves the kitchen and starts up the spiral staircase, portraits of his grandfather, great-grandfather, and their wives, staring at him from the wall, along with the framed letters from John Howard Paine and John Paul Jones. Outside the door of his and Ada's bedroom, he waits a moment to still his anger. He realizes he is really angry over what he anticipates, and not

76

simply over the fact of the lights being on all over the house and Cindy's vague responses. Once inside the room, he sees he is justified in his anger—what he anticipated is so.

Ada sits at her vanity in her slip, before the large leather-framed photograph of Dix, by the mirror. She has a glass in her hand but quickly pushes it under the green taffeta skirt of the dressing table when she sees him come in. She gets up unsteadily, trying to mask her consternation in a sudden vivaciousness.

"Oh, are you home, Pirk? I just got in and I was going to dress and—" She sways toward him, and Colonel, conscious of her breath, draws away with an almost unintentional gesture of distaste.

"What's come over you, Pirk? You'd think something was wrong with me, the way you're acting."

"Ada, you know I try to understand but I can't see why you have to—"

Ada looks at him with that specious expression, lips pursed slightly, eyebrow raised, eyes falsely surprised, and her choked voice reflects injured dignity. "Well, really, Pirk, are you accusing me of drinking? You know I hardly ever touch liquor. But tonight I thought I'd just have a glass of wine—I was so tired today that I thought it would help me relax. And it did."

"Ada . . ."

She turns back to the vanity, lifts the top of the powder box and begins to powder her nose with exaggerated care. She hiccups loudly and clamps her hand over her mouth.

"I ate asparagus this noon for lunch," she laughs. "Sparrow grass, as Cindy always says. It never agrees with me. I was just going down to feed Dickie. Dix has been gone the whole afternoon. I wonder where he is." She stands up cautiously. "I hope he'll come along to the barbecue. Vivie wants him to real bad. She asked special that he come."

"Dickie's being fed, Ada. You stay up here. I'll bathe him."

"That's my job. He's *my* grandson, after all."

"He's ours. I'll bathe him tonight."

"Ours, ours, ours," she says in a sing-song tone. "No, really, Pirk, you *will* make a scene if you can, won't you? Now I'm just going right on down and—"

"Please," Colonel says.

"Leave me alone. I'm very relaxed. I was just going down to feed Dickie."

"Listen to me."

She stumbles toward the door, but Colonel catches her by the arm. "I don't want Cindy to see you like this. Be reasonable, Ada. Do you want it all over town?"

"What do you mean by that?" Ada maneuvers out of his grasp, her voice becoming louder and tinged with hysteria. "Because I have one glass of wine or maybe two you're implying that I'm drunk. Me, drunk! I don't drink bourbon. You know as well as I do that you're the one who drinks bourbon in this family. I had two glasses of wine and I don't see anything wrong in that."

Colonel frowns; then his voice softens. He runs his hand along her bare arm. "Look, Ada, you get some rest, hmm? You've had a busy day. Now you rest yourself up and we'll see about whether we want to go to the barbecue or not, hmm?"

"Dix is invited. Vivie wants him to come real bad. She asked special." Ada sits down on the bed where Colonel steers her. "I worry about Dix and where he goes nights. If Suzie were only alive, I wouldn't have to worry. I worry about Dix."

"That's a good girl," Colonel says. "You get some rest."

"Suzie used to try and boss Dix like she was his mother or something instead of me, but I worry about Dix now. He alienates himself, doesn't he?"

"You get some rest, Ada, honey, there's a good girl." Gently Colonel pushes her head back on the pillow of the twin bed, pulls her feet out straight, and covers her with the comforter at the foot of the bed. "I'll be back up soon, Ada, honey. You rest."

When she shuts her eyes he knows she will sleep, and quickly, so as not to disturb her, he slips out the door.

On his way back down the stairs, Colonel wondered again how this problem had come upon his house. During the war years when Ada and he, and Dix, who was no more than a boy then, were traveling from one base to the next, both Colonel and Ada had downed more liquor than was their custom. Restored to civilian life, things quieted down and became as they were before in Paradise when he and Ada drank at parties. Sometimes, at a barbecue or on a special occasion they might even drink too much. But so did most people. It was only after

Dix married Suzie that Colonel noticed Ada was getting high more and more often.

For a short while after Suzie's death, she stopped abruptly; and seemed her old self again, but just as abruptly some six or seven months back, she resumed the habit.

She had had a brief lapse one afternoon when she had driven to Manteo with the Hoopers for the flower show. She had arrived home fairly drunk, but eager to snap herself out of it, and intent upon bathing little Dickie. There was an accident. Dix had come home to discover Dickie had been dropped from the bed, and he had said something to his mother about "being at it again"; while she had wept bitterly and sworn she was only trying to help. That was the point, Colonel guessed roughly, when she had returned to the bottle.

Colonel once again tries to understand the problem. Where did it start? And why? Somehow it was rooted in her relationship with Dix, he realizes, and in a certain insidious way it had developed into resentment over the fact of Colonel's closeness to his son and of Dix's tendency to take after his father. Still, neither Dix nor Colonel had ever excluded Ada from their lives until she had begun her drinking. Only now and then were there clues that she felt deserted by them—and by Suzie too.

There was that embarrassing time at the Legion picnic just after Dix's marriage, when Ada, dead sober in that moment when Storey Bailey walked up to Dix and Suzie and Colonel and Ada, sitting there on the blanket at the fairground, had blurted out: "Dix isn't at all like his father!" after Storey had said, "I swear, Dix, you sure favor your old man in every way."

And to make it worse, Ada had added: "Or he never would have married Suzie."

All of them had laughed it off bravely; but afterwards when Colonel and Ada were driving home alone—Suzie hadn't wanted to leave with them; so Dix had stayed on—Colonel had asked Ada: "What'd you ever mean saying a thing like that?"

And Ada had said, "It just popped out. I don't know why I said it."

"You're not jealous because my own son takes after me, honey?" Colonel had teased.

"Hardly," she'd answered.

"That was pretty mean to say about Suzie. I think they

should have waited too—but it wasn't nice, Ada. Suzie was hurt."

"I meant it another way," was all Ada said. Then tiredly, she added, "Let's change the subject, Pirk. I'm sorry for it. I can't worry it any more than that."

Once she started drinking in earnest, Colonel began to notice things that undermined his previous conceptions of his wife. Of course, she had always been whimsical and compulsive; even in the way she married him, after going with him less than two months; begging him to elope with her the Saturday after Thanksgiving, telling him then it was "now or never." And she had always been brighter than he was; quicker to criticize things, and hungrier for voiced affection. But the drinking had created in her times of unexplainable malevolence, times when the alcoholic fuse caused an explosion of unseemly anger.

"Don't you care about anything but crass politics?" she would accuse him suddenly when he would be simply discussing with Dix a bill before Congress or a local legal problem. "Don't you ever read literature?"

Or, "Sure, you were in the war," she would intrude on a conversation about veterans' rights, "right behind a desk, in Topeka, Grand Rapids, Washington, and all those other bloody battlegrounds!"

And how often would she say: "Pirk, you just roll over and grab a hold of them like they were cows teats. Can't you ever say anything nice?"

"I *love* you, honey," he'd tell her. "I tell you all the time I do."

"I like to know *what* you love about me," she'd say; and then anger him by adding, "and I'm afraid I do." He was never quite sure what she meant by that remark, but he knew she meant somehow to suggest a crudeness in him, a clumsiness, or an animal quality to his love for her. He resented that more than anything else; for often during those drunken interludes in their life, he had reached out for her more dutifully than desirefully; the reek of her stale liquor repulsed him as he tried to recapture what had been lost between them, with the one remaining consolation he knew he could give to her—his manhood, if he imagined some other faceless woman skillfully enough to enable him to have the body of the woman under him.

80

When he thought about it, he realized that before the drinking, their love-making had never been particularly inventive, prolonged, nor absorbing. Consistent, it had been, and, Colonel thought, comforting too. Perhaps that was the most appropriate adjective he could apply to Ada and him in bed together. But now even that was gone. They occupied twin beds, and neither spent any amount of time in the other's, save for the few nights Ada would ask him to "just hold me for a while," or those when he would go to her for relief, and she would let him.

Sometimes when Ada was very drunk she would dwell on the day she and Hollis Jordan were discovered in the woods, way back in time—too far back for Colonel to believe that that incident had anything to do with Ada's present condition. It was, to his mind, her way of shifting the focus off her present emotional problems to past ones. But what were the present ones? Menopause? Not yet; not nearly yet. A basic inability to fit into the idle warmth of the clubs and committees and social activities of the women of Paradise? She had never really fit in there, even though she had never known another home but Paradise. But she had compensated for it by being a superior cook, an avid reader, and a doting mother—and even though she wasn't "one of the girls" in Paradise, Ada had been truly respected and liked before all this. She had been happy . . . No, it's Dix somehow, Colonel thinks.

Walking into the kitchen, he stands by the table where Cindy is spooning the last of the spinach down Dickie's throat. He makes odd noises with his lips to attract the child's attention, and he talks to Dickie: "Hi, birdie. Oooh, git that worm down you before the other early bird comes along. Atta boy!"

Cindy says, "His appetite's sort of shacklin. D'you find Mrs. Pirkle, sir?"

"Umm-hmm. She's napping, so I won't wake her. I'll bathe Dickie."

"Well, I'm glad she's napping anyhow," says Cindy, not at all fooled by Colonel's offhand tone. "She could use a nap."

"You remember what I told you about those lights, Cindy," Colonel answers sharply. "When I take Dickie up for his bath, you turn them all off except in the living room and out here where you are!"

"Wasn't me had a mind to light up the place like a Christmas

81

tree," the girl murmurs. "Wasn't me turning them lights on one right after the other."

"Never mind who it was."

"I don't mind, Mr. Colonel, sir. I keep my mouth closed."

"Okay, Dickie-bird," Colonel says. "Let's climb the golden stairs to beddy-by."

"I ain't no broadcasting station," Cindy says.

"C'mon, Dickie-bird. Up we go!" Colonel reaches for the child, while Cindy wipes his mouth.

"One thing for sure," Cindy says as Colonel walks out of the kitchen. "I don't carry no tales back to school."

Colonel resists the impulse to tell her to shut up about it; then he stands still. Ada has come down the stairs, and stands there facing him at the landing; still dressed in her slip and barefoot. Walking past him as though he and the child do not exist, she goes into the kitchen, weaving.

Cindy moans: "Oh, now, Mrs. Pirkle, what you doing sashaying round like that?"

"Where's Dix, Cindy?" she asks, as Colonel stands holding Dickie in the doorway.

"I don't know where he's at, Mrs. Pirkle. You gonna catch your death with your feet all naked. You oughta go on back upstairs and put shoes on, ma'am, so as you can—"

"Oh, shut up," Ada says, lurching into a wall. "Make me a big cup of coffee."

"Ada, please. Go up and get a robe, Ada. Go up and lie down."

"You left all the lights on, Mrs. Pirkle, and Mr. Colonel—"

"Cindy, make her the coffee," Colonel commands. "Then go up and get her robe and slippers. I'll be down as soon as I get Dickie off."

Ada hiccups, turns around—focuses her eyes on her husband and grandson; then, giggling, she starts toward them. "Dere him is! Dere am itsy snitchy Dickie, isn't him?" She reaches out to touch the baby's cheek, but Colonel steps away.

"What're you trying to do, for Christ's sake!" Ada shouts. "He's *my* son!" She lurches forward again, bumping into Colonel and the child; and the sudden movement frightens the child, so that he begins to cry.

With drunken self-pity, Ada turns from them and starts back to the kitchen table, murmuring, "Look what he made me do. I scared the baby, Cindy. He made me scare my baby—" She sinks onto a kitchen chair and holds her head with her hands.

"Make her some coffee if she wants it," Colonel says. "I'll be down as soon as I can, Cindy."

"Lord, Lord," Cindy moans, as Ada sobs at the kitchen table, her face buried in the crook of her arm. "Working this house gonna turn me inta a nervous wretch. Lord, Lord."

Upstairs, Colonel undresses his grandson and soaps the child's body. He loves to bathe Dickie, the same as he had loved bathing Dix, when Dix was that age. With care he runs the cloth along the little dime-sized red birthmark beneath the baby's stomach, with wonder again at its perfect roundness, like a cherry embedded under the skin—a birthmark exactly like the one Dix has there. If only Ada could realize this feeling, he thinks, this fabulous feeling for her own blood, she would have less reason to ask questions of the bottom of a bottle.

From the hallway, Colonel can hear Cindy's voice drifting in, as she shuffles down to the bedroom to get Ada's robe and slippers, talking to herself the way she does when she's excited about something, going along talking to herself: "Lord, oh, Lord, dat woman sure done filled up on giggle soup today; down there shooting her mouf off, trying the worst way to git that coffee cup past them teeth. Lord, she sure walking out in high cotton this night . . ."

"Cindy!" Colonel calls out from the bathroom, "never mind the commentary, just do what you have to."

"Yes sir, Mr. Colonel sir, I'm studying it fast as I can . . . Lord, Lord, dat woman sure am feeling her oats; dat licker sure talk mighty loud when it get loose from de jug. Lord, Lord, Lord, this house gonna turn me inta a nervous wretch. . . ."

12

BRYAN POST sits at the tin table in the combination kitchen-bedroom of the Post shack, listening to his wife Bissy carry on while she fixes the hush-puppies; drinking his corn and thinking as how corn and only corn can get the threads and bobbins out of his head. Corn can make the mill seem far away as Egypt, and the hundreds and millions of empty bobbins it is his job as a doffer to cart from the spinning-room seem in his mind like stars, or drops of water in a river, or grains of sand in a field.

Bissy drops the patties into the smoking deep fat in which a catfish is frying, and talks more about how she had called up Daddy Tap Wood, the radio preacher from over in Manteo. She had called to request a hymn, as he allowed listeners to do, and he had promised to play "Lord On The Weeping Cross" for her; and he had thanked her. The call had taken two minutes and cost a quarter, and Bissy had had to walk clear down the road two miles to the Sinclair station to make it, but Bissy would have paid half a dollar and walked five to hear her tell it. "He just say, 'Why thank you, Bissy,' just as nice. He say, 'Why thank you, Bissy. I'm glad you done called, Bissy.' "

Bryan grunts, "Few minutes ago you tole it he just say, why thank you. Now you say he say the other too."

"Well he did say the other."

"Funny you just think to mention it."

"Corn's fried your brains you can't recall," Bissy says, "and you better had pour yourself back in that jug, nigger, if you spects to pick up our nephew from up North t'night."

"I don't see why you gotta spend hard-earned money calling up the preacher on the radio, if you ask me."

"I spend what I earn where I spend it," Bissy says sullenly, "just same as you, nigger . . . Now, g'wan and call in Claus and Marilyn Monroe. These hush-puppies gettin' brown as your behind."

Slowly, Bryan gets up, scratches his arm and raises it to gulp his corn. "You sure didnt' earn nothin' today," he says, wiping his mouth on the back of his hand.

"Somebody had to tote Marilyn to Doc James."

"Coulda picked in the afternoon, if you ask me."

"I pick soon as I can spell able . . . Call 'em now. We gone eat."

"Reason you can't spell able is you gotta be big shot callin' up on the telephone to the preacher."

"Call went right through in no time," Bissy Post says in a wistful tone, looking down at the hush-puppies, browning like winter oak leaves. "He just say, 'Why thank you, Bissy. Why thank you, Bissy,' just as *nice*. He say, 'Why thank you, Bissy. I'm glad you done called, Bissy. I hope you are well,' he say."

Bryan Post giggles and swats his wife's behind with his palm, as he passes her on his way out the door of the shack. "You sure do enlarge the facts of a matter," he says. "You sure do know how to relate and relate."

"Git on there!" Bissy snaps, "I'm not studying sass t'night."

Over the old black iron stove there is a calendar sent the Hoopers every year by the Paradise Feed Company. Miss Vivie always makes a present of it to Bissy, who follows its printed advice and predictions religiously, making Major read off the next day's weather and horoscope every night before bed.

Last night he had read:

A.M. Those of whom you are fond look to you for aid. You now can find right thing to do for them to bring them peace of mind. P.M. Get together with companions for cultural pursuits; music, art, literature. Weather: Cold with seasonable temperatures.

"You better take your coat to your pallet with you," she had told Major. "S'gone be cold, hah?"

And Major had said, "Aw Ma, Ma. Don't you know that calendar is printed up North!"

"Don't matter who prints it if it say the truth. I felt a chill all day."

"Ma, look," Major had said. "This calendar goes all over

85

the country. The Paradise Feed Company just tacks their name on the end. How you think someone can predict weather for all over the country, huh?"

Bissy Post had mulled that one over, going right on with her darning without answering her son.

"And those horoscopes are the same way. How you think the same thing's going to happen to everyone who looks up under Tuesday on the calendar?"

"Well, all I know," Bissy Post had told him, "is I'm not studying no trouble and don't want no one else in this house to. And whatever that means 'bout *aid* tomorrow, better not mean trouble!"

But trouble had come, just the way Bissy was sure it would; come down the hill hollering, and Bissy'd known the nature of the trouble the second she saw her child, the dirt on the back of her dress, known the nature of it before she saw the blood, and thought, Gawd Jesus, not so soon. Not so young.

"They said if I didn't show them they was gonna scalp me with a jack-knife," the child cried, "so I showed 'em and they held me down and took sticks and——"

"Hush, now, Marilyn Monroe," Bissy had soothed her, holding her naked brown body as she stood her in the tin pail in the kitchen and bathed her. "Hush and forget."

And old Hussie, sitting in the rocker and puffing on her corncob, declared, "I won't forget! *I* won't! A baby like that! You wait till I give Miz Hooper a piece 'bout that devil she raisin!"

"They hurt me, Mama. Hurt me awful!"

"Hush, honey, now," Bissy had whispered. "We gonna see the doc soon as you washed."

It had to happen some time; eventually, it had to. Bissy was just glad the first time had been a boy only a few years older than Marilyn Monroe; and not like it had been with Bissy, when she was just ten and a red-faced, fat, poor-white peckerwood, big as a bull, had caught hold of her in the woods on her way from school, forced her on the twig-blanketed ground under him and placed his mammoth hand across her face while he put pain in her she thought she'd die of; and afterwards, running and crying her way back to the shanties of Colored Town, Bissy, the girl, had thought, wait till my papa mop the floor up with that cracker for doin that——not knowing then what Bissy now knew: crackers can do what they please to a colored man's woman, and the colored man loves life better than to say a mumbling word. . . .

Bissy had stayed home from picking purposely, knowing Hussie was in a fit at it; thinking Hussie's fit won't do nothing but stir up trouble, and fearing to be up on Linoleum Hill when it started. She had listened on the radio to the kindly voice of Daddy Tap, feeling some vague reassurance in knowing there was someone bent on fixing the misery in this life, and going to call him up and ask for the hymn had somehow bolstered her spirits—even though her request had already been played, and the program over, by the time she returned home. Then when Bryan came from work she told him what little Thad had done; and she had felt almost completely restored to herself after they had talked about it this way:

"I'll go back up there to Hoopers place an' kill 'em!"

"Naw, Bryan. No good."

"Kill him and his kid, doing things like that to Marilyn Monroe!"

"You gotta calm, nigger. You gotta calm, cause no good's coming of it. The Lord'll show him when death stops him in the road and cuts him down."

"Yeah, Gawd don't need no feeler-uppers or knocker-downers in heaven. Gonna be a black Gawd sittin' judgment on white crackers 'at think black women made for maulin'!"

"They gonna burn. Hell gon smell of white skins burning like barbecue."

"I oughtta kill 'em but the Lord'll do it better, Gawd *knows* that, Bissy!"

"The Lord *will!*"

"The devil's got lots of cheese in hell, now all he need is crackers!"

"An' he gonna get plenty of them!"

"The Lord's writin' it down, sittin' up there an' lookin' down and writin' down everything he sees, and he already wrote in what happens to Marilyn Monroe. An ain't nobody gonna erase the writin'."

"I know it. I believe it."

"Has to be, Bissy. *Has* to!"

"*Couldn't* be no other way."

Thinking back on it, Bissy thinks Major sure gonna bust his gut when he hears it. Major just like Hussie, got fire burning in him. Can hide the fire but can't do nothing about the smoke; smoke's gotta come out in the open, same as with old Hus. Bissy worries thinking about it. It gonna get him into trouble yet. Major don't know he's black sometimes, Gawd help him; hung around with the James niggers and some of it rubbed off on him.

She pokes the hush-puppies and they siss at the grease; and she shouts so Bryan can hear her outside: "It's a mighty deaf nigger 'at don't hear de dinner-horn!"

"C'mon, Claus," Bryan Post's voice booms. "C'mon Marilyn Mon-roe. We got hush-puppies and catfish waitin' on us!"

Coming through the kitchen door, Claus Post asks: "Whatsa oven-belly bitch anyhow?"

"You hush dat language up," his father warns, "or I'll knock you looser quicker'n you kin say Gawd wid your mouth open!"

"That's what little Thad telled me I was when I tell him Hus say I cain't play with him no more cause what he done to my sister!"

"Hush, child!" Bissy says. "Hush! We gone have dinner right off, cause Daddy is gotta fetch your cousin from up North in the pickup."

Marilyn Monroe Post, still sucking on her dip stick, ambles over to the tin table and stands meditating, while Bryan pulls the orange crates, set on end, around the table. "Sit you down, now," he tells her and Claus, "and don't let me hear nothin' but the sound of forks on plates! We ain't studying conversation round here t'night."

"I'm a bitch," Marilyn Monroe Post announces. "Little Thad tole me that too before he hurt me."

"Child, hush!" Bissy tells her. "Hush! Now I got something good to talk about." She forks the hush-puppies onto plates stacked beside the old stove. "I bet you don't know the fact I talked to Mr. Tap Wood on the radio. Yes sir, bet you all didn't have no idea 'bout that."

"Sure she did," Bryan Post says. "She did, she did. An what'd he say, huh, Bissy? Re-late!"

Bissy beams, bringing the plates to the table. "He just say, 'Why thank you, Bissy,' just as nice. He say, 'Why thank you, Bissy. I'm glad you done called Bissy.' "

"He say more'n that, don't he?" Bryan says, fitting his handkerchief under his collar. "What else he say?"

"He say, 'I hope you are well, Bissy.' He say, 'I hope you and your family are right peart.' "

"Sure enough?" Claus asks.

"Sure enough he say that to your maw, boy. It come out right over the radio!"

Bissy sits herself on a crate beside her daughter. "Here, girl, now put that dip stick down and get at them hush-puppies, hmmm?"

"Doc James gave me this stick," Marilyn Monroe tells her father, "after he stopped the bleeding."

"Was you bleedin', sister? I never knew you was *bleedin'!*"

"What else did Tap Wood say, Bissy, huh? Relate!"

"T'morrow," Claus Post declares. "Ah'm gonna do de same thing ta his sister, 'n see how that go over wid dat dumb stupid snowflake!"

Suddenly, without warning, Bryan Post reaches out, grabs his son by the collar and shoves him off the crate, shouting, "You *nev*-er, say that! You nev-er open your big mouth wid dat talk! Nigger boy, you nev-er think dat thought! Goddam it damn! You hear?"

Shocked, incredulous, the twelve-year-old sits on the worn wooden floor staring up at his father, knuckling his eye the way he does before he cries, his eyes wide and frightened and injured.

"No, Gawd," Bissy moans, getting off her crate, stooping and pressing the boy's body against her own. "Gawd, Bryan, tell him another way. Don't beat facts in when all he wanna do is love his sister."

Standing now, his back turned on his family, head hung, Bryan Post mumbles, "Got to beat dat fact in. Got to be no mistake bout dat fact. Dat's sure."

"What else the preacher say, Mama?" Marilyn whines from the table.

Still kneeling with Claus pressed against her, rocking back and forth gently, now slowly, Bissy Post makes herself begin again, "He say, 'I hope you and your family are right peart—' "

"You say he say that already," the child whines. "You already *say* he say that."

"And he say God looking out over Claus Post, Marilyn

Monroe Post, Major Post, Bryan Post—the whole Post family, cause he say God knows we good people."

"Why, sure enough he say that," Bryan Post says softly, returning to the table, straddling the crate and raising his fork from his plate. "Sure enough," he murmurs, looking down at his food. "Relate it to 'em, honey. Relate. Relate."

13

At the airport where Millard is to change to the Dixie Airways for the rest of his trip, a porter stops him.

The porter says, "You going in the wrong door, boy."

"Isn't this where I go to get on another plane?"

"Over there." The porter points at a sign which reads For Colored Passengers Only. *"That door."*

Millard frowns up at the sign, thinks, Christ what the hell, laughs a puzzled laugh of dejection and walks into the airport offices through that door. Besides two ministers standing staring out the window at the runway, there are no other Negroes in this small room. At the baggage claim counter a white man stands, talking on the telephone. As Millard walks toward him he thinks how like a baby's the white man's voice is, rattling on in that slurry Southern accent.

"Yeah, now you know dat's a fact, isn't it?" the man is saying, giving a high, giggling laugh. "Why sho I am, hun-ny! Huh? Huh? Yeah? Well, wha you know, huh?" ending every sentence in a question.

Millard stands waiting for him to finish, stands holding his baggage claim ticket waiting. When finally the man finishes he doesn't look at Millard right away, but takes out a magazine and starts flipping the pages.

Millard says, "Is this where I get my baggage from the plane I was on, sir?"

"Now just a minute, boy," the white man says. "I be with you in just a pretty minute."

"Yes sir," Millard says, seeing his suitcase being rolled in on a cart then. "There's my bag now."

"Uh-huh. Well, you hold them horses, boy," the man says, turning the pages of the magazine.

A Negro porter puts the bag up on the ramp in front of Millard, and Millard starts to reach for it.

"Uh-uh, boy," the man says without taking his eyes from his magazine. "You got to wait until I take your ticket."

"I have to catch another plane, sir," Millard tells him. "I have to get on the Dixie Airways flight, sir."

"Well, you just be patient now, boy, hear?"

Millard's shoulders slump in exasperation. He shifts his weight from one foot to the other, waiting, watching the white man. Then he remembers the stickers in his pocket which he planned to paste on his cardboard suitcase, and he takes them out. The round one with the airline's name and the picture of the super-constellation, he turns over, licks, and then reaches out to slap on the old valise. The white man stops reading the magazine.

"What're you doing, boy?" he asks.

"Putting a sticker on my suitcase, sir."

"How do I know that's your suitcase. I haven't seen the ticket yet."

"Ticket's right here," Millard says, offering it to the man after he presses the sticker against the cardboard.

The man reaches down and pulls the sticker, still wet, off the bag. "I can't let you mark up baggage until I know it's yours." The man smiles sweetly at Millard. "You can understand that, can't you, boy?" He wads the sticker up in a ball and tosses it behind him.

"But here's my baggage check," Millard says.

"You should have showed me that in the first place, boy. You understand I can't let you do anything you want to do to baggage unless I know it belong to you." The man chuckles. He takes the check from Millard's hand. "Yeah, you're right. Your baggage all right, I reckon." He keeps his hand on the handle of Millard's bag then. "What you got in the grip, boy?"

"My clothes," Millard answers, bottling up his fury but afraid too.

"Zoot-suits, huh?"

"No," Millard says.

"Up North don't you colored boys wear zoot suits when you go out strutting, huh?"

"No," Millard says.

"You colored boys up North live it up, huh, don't you? Dance and carry on? Huh?"

Millard says, "No, sir. Please, sir, I want to catch my plane."

"Well, you go on and catch it, boy. It's been loading out on Gate sixteen for twenty minutes now. Oh, they know you're coming, boy. Don't you worry none about that."

"Gate Sixteen?" Millard says, reaching for his bag. The white man still holds on to it.

"That's right, boy. You 'member to take the seat up front now, so no one has to tell you, won't you, huh?"

"Up front?" Millard looks puzzled.

"Up over the motors, boy. You know about that, don't you? The colored generally prefer to sit up there. You know, boy?"

Millard understands then.

"Yes," he mumbles, "Yes—sir."

The white man lets go of Millard's bag and Millard picks it up. Pushing through the revolving door, Millard feels for the first time the breathless mugginess of the sticky weather. And when he feels the tears want to come in his eyes, he sinks his teeth hard into his lower lip, battling them back, fighting those goddam chicken tears with everything in him, until he tastes his own blood. And instead of swallowing it back inside of him, he spits it out on the sun-baked Southern soil to the right of the ramp to Gate Sixteen.

92

14

Walking away from the circle made by his guests around the fire, below the brow of Linoleum Hill, Thad Hooper sets off for the top of the hill where the stew and barbecue are cooking. It irritates him that the evening has started off badly, first with the petty incident between little Thad and the nigger kid, which had incited old Hussie's anger, as well as Major's, Thad guesses; and then with the inevitable scene between himself and Vivian, both before and after their lovemaking. Finally, Vivian had deliberately, Thad decides, put on that flimsy blue cotton for the party, put it on knowing full well how it shows her in the front, when she bends to talk to someone or serve someone or stand beside Major at the plank table, his tallness looking down on her, as if to flaunt the very thing Thad had criticized her for after they had risen from their bed late that afternoon and talked while they dressed.

"Can't see what you're getting at, Thad," she had complained. "Isn't it normal to feel like making love?"

"I'm not referring to that now. I'm talking about self-control in everything. The way you dress and take naps and—"

"But you were talking about *that*. You were trying to make me seem like some kind of loathsome—"

"Vivian, please! Don't try to begin an argument."

"No, now let me talk. Let me say what's on my mind. You used the word *wiggle*, Thad. You said you didn't like it when I got to wiggling like a bitch in heat. What did that mean? I don't know what that meant."

"I didn't say that. You're twisting what I said."

"You said *wiggle*. You said I *wiggle*. What does it mean?"

"God damn it, Vivian, you *know*, honey! I just mean people have to—people can't go around without any self-control! You're a grown lady!"

"And grown ladies don't wiggle in their husband's embrace, ah?"

"Vivie, honey, now, *damn!* I just mean you have this little thing about you that is—well, sometimes it's right vulgar."

"Oh, that's good!" She had laughed sardonically. "That one's rich! You stand there and tell me that, and I like to died laughing. You stand there and say a thing like that to me, when you just get through ordering me on to the bed like some tart up in Mary Jane Frances Alexander's cat house! That's good! That's typical! If it's your idea to go to bed, everything's right fine. But if it's mine you manage to make me ashamed for getting the idea in the first place, and then when you've managed to do that and I'm out of the mood, you order me onto my back!"

"Vivian!"

"Well, isn't that true?"

"Vivian, I just—I get sick—sick inside when you speak that way. Use words like that. I don't know what comes over you sometimes. Sometimes I can't believe my ears, or my eyes. Vivian, I seriously mean it. There's something in you that's got to be bridled. Some kind of little worm that's—"

"*Wiggling?*" she'd interrupted him, laughing bitterly.

"All right. All right. Please. Please, not today. Today of all days."

And then she had said the cruelest thing of all. "Oh, yes, lest we forget that paragon of virtue, Thelma Ann Hooper!"

That had hurt. It still hurt. To bring his sister into filthy talk in the bedroom. To mention her name and call up to Thad's screen of memory the vision of the sweetness of the child, his twin, his sister in the womb, and the agony her loss had caused, the recurrent agony pricked by nostalgia for the time when they were young together, growing up as one, remembering only last Sunday in church the robbed and forsaken feeling that had crept through him as Joh read from Solomon's Songs: *How fair is thy love, my sister, my spouse! how much better is thy love than wine! and the smell of thine ointments than all spices!*

It was not anything Vivian could comprehend. It was something, Thad believes, few could appreciate—to lose half of yourself, to have what was joined to you sliced and stolen as though you had done something to deserve it, as though it

94

were a punishment for something you had done. And to ask why all your life and never find an answer. But Thel dead, her body rotten under clay, the young body of a girl given to the dirt while you stand helpless. Why?

In the darkness Thad Hooper frowns, chasing away these thoughts, forcing himself to concentrate on the business at hand—right now, on Hus, how he must handle her and cope with her stubborn wrath. Hooper contends there's no harmony in a house in which the servants are disgruntled; an ornery nigger can create chaos, and while Major is easily enough threatened back into toeing the mark, Hussie isn't. If she's mad enough, the stew kettle will fall to the ground accidentally, the contents spilled and wasted; the pig will slip off the spit into the dust at its side; or some other damage will happen "by mistake" in the preparations for the evening.

At the top of the hill, Hooper mops his brow with the sleeve of his blue wool sweater; then strolls toward the fire and the pit where Hussie stands stirring the stew.

He calls, "Hi, Hus, how you?"

Hus doesn't answer him; puffs of white smoke start from her corncob and spiral up into the night air. She stirs more vigorously, a squat little black woman with wild white woolly hair cropped short and close like a man's. She is black and gnarled and sassy, an "independent Nigra" those in Paradise describe her, and smile tolerantly at that fact, for Hussie Post is very old, born, as she recalls, on the first clear Sunday after General Lee surrendered.

Thad Hooper grins as he comes closer to her; grins and stands arms akimbo as he stares down into the big iron kettle where the Brunswick stew is cooking; and in the pit beside it, the pig roasting over the embers. He and Hussie Post are the only two in sight; the guests are all down below the brow of the hill, and Major too, capturing water from the spring for them to use to chase the bourbon, and helping set up the plank table for eating.

"Hey now, Hus—you mad at me? Huh?" Thad asks as he watches her manipulate the long-handled ladle.

Hus shrugs; she won't answer him.

"Now, didn't you and me always get along, Hussie Post? Didn't we, hmm? 'Member last week when you was ailing and Bissy mentioned to me 'bout that leak in you-all's roof?

95

Didn't I see it got fixed so the rain isn't going to leak in there any more?"

The old woman looks up from the stew to Hooper, takes her pipe out of her mouth, and spits over her shoulder. "Dat roof didn't leak in dere, Mr. Thad," she says. "When it rained it rained in dere, and it leaked outside."

"Well, I got it fixed, didn't I?" Thad Hooper answers, guffawing, always breaking up over Hussie's wry humor. "Now didn't I, Hus?"

"I spect you did, Mr. Thad."

"You and me always got along, Hus, didn't we? Now what'd I do to make you mad at me, hmm?"

"If you knock de nose, Mr. Thad, the eye cry."

The Negro proverb is well known to Hooper. Hurt one in the family, hurt all. He sticks his large hands down into the pockets of his khaki and rocks back and forth gently on his heels, watching the moon off in the sky gilding the cotton fields and outlining the willowy branches of the black pines and dogwoods.

"I spoke to little Thad, Hus," he says, "but now you know kids. They get at that age. An' if a little girl tease 'em, they going to do as they please with her."

"White kids do as they please; colored do as they can."

"Hussie, I'm surprised at you talking that way! You lived in Paradise all your life, now haven't you? You know this is a right friendly town to all folks. We always looked out for you and your family, now, you *know* that. Why, kids get into all sorts of things, Hus, but it don't stop folks from getting along."

"Little girl had to go to the doctor," Hus grumbles.

Thad smiles. "Oh? Well, now why didn't you say so in the first place, Hus?"

"I tole Miz Hooper all 'bout it, Mr. Thad."

"Well, Mrs. Hooper should have told you we'll pay Doc James whatever he charged you, Hus. Don't be worrying about that, for heaven's sake. We'll pay that bill, Hus. Even though little Thad was only *half* to blame. But you got to tell the little girl not to be asking for trouble. Hear?"

Hussy answers, "Doc James didn't charge nothin'."

"Well, then, why are we carrying on so about it, hmmm? Tell you what, Hus. I'm going to see you get a dollar for your trouble tonight. Mrs. Hooper and I appreciate your

96

coming up here to do this for us when you been so sick and all, Hus."

"Got no choice 'bout earnin' a livin' if I ain't studying dyin', Mr. Thad," Hus says.

Thad Hooper chuckles. "Yeah, you're right there, all right, Hussie. There's none of us that has."

He stands quietly beside the old woman, watching the ladle turn up chicken and corn and squirrel, and smelling the pungent aroma of the mustard and vinegar and sugar; red pepper and celery, all intermingling with the good odor of the pig nearby in the pit.

"Sure smells good," he says.

He glances at the old woman, whose expression is stony, her eyes fixed steadily on the stew's liquid, the pipe puffing in short quick clouds of white smoke, her wizened brow wrinkled in one long frown. Reaching into his back pocket, Thad Hooper feels for his wallet, pulls it out with a flourish, holding it up to the fire's light and picking out a dollar. With a quick movement of his long arm, he shoves the money into the pocket of Hussie's patched black apron. Hussie ignores the gesture, bland and indifferent as before.

"Yes sir, Hussie!" Hooper says putting the wallet back. "It sure smells good." He stands there a moment longer. "You sure fix the best stew around here, Hus," he says. "Yeah, you *do!*"

Then finally he turns away from the pot and the pit and the old Negro woman, and ambles back down the hill to the spring, whistling a little and snapping his fingers.

When he is out of sight, Hussie Post hawks again, aiming the spittle so it lands inside the kettle; puts her pipe back between her gums, and wields the ladle in the blending of the stew.

Besides the Hoopers that night at the barbecue, there are Joh and Guessie Greene, Bill and Marianne Ficklin, Storey and Kate Bailey, and Colonel Pirkle, who came without Ada. All of them, except Vivian, sit in the circle with its campfire center, swirl whisky and talk. Over at the plank table, Vivian helps Major Post set out the paper plates and silverware, napkins, and salt and peppers. They stand beside one another near the queen-of-China trees, two candles giving them light; and the moon off in the west helping.

"You seem solemn, Major," she says, handing him a stack of plates. "I'm sorry. Sorry you're solemn, and sorry you have a reason to be."

"I always thought well of *you,* Miz Hooper."

"We've always gotten along, haven't we, Major?"

"Yes, ma'am."

"Major, you have a good mind, don't you? What I mean is, you're more intelligent than most nig—nigra people, aren't you?"

"I don't know that's smart to own up to, Miz Hooper."

"Well, *do* you know what I mean when I say that I don't condone little Thad's behavior?" She hesitates; wondering if she should have brought up the subject to this boy, no more than a boy, really; still, with his grown-up ways, more like a white man than a colored boy, but nigger-like in his sullen, close-mouthed resenting. "By condone, I mean—"

Major interrupts. "I know the meaning of *condone,* ma'am. You don't have to explain."

"Major, I didn't question that." She is irritated for even having broached the subject now; smarting at his defensive hint of belligerence and his glum tone. "You make it hard for anyone to talk with you."

"I'm sorry, Miz Hooper. I know that. And I know you mean well—you more than anyone around here. I didn't mean to sound like I did. I just get the anger all boiled up in me sometimes. When my grandmother told me about my sister, I just saw red, ma'am, and I still see it."

"Of course, I'm not saying little Thad was all to blame," Vivian Hooper says, "but no matter who had what share in the blame, I regret the incident."

Major says nothing to that and she thinks she detects some stiffening in his attitude again, a sudden withdrawal which is difficult for her to appreciate. This spasmodic hostility which lately seems almost a trait of Major's irks Vivian Hooper. It's just as though Major were totally unwilling to be accepted as an above-average colored person, wanting, instead, acceptance as a white. Perhaps Thad is right in his theory that regardless of the Negro's brain power, and despite the fact a few seem to possess uncommon intelligence, a white's never got to let them think they're anything but black; particularly in places like Paradise where the niggers outnumber the whites four to one. A white's got to treat a nigger like a nigger, or the nigger will lose respect for the white and start to take advantage of the white, drop the "sir" and "ma'am" and show his shoulder to the white, and sass him. And if enough of them got away with it, if enough whites dropped their guards, the niggers could just *take over*.

But Vivian Hooper likes Major and wants to treat him right; yet he has an annoying effect on her which seems to result in her feeling somehow obliged to apologize to him for any little thing that goes wrong—like last week, going out of her way to explain to Major why the roofer hadn't been able to get to their shack on Monday; had to postpone patching their roof until Wednesday, and Major answering bluntly: "Well, Miz Hooper, I'm sorrier than you, cause Hus is getting rained on. Could just as well find a roofer who could come on time if we had the money!" knowing Thad had chosen Ed Blake to do the job because Ed owed Thad a favor and wouldn't charge him. Major's reactions to her attempts to placate him—and why did he somehow make her feel she had to!—inevitably make her regret she puts herself in the position of patronizing this nigger.

Between them a silence hangs now; Major seems to slam everything she hands him onto the plank table, in a contemptuous gesture; letting the forks she had just given him fall out of his hands and clank against the wood; some landing on the ground under the table. She sighs.

"Pick those up, Major," she says tersely. "Now they'll have to be washed."

"Yes, ma'am." He bends to retrieve them slowly. Then, pausing as he holds them, waiting for her to notice he has stopped what they are doing together, he says when she glances over at him, "Miz Hooper?"

"Well?"

"I'd just like to say one thing."

Suddenly in that second before Vivian Hooper starts to answer Major, intending to say: "All right, Major, but hurry. We have guests waiting and I can't be here helping you the whole time," Thad's voice cracks the silence.

"Hey, boy, what the hell you think this is?"

Major turns and stares at Hooper. "Sir?"

"People back there waiting for some more spring water, Major!"

99

"I was helping Miz Hooper, sir."

"You mean she was helping you."

"Yes, sir." He speaks tiredly again, perpetually tired and resigned in his tone, his shoulders sagging, stance impatient and slumping.

"You get that jug and get on back there, Major. When you finish with that, you can do the rest of what's here by yourself. Mrs. Hooper don't need to be overseeing the job!"

"Yes, sir."

Major puts the forks on the table, and goes to lug the jug down to the campfire. When he is out of hearing distance, Hooper says: "I'm getting damn tired of that boy. Working for that Northerner hasn't done him any good."

"Shhh, honey, Marianne'll hear."

Hooper regards her coldly. "What you doing back here in the bushes with him anyway?"

"No, Thad, don't start—"

"How come you decided to wear *that?*" He flicks his thumb against her flesh above her bosom.

She looks down at the blue cotton dress, its neck cut in an expansive oval shape dipping down near the crease of the beginning of her breasts, its waist tight, the skirt full and three times petticoated underneath.

"There's nothing wrong with it," she says. "It's pretty, I think."

"For some kind of ballroom, maybe. Not an outdoor barbecue."

"I suppose I should be buttoned up to the neck."

"Wouldn't hurt. If you're gonna be back in the bushes helping a nigger!"

"Thank you."

"You asked for it. Viv, you keep asking for it—for it and a lot of its."

"What started you off today, Thad. Can you tell me that?"

"I come home on a day like today and get sassed by an uppity nigger because my kid done to his sister what he's probably done to her three nights a week and all day Sunday, and then I walk upstairs and get worse sass out of the mother of my children, lying around half naked on the bed with the door wide open!"

Vivian Hooper shuts her eyes and thinks, God help his lies, stands impassively. She knows he has more to say.

"And I'm never going to forget what you insinuated about Thel; what you insinuated about me and Thel."

"Huh?" She opens her eyes immediately, staring incredulously at her husband's fury-ridden face. "What, Thad?"

"That's right, act like you didn't say anything of the kind. The way you act about everything! Pretend you're just little Miss Innocence! Well, we know better, don't we, Vivian?" He smiles sardonically as he stands in front of her, looking down at her. *"Don't* we?"

"I wish I knew what's eating at you, Thad. I don't don't know when you've ever carried on this way this long."

"Oh, yeah. Yeah-uh! You don't know what's eating me. You make all sorts of dirty insinuations about Thel not being virtuous, and you—"

"My God, I never said that—"

"Shut up, will you! Will you close your mouth like a lady should? If you kept it shut you wouldn't let what's in you out for people to see and just get sick at. Well, Vivian, let me tell you something. I'm going to forgive what you said about Thel because I have to. I'm married to you, and you're mother to my kids. I'm obliged to forgive the remark, but I'm never going to forget it."

They look at one another silently. From behind them the voices of their guests sound in the night's cool air, and the slight breeze rustles the branches of the queen-of-China trees; the campfire crackles in the background, and the candles fight the frail wind whipping them.

Thad Hooper says: "I want that dress off before you rejoin our guests."

She puts her hand on the round button at her bosom. "Yes, Thad, I'll take it off right now."

With a sudden swift movement of his arm, his palm cracks across her jaw, the impact of it sending her to the ground.

Behind him, Major Post's voice says: "They got all the water they need now, Mr. Hooper. I'll finish up here."

Hooper stalks past the startled boy wordlessly.

For a moment Major just looks down at her, sitting on the ground, her hands covering her face. Then he goes over to her, asks gently, "Miz Hooper? Can I help, ma'am?"

"He's mean." She seems to say it to herself, though she says, "Major, he's mean, and his mind is rotten. Oh God."

"Can I help you, ma'am?" He bends a little, as if to offer his

101

hand to pull her back to her feet, but waiting for her permission.

"He hurt me, Major. He really hurt me."

"Are you hurt, ma'am? Can I—"

"Yes, I'm hurt. I'm really hurt. I can't be doctored for this one, Major. Here, Major—here, help me—" She gives him her hand, and the boy takes it, tugs her up, stands beside her as she pushes back the wisps of raven hair that have fallen around her face. She rubs her cheeks with her palms, and the spot on her jaw where Thad Hooper had struck her. She stands then as though thinking very hard, oblivious to anything else, one hand supporting her as she leans against the plank table, the other dangling listlessly at her side.

Major waits for a while behind her. Then he says softly: "Is there anything I can do, ma'am?"

"Hmm?" She looks at him. "No. No, there's nothing."

"I'm real sorry, Miz Hooper."

She purses her lips, pondering a moment. Then removes her hand from the table and straightens herself.

"I'll wash off these forks, Miz Hooper," Major says. "Then I guess Hus will be fixing to serve."

"Yes," Vivian Hooper says. "I'm going on up to the house. Yes, tell Hus to go ahead and serve when she's ready, Major."

"You want us to wait on you, don't you, Miz Hooper?"

"No."

As Thad Hooper enters the circle, he seats himself between Storey and Kate Bailey, slapping Storey across the back. "Hey, boy, you all tanked up on that bourbon? Hi, Kate. You look mighty pretty tonight."

"Where's Viv?" Storey asks.

Thad says, "She'll be along. How's the band coming, Kate?"

Kate Bailey's thin face brightens at the mention of the band. She sits cross-legged, her yellow cotton skirt smoothed over her knees, the matching blouse open at the neck where there is a double strand of white beads which her fingers touch lightly as she talks.

"We all hope Vivie will take up an instrument one of these days, Thad."

"Why, I was mentioning only this afternoon I thought she should."

"Band does a whale of good," Storey muses. "But I don't know. I just can't see Viv tooting a horn."

His wife glances at him questioningly. "Now, that's a right silly thing to say, Storey."

"Oh, I don't mean it no way special. It's just that Viv is so—"

"I guess you think she's too wild, ah, Stor?" Hooper laughs.

"Hell, no, I didn't mean nothing of the kind. Wild? Viv?"

"Some get that impression. Girl can't help because she's pretty," Hooper says.

"G'wan, Thad. Viv wild?"

"Sure. Some think so, I guess."

Kate says, "Why it's quite to the contrary. She seems too much like a city lady, is what Storey means, I guess. Though, law, we got Marianne Ficklin playing in our band, and she's from New York City."

"Where *is* Viv anyway, Thad?"

"You're mighty impatient. Guess I got to look out for you." Hooper laughs again and nudges Kate. "How about that, Kate? You and me got to watch out we don't get cut right outa the picture."

"What we really need," Kate says, "is a saxophone player. It'd improve us a whole lot."

"I was by to see you s'afternoon, Thad. Got off early over at the mill. Viv tell you?"

"Naw, she didn't. See what I mean? I got to watch right sharp 'fore my best buddy cuts me out."

"Of course Clara Sell plays sax some, but tuba's her specialty and we really need both."

"Yeah, I was by around three o'clock. Viv told me you was up to the grave."

"You know, Storey, it's funny. You're the only one that ever calls her that, Viv. . ." Hooper chuckles. "Sort of like a pet name."

"Oh, I always called her that. From way back I have."

"Hear that, Kate?" Hooper grins at Storey's wife, who looks at him somewhat bemused. "I think way back they were kind of sweet on each other."

Kate Bailey shrugs; puzzled at the way Thad is laboring the joke.

"Aw, hell, Thad! You was always my idol, f'Chrissake."

"Why all this talk suddenly?" Kate says.

103

"We're just teasing," Thad answers.

Kate says, "Maybe I can go and help Vivie?"

"To tell you the truth, Kate, Vivie's in a little tizzy, sort of. Oh, she'll get over it. She'll be along soon enough."

"You and her had a spat?" Bailey asks.

"Naw, nothing like that. Just some words."

"Maybe we all ought to sing," Kate suggests, "and pep everybody up."

Opposite the Baileys and Thad, across the fire, Joh, Guessie, the Ficklins and Colonel Pirkle discuss the moonshine crackdown. Marianne Ficklin's thoughts wander from Colonel's words— ". . . but out at the one I was visiting this afternoon they got a number ten upright boiler in good condition, and a two-hundred gallon pre-heater and pre-heater unit . . ."—to: thoughts of Major Post, as her eyes follow the dark, tall, sturdy figure of the young boy, the young black boy-man, as he goes back up the hill from the spring, lugging the stew pail. Big nigger, she thinks; big virile strong kind that push against you up North; knee you on a subway with their big strong knees in you. And she thinks of how this morning he was afraid to take a cool drink, so scared he left the ashcans on the lawn and went, scared because he's wild and he knows he's wild with that nigger blood pulsing through his big body. And she thinks of how tomorrow he will come to the house, cap in hand. "What do you want me to do, ma'am?" and of how she could say, "What would you like to do, Major? If you could. Tell me. Go on, Major. I dare you." Big strong, kneeing nigger, the kind that puts his knee right in you during a rush hour—once she had let one do it, just to see. Get a black ape out of the Alabama cotton fields and put him on the 8th Avenue at 5:15 any evening and the nigger in him can't help finding a white girl to rub against; it's all hidden down here behind the goddam sneaking-around servility. "Yes, Miz Ficklin"—but underneath thinking, I got something you want bad, baby. South *or* North, never mind, big strong kneeing niggers know what they got and what you want.

". . . don't you think so, Marianne?" Colonel Pirkle's voice crashes through the wall of thoughts.

"I certainly do, Colonel," she answers quickly. "And before I forget, Colonel. I think your editorial about getting rid of the Naked Hag, in last Wednesday's journal was very well put!"

"Well," Colonel says, "thank you. The way I figure, we got to do something and do it fast. Now, what the Supreme Court says we should do *isn't* that something, to my way of thinking. Not going to solve the problem by a decree which overnight throws down a long line of Supreme Court decisions under which the separate schools were built in the first place!"

Bill Ficklin says: "Hell, Colonel, in a way we have to do things overnight or they'll never get done. You *know* that. You think we'd ever desegregate our schools if such a decree weren't made?"

"Eventually, yes. Yes, Fick. Every generation we've narrowed the gulf between the niggers and us. But the Supreme Court's got no right to insist that in every place, and without regard to circumstances, the whole burden of solving the most difficult of social and political problems, should be thrown at one single generation of school children. You oughtta know that, Fick, as superintendent. You oughtta know what'd happen if we were desegregated in Paradise tomorrow. Why hell, there'd be fifteen black niggers to every white kid. How you think it'd work out?"

"It'd sure be a mess," Marianne Ficklin says.

"That's why I say what we got to do is build a new, modern, good nigger school. And make the white school a private school. Hell, we're good Southerners; we're obliged to take care of our niggers!"

"But will we?" Ficklin says. "That's all."

Guessie Green, who has been listening silently, says in her mild, soft tone, "I believe we *will*. In Paradise we've always loved our Nigraws; we've been tolerant of all their traits, and loved them just like they were our own children."

Her husband, the reverend, nods in agreement. "It's all in the Bible. The Lord said of the children of Cain that he'd put a mark on 'em and all their children would be the servants of servants. We're God's servants and they're our servants, and it's the Christian thing to do to look out for our help, cause we're all good folks here in Paradise. Not like some Southern villages. We're Christians." He puts his arm around his wife affectionately. "Guessie and I were talking driving out here. The only way to sell tolerance of the Nigraw

105

is to be tolerant of his traits. And we got to sell tolerance, cause it's Christian."

Colonel muses, looking into the fire. "Well," he says, "I don't know about Christian or not Christian. The way I feel is folks got to stand by their own, that's all. I believe a man's got to stand by his own."

"Amen!" Joh exclaims. "That's selling my product, Colonel. Amen!"

At the top of Linoleum Hill, Major pauses, the pail hanging in his hand. He looks down on the circle lit by the fire, listens to the noise white folks make, and thinks of Mrs. Hooper. *I'm really hurt; I can't be doctored for this one, Major.* He says in his mind, neither can my sister, white lady, not by Doc James, not by any doctor. But don't you think little Mister Thad is all to blame, no, like you said not *all* to blame; but the other half ain't sister's fault either, like you think. Blame's other name is South, the land where a proud Negro man's got to hold his head up cause if he look down he sees his sister on the ground under a cracker he feels like killing, but can't kill, can't even say nothin' to, or he gets himself killed and takes food outa his sister's mouth. A dead nigger can't keep the cowpeas and fatback on the table, and if the nigger can't feed his own, the white man ain't going to.

Like Hus said when she told him about Marilyn Monroe and he told Hus he'd wring that white neck for little Thad: "Sure enough, Major, s'good idea to choke that little devil, but you'd go and get your own neck a rope and what good that do for us? Posts ain't got no corner on brains as 'tis, widout you gettin' your neck in a noose."

And, "Oh, yeah," Major had said. "Oh, yeah! Where there's life there's hope. Where's there's a tree, there's a rope."

"My, my," Hus had said. "How smart you're gettin' to be."

When he thinks mad, Major thinks it in that way of his that makes it more ironical to use the words and expressions and easy-sounding jargon the white man thinks *niggers* use; because when he thinks mad there's always a white man behind the curtain, raise the curtain and find the reason: white man jumped a colored girl in an *alley, Lord, couldn't say a mumbalin' word;* white man stared a colored boy off the sidewalk to the gutter, *keep him in his place, damn coon;*

106

white man built a new white school that looks like a goddam palace, gave the old desks to the colored barn on the hill, *see how good we is to our little black Samboes learning their wool head the A.B.C.'s so they can spell cotton some day;* white man complained, *Nigger what the hell you mean you only picked a hundred and seventy pounds t'day, you know we're in a hurry, God damn it, now git back, you ain't through by a long shot!* Sing out *Can't pick cotton, massa—whine it like a nigger would—Cotton seed am rotten, haw, haw, haw!* Raise the curtain, Rastus, and find the reason, but *keep yo big mouf shut!*

I'm sorry for you, Miz Hooper, Major thinks—turning from his view below him at the brow of the hill, heading to Hus with the stew pail—but my tear ducts ain't workin' or somethin'. Maybe nigger ducts done gone dry back in Year One. Lawd, dog-gawd, she sure got herself a swat though. Big goddam bull dog with his boy, boy, "Hey, boy! You! *Nigger!*"

Trudging toward his grandmother, the old lady watches him, studying him while he sets the pail down beside her with a clatter and a *whew!*

"Yeah, Major, you don't look any other way but like you was gonna cut somebody up in small pieces and send 'em to the coroner in a crocus sack, col-lect."

"G'wan, Gran, I love slavery. Ain't had so much fun since the hogs et up Harriet Tubman!"

"Here." Hussie pokes her pipe toward the stew. "Take a spit, Major. Get the taste outa yo mouth."

"Gran, I'm going to worry that stew some, but not by *spittin'* in it, I tell you. It's not spit I'm intending for that stew."

The old lady looks up at him. "You ain't goin' to do nothin' else in it while *I'm* lookin'," she says with a gleam in her eye, poker-faced. "So you gotta hold yourself till I turns around."

While the moon comes up over Linoleum Hill and a clock strikes eight in Paradise, down below the brow of the hill Kate Bailey leads them singing:

Still long-ing for the old plan-ta-shun
And for the old folks at home....

107

15

Jim Crow's brass rail divides the grimy yellow-brick-walled station; sign says Manteo *over the paint-peeling wooden ticket window on the white side, and the rows of wooden benches, all empty.*

And a dopey-eyed old Negro porter standing by the bulletin boards that post the train schedules, peers out disconsolately from the peak of a faded red cap, and asks Millard Post: "You looking fo somethin' particular?"

"I just got off the bus from Athens. I'm supposed to be met here."

The old man shrugs, spits a yellow stream of chaw over his shoulder into the spittoon, then shuffles along the floor that reeks of coal-tar disinfectant, to the door, and out.

Millard glances at the clock. Nine-thirty. Bus was late, maybe they came and went already thinking he wasn't coming after all, leaving him stranded in the Manteo station—Christ!

The ticket window on the white side is open; on his side, closed. Millard sees a man standing behind the bars of the open window, flicking through a copy of the Atlanta Constitution, *an eye shield hiding his face and his view of Millard.*

Millard says, "Sir?" Millard says, "Pardon me, sir. I wonder if you could tell me—"

But the man does not raise his head from the newspaper.

Millard sets his suitcase down; looks around him and sees no one else. He looks at the benches, then again at the clock, frowns, and finally walks by the brass rail and up to the window.

"Sir?"

The man raises his head slowly, seeing Millard for the first time.

"What're you doing over here?" he demands, pushing his eye shield back on his head. "This isn't the colored side."

"Yes, sir, I know, but—"

"Well, then, what're you doing here? Get on back, boy."

"I have a question, sir. I just want to know something."

"Look, dark boy, you got no business wanting to know something over here. Now make tracks! You go over there if you want to know something," he says, pointing a skinny finger at the opposite side of the station.

Millard says, "Yes, sir."

He turns and goes back behind the rail, stands looking around him, then picks his suitcase up and carries it to the wooden bench. The white man at the ticket window across from him disappears from sight. Millard sits down, exhausted, weeping-Jesus miserable. He shuts his eyes, rubs them with his hand and then just sits. Wonders what in hell to do now; what in hell should I do?

Fifteen minutes drag up the clock before a door opens on the white side, the man with the eye shield comes out; crosses the rail, and comes up to Millard.

"You're not from around here, are you, boy?"

"No, sir."

"You're from up North, aren't you?"

"Yes, sir."

"You like neckties, boy?"

Millard's hand touches his necktie unconsciously, straightens the knot in it. Must look plenty ugly to this white man, ugly and sloppy after a day's traveling.

"Yes, sir," Millard says. "I've been a day traveling."

"I didn't ask you that. I asked you about your necktie."

"Yes, sir, I know. I straightened it."

The white man raises an eyebrow, skinny little white man, standing in his shirt sleeves eying Millard, a burnt-down cigarette caught between his long, bony fingers. "Around here there's an expression, boy. They say around here a nigger with a pocket handkerchief better be looked after. Same with neckties, I reckon."

Millard just looks at him, scared.

"I wouldn't wear that around here if I was you, boy. Folks going to get the wrong idea about you, boy."

"Yes, sir," Millard says weakly, and pauses while the white man looks at him, looks away from the white man, then slowly undoes his necktie, bunches it up in his hand, and shoves it into his coat pocket.

"You get that suit up North?"

"Yes, sir. In New York," Millard says; sweat on his brow —oh Jesus, what'd I do?

"You must be a big shot coming from up in N'yawk, huh, boy?"

"No, sir!"

"I hear the buildings in N'yawk are so tall they rock. That true?"

"No, sir."

"I hear the niggers up there act just about as tall and loose as those tall buildings that rock. That true?"

"No, sir."

"You know in some places you walk over to the white side wanting to learn information, they learn it to you."

"Please, sir, I'm sorry, sir."

"Oh, I'm not saying this place is like the next. I'm just saying some places don't cotton to pocket-handkerchief niggers." The skinny man drops his cigarette, grinds it out with his heel, and regards Millard thoughtfully. "But you just don't know no better. Up there they don't learn niggers how to act none."

"Yes, sir."

"All you gotta do down here to get along, boy, is remember you're a nigger. We got nothin' against niggers."

"Yes, sir."

"Treat our niggers better than they do up North, but our niggers are niggers and our niggers know it."

"Yes, sir."

"I'm tellin' you for your own good. That little nigger boy works here as a porter been here long as I have, and I feel right fond of that boy and he'll tell you so himself, but I don't like a nigger don't know how to keep his place. That kind of nigger stirs up trouble." ·

"Yes, sir. Thank you, sir."

"You're welcome, boy. Now what you want to know?"

Millard feels a wave of warm relief flood through him, feels almost grateful to this white man. He says softly, *"I was supposed to be met, sir, by my uncle. I was late. I wondered if he came and went."*

"Who's he?"

"Mr. Post, sir."

"I don't know no mister niggers, boy. And I don't know

no niggers that got last names. Now you got to learn yourself how to conduct proper. What's your uncle's first name?"

"Bryan, sir."

"Nickname?"

"I—I don't know, sir."

"An' he's from here in Manteo? What's he do?"

"No, sir, he's from Paradise."

The skinny man sighs. "Hell, whyn't you say so in the first place! Naw, I wouldn't know him anyways. But I don't guess he's been around here. Not tonight. Been real quiet."

"Can I get to Paradise on a bus, sir?"

"Naw, hell no! Only one a day goes there." The skinny man starts to walk away, says before he turns, "You best hitch or walk, dark boy. You g'wan out on the highway and get along's best you can. It's twenty miles, but there's trucks on the route this time night. Sometimes those drivers like company." He looks again at Millard. "But if you're hitching, you better get that New York coat off'n your back and roll up them sleeves, or you're not gonna get no place, nigger, but into a peck of trouble."

"Yes, sir," Millard says. "Thank you, sir."

"You got a long way further than Paradise to go, nigger. Better not be forgetting it."

"Yes, sir," Millard says. "Thank you, sir."

There's the sound of a door slamming, the sudden eery emptiness of a combination train-and-bus station in a small strange town—how many miles from home?—and a clock ticking too loud, and Jim Crow's brass rail shining so Millard Post can see his face in it, at night, in Manteo, Georgia, U.S.A.

Millard picks up his suitcase.

16

"Just what would I be giving up?" he says, knowing even his tone bespeaks the futility of trying to make her believe that what he is saying *is* possible; trying to make himself believe it too, as though now at this moment when they have finished and rest lying beside one another in the Naked Hag, he must promise her something more, and make himself believe he means to keep the promise. And I *do*, Dix thinks, and feels the softness of her long fingers explore his flank, creep upward languorously, loving his flesh.

"Hush, Dixon, darling, hmm? Hush and let's not talk about it now. What's this?"

"A birthmark . . . We've got to talk about it. We can go up North."

"I never noticed. Cute. Looks like a little strawberry."

"Barbara, I mean it. I'm not a kid. Younger than you, maybe, but not a kid. You know it too."

"Yes indeed, darling. You have a child too, hmm, Dixon? You don't want to forget that."

"We'll take him with us."

"Lift up, baby, will you? I want to pull the blanket around us. This is a chilly barn, isn't it?"

"Won't you even listen?"

"Oh, should I, Dixon?"

"I swear we could. I swear it!"

The moon coming in the window high above them is girdled with a crystal rim, giving its light to their bodies, both young and supple and white-looking in the white night rays; but the floor of the Naked Hag is hard as life, Barbara James muses. Out of the beaver-wood walls, and belly stoves with their black claw legs, the blackboards with their chalk dust smell, and the worn hand-me-down desks from the white school, they have made a boudoir; and out of Dixon Pirkle's

112

auto robe, the love bed, with the cracked plaster ceiling its canopy.

She is a small, slender girl of twenty-six, with light golden skin and straight black hair; wide brown eyes, and lips that curve generously through her delicately featured, fair, lovely face.

Pulling the blanket's edge half over her body, she covers one side, leaving the half next to Dix uncovered, showing in the moonlight the crescent thigh, smooth-skinned slim waist, and one of the round pendulous breasts, wondering how long in time it will be before Dixon forgets to mention going up North together so they can live man and wife. Thinking just thank God for Dixon and me being together now; letting her palm travel the strong hardness of his stomach, and not expecting any more than this ever. Thinking that even this is ephemeral, will be taken away too, soon, like everything else, like in the beginning her mother was, and like, as she grew, her color was taken away—she was white in color, but it was taken away by fact; she was Negro. And like Neal was taken, taken away by war, his young, good body made dead by a bullet, his fine mind just stopped, useless.

After college, when she had come back to Paradise to teach at the Naked Hag, her hope had been taken away, too, many times—a day when a student shouted defiantly, "Well what we need an education *fo?* So we gonna be educated cotton-pickers?" Life in back county land left little honest optimism, that day and other days. And a night Doc Sell made an appointment with Barbara James to meet him at his house to talk about new books for the shelf in the Naked Hag, laughingly called the library; and when she went there, and found him alone there with books not on his mind at all, and a two-word greeting when the door shut behind her and he stood leering at her: "Get naked!" She had known optimism was white man's cake, not food for colored, known it that night even while she tried to keep hope married to reason.

Arguing: "Now, Doctor Sell, sir, you're a good man, sir. You don't——" "Get naked, *teacher,* and teach me every way you know to do it. We got all night to do it in and you gonna stay here!"

Pleading: "Please, Doctor Sell, please have some pity!"

113

"I swear I'll rip every stitch of clothing you got on your frame *off* your frame if you don't get busy."

Thinly threatening: "If anyone ever found out, Doctor Sell, sir, they wouldn't like what you're trying to do, sir."

"Didn't them niggers teach you the facts of life in that black college you went to, *teacher?* You think you're white? Who the hell'd blink an eye if they heard you come up to my house and got naked and spread your nigger legs for me? Here, I'll rip 'em off you—" He reached for her—

Resignedly: "I'm sorry you're doing this to me, Doctor Sell. I never thought you were that kind."

"Any man's the kind when it comes to gettin' what a nigger gal can give. Hurry it, up, teacher! Work them hands faster on them buttons!"

Dix Pirkle moves beside her, fumbling on the floor for his shirt and the pack of cigarettes in the pocket; he takes one and sticks it in his mouth and scratches a match. "Barbara?"

"Hmmm?"

"What are you thinking about? You're so quiet all of a sudden."

"Just being quiet. Not thinking, Dixon."

"I mean what I say about us going up North, Barbara. Don't you believe that?" He leans on his side, propping himself on his elbow, watching her as she lies on her back; the blue smoke from his cigarette dancing up above them. "And as far as Dickie's concerned, any place would be better than home is now . . . That's why I was late again tonight, honey. My mother!"

"Drinking more, Dixon?"

"Yeah. Yes. God . . . She was already flying when I got home from Joh Greene's. Then Dad went off to Hoopers' without her, and I had to see that Cindy'd stay with Dickie. My mother was acting real crazy; not drunk—crazy. You know what she was doing, Barbara?"

"What, darling?" She reaches out again to touch him, his fingers close tightly on hers.

"Well, she was calling someone up in the telephone. She'd get him to answer, listen to him say hello, hello; then she'd hang up, wait, and do it all over again. I heard it on the extension."

"Calling who?"

114

"I don't know. Christ, she probably didn't know either. Just bothering the bejesus out of someone. Real insane-acting."

"Poor Dixon."

"And I got mad at her before that, when Dad was leaving for the barbecue. I got mad because Dad said maybe he wouldn't go, maybe he hadn't ought to; and she said, 'You go on. Dixon and me are going to spend an evening without you.' I said, 'I wouldn't spend an evening with you if I had to go to hell to keep from it!' " Dix sucks in on the cigarette; sighs the smoke out, shaking his head. "I shouldn't have said that. I know I shouldn't have, but God, I love my dad. In a lot of ways Colonel's narrow, but I love him, Barbara. You don't know!"

"I think I do, Dixon," she says. "I feel the same about mine."

Her words conjure up in Dix's mind a vision of the doctor; a remembrance of how the doctor was conspicuous in the white people's eyes when Dix was a kid, and the Jameses first moved to Paradise. He sees the small Negro as he saw him hundreds of times, heading down to The Toe for that strange one street in The Toe where the better-off colored live, colored whose backyards aren't waving white folks' wash every Monday, and colored whose hands don't pick cotton, or clutch scrub brushes and mop handles for a living: a colored plumber, a colored insurance man, a colored dentist; oddities in Paradise—and oddest of all, mild-mannered, wise and gentle Doctor Edward James, carrying a black physician's bag, smiling at passersby and speaking in that same way all the Jameses speak, casually and affably, but not presumptuously so, without the hesitating lapses, the slurring inflections and the haphazard Negro expressions coloring his sentences; and remembering Clint Green or some other boy in Paradise pointing him out to Dix, "See him?"

"Yeah?"

"That nigger's a doctor."

"Yeah?"

"Yeah, he's a bona fide M.D.—that nigger!"

"No kidding."

"Yeah, he's got a degree in medicine."

Dix remembering that as he lies after love with the daughter of Paradise's one colored doctor, feeling a sudden aliena-

115

tion from Barbara James then as she said: *"I feel the same about mine."* Thinking of the worlds apart they are from one another, wondering with some unaccountable awe why it is that her mention of herself as a daughter who has a father she loves, just as Dix loves his own, wedges their two worlds even wider apart. It suddenly shows Dix in a new light with her, brighter than the moonlight bathing their satiated limbs, love-wearied and young; a new harsh light that calls color, not even seen, into view: black as opposed to white. Her black family; his white one; forgotten by them both in those moments they had fed on one another's lips and stayed kissing in exquisite pulsation through to the long last kiss; forgotten in the lingering aftermath, as they stayed together in that fond and late embrace; and forgotten, but pushing for recollection, in their conversation when they drew away from each other's worshipped bodies, and Dix swore to himself he could take her North with him the way he was saying he would; marry her; be husband to her. . . .

Silently watching the smoke from his cigarette curl above their intertwined hands, Dix imagines voices of people he won't know any longer say in the future: "Sure, Dix Pirkle went and married that colored doctor's daughter. Went on up North with her, f'Chrissake. Imagine Dix and a nigger living under the same roof like anybody ought to do it! Wonder what color their kid'll be?" And Joh's voice crouching in his memory, whispering: *A man that turns a colored girl, a decent, intelligent, fine colored girl into the object of his lust, turns that lovely girl, whose color is not his, into a nigger in the eyes of all the world.*

I don't want Barbara just for that! I think of Barbara James the way I'd think of—well—Suzie!

Suzie. Suzie and their tender, ripe love marriage, Dix thinks of it with a certain aching sadness; Suzie sweet and naive and silly, whom he had loved less passionately, but more proudly, than he loves this girl beside him. Suzie whom he could take by the hand into the sunlight and see Paradise smile on them together; innocent, shy Suzie, whom Dix had never seen naked in a bright light until he stared at the dead flesh of her corpse, that morning, when she died in the upstairs bedroom and a nurse in white bathed her for the grave.

Suzie and the long dragging days and weeks immediately after Joh had blessed her coffin into physical oblivion; the

116

dragging days and weeks that Dix emerged from, in time, for the sake of his son, wrecking his grief then in work, consoling himself in "causes," until the afternoon he drove the hill to the Naked Beggar-Hag to interview a colored teacher, and found a white-looking, lovely woman.

"Yes, I'm Barbara James. Are you Mr. Pirkle?" and said for the first time ever to any Negro, "Yes, ma'am. I am." He remembered even as he said it, a voice from his boyhood: "My God, Dix, do you know what happened to me today? I was hurrying down Church Street not looking where I was going and I bumped into a woman, and I said, 'Oh, excuse me, ma'am, and my God, Dix, I'd a like to died when I looked up and saw she was a nigger I was ma'am-ing.'"

An interview, and another; and then a committee formed with Negroes and whites looking across a table at one another in the county courthouse, with fund-raising talk; and Dix Pirkle's eyes fixed on the pure, strong face of Barbara James, until, aware of it, her eyes met his, and Race couldn't stop them looking at one another that way; and Race couldn't tell them they were wrong in thinking more was going to come out of that committee meeting than a proposed program of action for building a new Naked Hag, and a vote of confidence; because that night Dix dropped her off in his car in The Toe, neither one saying a blessed word to the other until she was halfway out of the back seat.

Then: "Barbara?"

"Yes, Mr. Pirkle," she said, not looking at him but at the pavement of Brockton Road; his motor running; headlights on, ready to go on.

"If you'd like—it's a nice night. We could drive."

"I don't think so, thank you, Mr. Pirkle."

"You could call me Dix. I wish you'd call me Dix."

"I don't think I can do that either, Mr. Pirkle."

"I'm sorry. I'm—s-sorry."

"So am I," she had said; and that should have been the end of it. She had gone up the gravel path and into the house; and Dix had driven on home; and it should have stopped there.

But the next afternoon Dix had an errand near the hill right at the close of school time; and he "happened" on her walking down the hill, and drove her home again. That time and times after that, until one night she agreed to meet him out near Awful Dark Woods, and both were so uncommonly shy and silent walking near where he had parked his car in the shadows of the black pines that each one knew it would be a long time and a lot of trouble before their love would feel real, before they would even speak of it, or do one single thing for it but realize it.

I don't want Barbara just for that! Dix hears his own words, spoken that afternoon, echo again as he lies smoking beside her; thinks of what else he wants her for; a wife living with him, where? Once he had said: "We could go somewhere nobody'd know. You could pass, Barbara. You're white enough to! Who'd ever know?" And she'd said, "The only two that really matter, Dix. Us. We'd know."

A mother to Dickie? Yes; with her goodness growing around his son; a goodness better than he could give his son—stronger, and his own stronger for it; and the subtle, sharp clean keenness of her mind; this and the infinitesimal little things about Barbara James he wanted her for. God, what kind of a belly laugh is sounding in hell for the joke of her blackness and Dix Pirkle's whiteness making stripes out of them that can't be people, black and white stripes; a study in color contrast, instead of just the one difference that there is between a man and his woman. . . .

"We both think a lot of our fathers, Dixon," she says suddenly after the silence had seemed to sink in and set on them. "That's just one reason we shouldn't expect more. It'd kill them both."

"Your too?" Dix could bite off his tongue for saying it.

"Of course, mine! Dixon, my father is very proud."

"I didn't mean it."

"Meant it, but didn't mean to say it. Aw, Dixon, it'd be so long; even if we did have a chance outside Paradise, it'd take so long for *us* to get used to it. And maybe we wouldn't. I love my people almost as much as I love you. You're the same way."

"I never think of *my* people. I never think of that."

"You don't *have* to," she says, rising a little, leaning into him, her finger touching his cigarette. "Let me have the last drag on it, darling. No, let's just thank God for what we got now."

118

He frowns, watching her take the smoke. "If we only knew who saw us, who told Joh. Oh, Joh won't say anything to anyone but me, but I wonder who saw us, Barbara, that'd give us trouble."

"I don't know." She tamps the burnt-down cigarette on the concrete, touching him again lightly on the chest. "You're too skinny, Dixon, you need more fat on you, baby. No, I don't know. We should have thought to come here and not go there. We went there too much; our luck gave out."

"Joh thinks last night was the first time."

"My Dad too. Thinks it was Hollis Jordan." Barbara gives a little high hoot. "Gawd, *him!* Dad sure hates him."

"Why him?"

"Cause of the woods, sugar. Because he lives up there, I guess. I should have let you drive me on into The Toe, but I was afraid to. You have too often as it is."

"What would he say if he knew it was me, honey?"

"Dixon, I don't know. He just hates Hollis, though. Don't know why."

"Nobody likes him much. He didn't fight in the war."

"He's crazy, I guess." She runs her finger across Dix Pirkle's lips, slowly, lovingly, gently. "Dixon, they're going to take it away from us some time, but be glad about now, baby. Don't be sad about right now, cause there's nothing we can do for it, baby. Hmm?"

She leans on him, her fingers reaching up to tangle with his hair, while her mouth leans his in a soft, searching way, until his arms pull her into him.

"We got to get out of Paradise, Barbara," he whispers; her breasts crushing against his chest, the moonlight glistening in jagged shadows across her golden-soft buttocks and his hands pressing them; white on black, stripes in the light of the night. "We got to!"

"Hush, Dixon . . ."

"Barbara . . ."

"Baby, hush now. Don't talk."

119

17

THE HIGHWAY snakes through back-country land, dark in the night as the car careens past deserted cotton fields, dimly lit farm houses, Sinclair stations, gas and pop stands, and the stretch of black pines, lonely-looking shadows sticking out of the earth; while over the radio the interminable sound of hillbilly tunes, peppered with spot announcements for anti-acid pills.

Hollis Jordan reaches over and snaps off the button, drives silently thinking, Of course it was her, couldn't mistake that giggling on the fourth call. Just giggling—not saying anything; drunk, no doubt. Gawd, Ada, what's to become of all of us!

Thinking: Why can't Ada just let it go; it happened too far back to be still bugging her. Thinking that and remembering how for years after she married Colonel it was just, "Hello, Hollis," and "well, hello, Ada," whenever they met in Paradise; except for two times. And tonight, giggling at him over the telephone—the third time.

The first time was a while after Dixon Pirkle married Suzie Barr, and Ada appeared outside Hollis's house one afternoon like a ghost, sitting in her car looking at his house until he came down off the porch and walked over to her.

He said, "Why, hello, Ada. What brings you out this way?"

"Dixon got married, you know, Hollis. He's a *doer.*"

Then he noticed, as he leaned his arms on the edge of the car's window, that Ada had been drinking; her breath reeked of liquor.

"I'm glad to hear it," he said.

"You were never a doer, were you, Hollis? Never as long as you lived did anything about anything—did you, Hollis?"

"Ada, Ada, it was a long, long time ago. Now don't you think you better drive on home?"

He was surprised, no, shocked, to see Ada there, and to see

her that way. The last time he had seen Ada Adams alone had been the night after Thanksgiving, Gawd—eighteen years past, in Athens, when he'd gone there some weeks after old man Adams and young Hooper had come across them up in the wood's clearing. She'd phoned him, asking him to come, and he'd gone, spent a night with her in a motel outside the city, registering as Mr. and Mrs. Marsden. They'd eaten bacon and eggs the next morning in a greasy diner in Watkinsville, and Ada had announced, "I want to marry you, Hollis. I want to do it today. Drive to Macon and do it."

"Ada, I can't do that. Not now. Not just yet."

"Now or never, Hollis Jordan," she had said.

"Can't be now, Ada. I got a lot to take care of. You don't know anything about me. I got to—"

But she had interrupted him. "Dick Pirkle's been chasing after me, Hollis. I could marry him."

"Ada, if all you want to do is get married—to anyone, so long as you get married—then you best marry Dick Pirkle."

"I want to marry you."

"I couldn't take care of you, Ada. You don't know some things."

"When could we get married, Hollis?"

"Ada, I just don't know."

Eighteen years past they had fought about that; and eighteen years past plus two days, Ada had "showed" him, like she'd said she would; married Colonel, eloped with him; and never said another thing to Hollis Jordan but what people living in the same town say to one another when they just know one another "casually."

Until that afternoon.

"I never regretted marrying Colonel Pirkle, Hollis," she said.

"I don't suppose you did. Colonel's a good man."

"I did it on impulse. I was crazy in those days, wild—didn't know what I wanted. But I've had a happy life with Colonel, and I've had Dix. It's more than you've had, Hollis."

"Ada, I don't deny it, but I don't see the sense in going into it, or why you want to. You better go on home now, hadn't you?"

"When Colonel went to war, I was proud, Hollis."

"All right, Ada, all right."

"A lot prouder than that day we were caught up in the

121

woods, you know," she said, giggling. "Gawd, we shook them up that day, all right. I was a stupid kid. When the war came along and Colonel enlisted, I was proud. You know, Hollis, I often wonder how I'da felt had I married you and the war came along."

"I'm going back in the house now, Ada. I didn't know you bore me malice after all this time. Don't know why you should, but you better go on home now."

She'd turned the key in the ignition; gunning the motor. "Turn your back on it, like always, Hollis," she said. Then she'd started the car going; leaving as suddenly as she'd arrived; zigzagging down the hill toward the crossing. . . .

Jordan often wondered what Ada would have said back when she wanted to marry him, if he had just told her: "Look, Ada, I *am* married, in a sense." Told her that right out and then added, "She's living back in Juddville, where I come from. We were very much in love, Ada, but something happened— she lost a child in birth, and it changed things. I haven't seen her since."

He *could* have told her that without telling her any of the rest of it; without telling her how he left Juddville, left the sprawling plantation he'd helped his father run, and come to Paradise, just picking any place that sounded nice. He left Juddville on a summer's morning after a talk with his father there on the lawn outside their home, near the old white post by the driveway, where a storm flag of the Confederate Cruiser, *Shenandoah*, still waved; and his father said, "And I don't care where you go, Hollis, or what you do after today. You'll still get the income your great-grandfather Henry left you; that I can't do anything about, and I'd get it from you if I could—but you'll not live high off the hog on that. You've murdered a baby, and ruined a good woman's life with your prodigal ways. You've broken every tradition the Jordan name ever stood for. There's not much left for me to say except good-by."

He could have told her too that Kathryn, his wife, had lost their child because he'd kicked her in the belly. But he would have had to tell her a lot of other things to tell her that; filthy, rotten, drunken things he'd done when he was Mitchell Jordan's heir, cock of the walk in Juddville.

What was it Joh Greene had said to Hollis this morning, when Hollis had gone to him to tell him Dix Pirkle was

122

courting trouble, Dix Pirkle needed to be advised. "You know, Hollis, you're a many-faceted human personality, but I think there's something deep inside you protesting evil; protesting and wanting to do something about it," Joh had said, "and I think one day you'll buy my product without me even giving you a sales pitch."

"I didn't tell you this just for Dix Pirkle's sake," Hollis had said. "I don't know why the Christ I did tell you exactly."

"Some day you're going to use the Son of our Lord's name in a prayer, Hollis Jordan; not just to cuss with. But I'm glad you told me about Dix. I'll have a talk with him."

Hollis Jordan squints at the road in front of him, imagining for a moment that far down the road he sees someone, then deciding, no. He resumes his thoughts, recalling the second time he had seen Ada alone—drunk too, just like the first time—just like she must have been tonight calling him that way and giggling without saying anything. Oh, he knew her giggle; no mistaking that. But about tonight, he wondered had Joh broken his promise and gone and told Ada about Dix and the James girl? Had that been the reason why Ada had started up again tonight?

The second time had been as sudden and short-lived as the first time. Happened in the early evening, dusk hour, when Hollis Jordan had been in town on a Saturday buying supplies, and had met Ada at the parking lot, fumbling with her car keys, trying to open her door, smelling again like liquor and smirking up at him when he tried to help her.

"Why, here's Hollis Jordan," she had said. "Johnny-on-the-spot. That's not like you, Hollis, to be Johnny-on-the-spot."

"Let me help you with your keys, Ada. Ada, you shouldn't drive home the way you are now."

"God provides, Hollis, for drunkards. You know that's what I am, don't you? Everyone knows that's what I am."

"I don't know anything but that you hadn't ought to drive, Ada. I'll drive you."

"And cause scandal again. Naw, Hollis."

And then she said something peculiar to him—how had she put it? She had turned and looked at him, smiling that funny, ironical smile she had, and she had said it in a flat, almost accusing tone, "Hollis, tell me something. Do you—"

Jordan's musings halt instantly then, and he slams the breaks on, brings the car to a screeching, tire-burning stop, then backs up. Through his rear-view mirror he sees the figure of a boy in the road. He hadn't imagined it, and as he nears the figure, he sees the colored boy standing there, holding a suitcase.

He says, "I damn near run you down, boy. What the hell you doing?"

"I'm hitching to Paradise," the boy answers, standing by his suitcase, not moving toward the car.

"Well, come on then!"

"Yes, sir! You going to Paradise?"

"Come on!"

The boy lugs the suitcase into the car; into the back seat. Hollis Jordan says, "Leave it back there and sit up here with me."

"Yes, sir."

"What you doing off the main road anyhow?"

"I thought I was on the highway, sir."

"Naw, boy, you're on a back road."

"I started walking on the highway, sir, from Manteo."

"Well, you got off it. You must have walked about five miles. Where you headed?"

"My uncle's Bryan Post, sir. I guess you might not know him. He's from Paradise, and he was supposed to meet me, but he didn't show." The boy adds, "My bus was late. Guess he didn't wait."

"So that's where he was headed, hah?"

"You know him?"

"Sure, boy, I know him. He had a little trouble. He was driving the Hoopers' pickup and he drove it up a tree. Oh, he's all right, boy, don't worry about that. Just likes his corn, I guess. Yeah, I passed the wreck a while back, just beyond Hooper's Place."

"You kidding me, sir?"

"Kidding you?" Hollis Jordan glances over at the boy. "What the hell'd I tell you something like that for if it weren't true? Hah?"

"I don't know. I just—" His voice trails off, and he sits there dumbly, rubbing his hands together in his lap.

"Told you you don't have to *worry* about him. He got out okay. Just made a mess of the pickup . . . You related?"

"Yes, sir. He's my uncle—only I never met him."

"You from up North?"

"Yes, sir."

"I thought you had a Northern accent. Well, you'll be in Paradise in a bit now, boy. I'm not sure just where the Posts live in The Toe, but I'll drop you at the Hoopers'. They work for the Hoopers mostly."

The boy says nothing to that. Jordan glances at him, sees him rubbing his hands together more frantically.

"You have a nice trip down?" he asks.

"It was all right," the boy mumbles.

"Those are the lights off in the distance, boy—see, way off there? That's Paradise."

The boy looks out the car window, off to the left between the black pines and the hills, watching the dark-looking land silently, not saying anything. Jordan scratches a match and touches it to a cigarette he pulls from his wool shirt pocket; then flips the radio on again: ". . . because Alkalino clears up sour stomach in fractions of a minute, listeners, when due to hyperacidity," the announcer is saying. Hollis lets his mind sink back again into the deep cushions of memory, recalling now how Ada had put it that day in the parking lot; and wondering whatever had possessed Ada to think of a thing like that after all these years:

"Hollis, tell me something. Do you still have that little birthmark that runs in you-all's family on the male side?"

18

At eleven-thirty in Paradise, down in the brow below Linoleum Hill, Kate Bailey says it seems a shame.

"Yes, it does," Colonel sighs. "It all started off so nice, too."

"And I never tasted Brunswick stew that good, did you, Guessie?"

"Law, no. Hus must have some secret ingredient."

"Seems a shame," Kate repeats. "But maybe Storey can do something about *Vivie* anyway. How'd she get in such a temper? It isn't like her, do you think, Marianne?"

"Hmm?" Marianne Ficklin looks away from Major Post's shadow, off by the queen-of-China trees, where he's clearing the plank table. He sure is mad, she thinks; he sure got mad when Thad Hooper told him hell, no, he couldn't leave the barbecue and go down to The Toe to see what become of Black Bryan in the wreck. Thad said, "Don't you worry, boy, *he* ain't hurt! Fellow who called said only thing hurt is my pickup and a black-gum. Don't you worry, Major, the way your old man was feeling he couldn't feel hurt if he had it!" That sure made Major Post's black eyes flash up, sure made his jaw set hard, big hard-looking nigger boy, mad like sixty, he is, Marianne Ficklin thinks; and answers Kate: "What'd you say, honey?"

"I said I never saw Vivie in such a temper. Did you?"

"Naw, Gawd, Thad sure got his hands full tonight. First Vivie, and then Major Post's pa wrecking his pickup. Major Post's sure burning, isn't he?"

"What's he like as a worker, Marianne?" Joh Greene pokes the dying campfire with a stick, sparking it. "I got some odd jobs around the rectory needs looking at. Thinking of hiring Major."

"He does his work, but he's sullen. It's as though he had something smoldering inside of him."

Bill Ficklin smiles. "Marianne here thinks any colored boy that can count beyond ten is thinking dark thoughts. Major's just brighter than most. Probably resents having to tote for a living."

"What do you know about it, Fick?" his wife says sharply. "Do you have him around all morning? Even now, lookit him. Slamming things around back there."

"He's angry," Colonel Pirkle says. "Boy wanted to see for sure that his father got out of the wreck. Thad should have let him go. Don't know what's got into Thad tonight. Boy got a cousin coming in over at Manteo, too. Worried about his cousin. It isn't like Thad to be so hard on one of his niggers."

"Aw, Thad's had more than his share of bother tonight," Joh Greene says. "And it seems to me Bryan Post is always wrecking something that belongs to him."

"Still, the boy can't be blamed for being concerned about his family. Thad should have let him go."

"I make a motion we *all* go soon. Party's sort of broken up." Joh Greene tosses the stick onto the campfire. "Ought to make it an early evening."

"We got to wait for Thad to come back. Shouldn't be long now. He just had to check and see that the pickup isn't obstructing any part of the highway. I swear I don't blame him for getting hot under the collar. Nice enough of him to lend Bryan Post the car. Now he has to leave his party and go investigate the damage."

"Maybe Storey can get Vivie out of her mood before he gets back," Kate says. "That'd make Thad feel better. Storey has a way with her. Maybe I ought to run up to the house and help him."

Then for a while they sit around the died-down campfire, lost in their individual thoughts; crickets squeak down in the brambles by the spring, brambles rustle in the slight breeze of the underbrush behind them; and the ashes of twigs and burnt-up paper supper plates, autumn leaves and scrub logs, dry and flake in the fire's grave before them, with the few remaining coals still hot and giving glow. All of them think inside themselves for that lazy interlude at the end of the evening.

Colonel wonders what he'll find when he gets back home—

127

Ada drunk still?—wondering vaguely where Dix has been spending his nights lately; reminding himself it's been a long time since Dix and he have had a talk; ought to do something about that. Used to talk a lot together about life and all, but Ada makes everything so tense in the house when she's at it. How did this problem come on him; why?

Guessie Greene, beside Colonel, vaguely planning the menu for the church social on Friday. Fried fish, let's see, and hush-puppies, slaw, potato chips, pickles, apple cobbler and coffee. Got to remember to take her red silk down to be cleaned in time . . .

Bill Ficklin ponders the reason for Marianne's irritability, increasing daily; not just in small matters, like this morning's with Major, but in larger, more important ones. Like last week's argument, which had started off as a silly discussion about small towns and large cities—the dullness, she had complained, of small towns; and then the talk had grown and expanded until Ficklin had realized she was criticizing him for something, blaming him for something. Then finally she had snarled: "I'm still young! I'm not ready to decay here along with last year's crops!" He guesses maybe they should go someplace on their vacation next year—save, so they can afford to take a trip, maybe even to Europe. No, he'd never save that much from his salary, but New Orleans, maybe. Someplace exciting . . .

And Joh Greene remembers it's been a long time since he's given his "apples" sales pitch on a Sunday. Everybody's heard it; still, won't hurt to say it again and again, same way singing commercials on the radio start to sink in on the unconscious. There's a lot of value to repetition; just keep on saying it. Ought to drive down to The Toe and have a talk with Doc James too; he's a sensible Nigraw, don't want trouble any more than the rest of us in Paradise; he'd keep it under his hat too, no sense Colonel knowing anything about Dix and the James girl. Colonel's got his hands full already with Ada. But Doc don't want trouble; he'd know to keep the girl on close rein, put an end to it right here and now, before it's too late. Nip it in the bud.

Vivie ought to take up an instrument, Kate Bailey decides; no reason a woman's got to think about herself to a point she gets herself out of control, embarrassing Thad before the guests that way—not showing up at all at the barbecue. Band could

128

use a saxaphone. Poor Storey up there at the house trying to talk reason into her; ought to get up there and help him. Saxophone'd be a good thing for Vivie Hooper, and the Bigger Band sure'd sound fine!

Black eyes and a hard-set jaw; big hard-looking nigger boy; what'd you like to do if you could, Marianne Ficklin thinks; what'd you like to do, buck? If you could—what'd you like to?

At eleven-thirty in Paradise, up on the road near Awful Dark Woods, driving slowly, Doc James watches the land around him. "See anything, Myra?"

"Aw, Ed, I don't think you're right about Barbara."

"Then why didn't she tell me the truth about last night?"

"I think she just objected to having to explain her every move, Ed, that's all. She's not a child, like Betty. She's a grown lady."

The doctor shakes his head. "No, Myra," he says, studying the darkness carefully through the car's windows. "No, Barb and I have always been close. She's doing something she's ashamed of. She's doing something with a white man."

"Ed, it won't do any good even if we find them up here together. Don't you know that by now?"

"Hollis Jordan'll listen to *me!* That's one white man I don't have any qualms about speaking up to!"

"And if it's not him?"

"I've got a hunch it is. When I saw him the other night, and then picked Barbara up right after, I had a funny feeling —even before I saw Neal sitting on the porch. I got that same feeling tonight, Myra, when Barb sneaked off again; and a few minutes back, when we passed Jordan's house and saw it dark. I got a hunch they're together right now."

"Just because of Juddville, Ed?"

"That, and other things too. It couldn't be anyone else."

"Be hard to find them around up here even if you're right, Ed."

Doc James says, "Just keep looking, Myra. We've got to just keep looking."

At eleven-thirty, down in the two-story yellow frame house on East Church Street, Cindy walks into the large upstairs bedroom, mumbling as she views the debris; the neck of the phone dangling from its hook, an overturned wine bottle, clothes strewn along the floor, a photograph of Mister Dix dropped beside the mauve stuffed chair Miz Pirkle slumps in asleep. Cindy mumbles, "Lord, Lord, this place looks like a hooraw's nest. Miz Pirkle sure raised herself some hell t'night and put a chunk under it at that. She sure carry on wid dat giggle soup, she do; she walk out in high cotton all right."

The colored girl stares down at her mistress; then touches her shoulders. "Miz Pirkle, ma'am?" . . . "Miz Pirkle, ma'am?"

"Done passed out." Cindy frowns. "Lord, Lord!" She calls again, "Miz Pirkle, ma'am. Hey, dere—"

"It must be late, Storey," she says, sitting beside him on the shell-shaped violet-splotched couch in the living room.

"Only eleven-thirty, Vivs." With his finger he traces a pattern in the cotton covering of the couch, and continues tracing as he talks, making a series of spirals. "No. Don't you see?" he continues. "I'm not saying Thad's perfect—nothing like that at all—but just that he's good, Vivs. He's like Kate. There's a basic goodness about him; he's strong, do you know what I mean? He knows what he stands for. Principles! Some of us just—well, just don't know how to keep ahold of ourselves. Some of us get sloppy—" Storey Bailey stops himself as his finger uncontrollably comes in contact with the flesh of her arm; he withdraws it suddenly and heaves his breath out, sighing, "Hell! Hell, I don't know. I had a lot to drink!"

She sets the coffee cup down on the round antique end table beside the couch; looking over at the opposite wall; at the black wood-framed Currier and Ives print above the shelf of cactus and ivy plants. "Do you remember that night at Mike's, Storey?" she asks him abruptly.

"Remember it?" he answers, feigning nonchalance, showing some considerable embarrassment; shrugging, "Sure, I suppose. It was a long time ago though."

"I always wondered why you changed; changed the minute you stepped out of the car and went inside. I always wondered why you had to talk nasty, Storey. I never figured it out . . . I suppose it was because of Thad."

"In a way. You were his girl . . . Still, you started it— started all that nasty talk and I couldn't stand you telling me I was rotten. It made me sore because I thought then that you were as much to blame as I was . . . It was you who changed so quickly." He shakes his head. "Aw, we were only just kids, Vivs. What the—"

She stares down at her nails, polished bright red, long and tapered; studying them. "When I went into Mike's and heard your conversation, I wanted to die."

"My conversation?"

"I heard what you said. I didn't know why you wanted to talk that way about me. It wasn't like you. I was shocked."

"You must be crazy, Vivs. I didn't say anything at all to Mike! What'd I say?"

"No—no, let's not go into it. It was too long ago. There's no sense going over it."

"But you're mistaken."

"All right, Storey. Let's not talk about that. We were both such kids. You with your crush on Thad, and me with mine on you . . . We were kids, that's all."

"Yours on me?" He looks at her. "Huh? Gawd, *I* didn't know anything about yours on me."

She stands up, her hands in the pockets of the blue cotton dress, stands staring out the window at the light up at the barbecue pit off in the distance. "Poor Hus worked late tonight." She sighs. "No, Storey, I don't know. I don't know that you and I wouldn't have worked out better than—"

"Don't say something like that, Vivs."

"All right, don't worry. I'm not going to."

She reaches to the end table for a cigarette, and Storey rises from the couch, goes over beside her and lights a match, touching it to the cigarette. "I swear I never knew about any crush you ever had on me, Vivs . . . Why, Thad was such a—"

"That's why you never knew. You were too busy worshipping Thad. Oh well, what's the sense in going on about it . . . it's pointless." Sucking on the cigarette for a moment, she is silent. Then she adds, "That night in the car with you . . . I never felt that way . . . I don't know."

He reaches his hand out and touches her arm lightly. "Vivs —Vivs." His hand grips her arm now, but she pulls herself away.

"And Thad." She gives a dry little laugh. "Poor man! I never loved him. Respected him, yes. Oh God, didn't everyone? He was so good, wasn't he? He was so damnably respectable, huh, Storey, wasn't he? But—"

"Vivs—"

"No, don't, Storey." She moves away from him, from his

131

hand on hers. "I tried to love him. You know I even felt there was something wrong, *bad*, about not being able to love him, but I couldn't ever be myself around him. He wanted me to be someone else—I don't know—Thel, maybe. Dear sweet Virgin Thel, maybe. But I was his wife—" suddenly, dropping her head, beginning to weep.

"I never should have come up here," Storey says. "I was a fool. I should have let you alone to get over it by yourself. You don't mean all this. Vivs. I never should have—"

"Never should have what?" Vivian Hooper says, the tears starting down her cheeks, her hand reaching up to push them way in an irritated gesture. "Listened to this? Because it's true and it doesn't have a pleasant sound? If I can't tell you, Storey, who can I tell? Joh Greene? Guessie? Maybe I should tell Ada; *she'd* listen, if I'd give her a drink. No, Storey, the only one I can tell is you. I can tell you that I'm not some pure little Southern belle that does it because it's part of her marital duties and not because she likes to do it. I *like* to do it, hear? Yes, and that shocks Thad Hooper, that I like to do it. But you knew it all along, didn't you, Storey. Knew it before Thad knew it. You—"

"Vivs, Vivian, Gawd, you must stop this!"

"And it's awful for Thad," she continues unheedingly, "because he thinks it's dirty, thinks I need to be held in check, because if I'm like that with him, I must be like that with any man. I must want to do it with any man just as badly as I want to with him, because he thinks a woman that likes to do it has something wrong with her. Thinks she's wanton or oversexed or something; thinks she has to dress like she's putting on armour to protect her from the way she is; thinks—"

"Vivs, oh, Vivs!" He puts his arm around her now. "My Vivs," he whispers. She chokes up with sobs and begins crying so hard that Storey Bailey has to hold her tightly at the shoulders, feeling her tremble, some of her trembling communicating itself to him. He says, "Vivs. Oh, Gawd, we can't let nothing happen. We got to get a hold of ourselves." He feels her black soft hair touch his cheek. "Oh, Vivs, Gawd!"

"Let me go, Storey. I didn't want it to happen; it's the last thing I wanted. Please let me go."

"Not yet," he tells her. "Wait now. Wait till we can stop this. My Gawd, I think all the world of Thad. I can't stand

132

to see you like this. I think all the world of Thad. I always have."

"And you hate me for saying bad things about your idol."

"No, no." His lips touched her hair. "No, Vivs, I've always—"

"Don't do that, Storey."

"I can't help it. What do you think I want to do, hearing you talk this way? I can't help it, Vivs. I think the world and all of Thad, but—" He turns her to him, lifts her face. For a moment she tries to turn it away; and then with a stifled cry, half whimper, half moan, she puts her mouth over his, as he takes her against him in a sudden, swift, powerful movement of hungering delight. . . .

Watching from the veranda, Kate Bailey, arriving then to see this, stands startled some slow seconds; then turns, walks with deliberate gait back down the steps she has come up, waits wringing her hands, and then straightening, calls, forcing calmness, "Storey? Yoo-hoo, Stor-ey! Vivie!" in a high musical tone that grows shrill in the night as she calls again, "Yoo hoo! Party's breaking up, honey!" and it sounds loud to her under the moon; like some inevitable, unnecessary noise.

"It's twenty to twelve, boy," the man tells Millard Post, as Millard slams the car door after him, "but there's lights on up there still—and hey, I think that's one of the Posts heading down this way."

Millard looks toward the Hooper house at the small, dark figure descending the hill, then waves at the man. "Thanks for the ride."

"S'all right," the man says as the car moves on.

Millard picks up his suitcase and walks slowly toward the old woman; trying to see her clearly in the half light.

He calls, "Hey!"

"Hey, yoself!" she calls back, an old woman coming closer, bent over carrying a brown shopping bag and a black apron over her arm.

"I'm looking for Bryan Post's family," Millard says as she comes up to him.

"You don't have to look far beyond me. I'm Hus."

"You my grandmother?" Millard stares at the old woman incredulously.

"You Henry's boy?"

"Yes, ma'am . . . I thought you were dying."

"Got no time to do that in," she says, still studying him.

Millard Post says, "Well—well, I'm here."

19

For the first time now, the tears are unleashed and running hotly down his cheeks in the darkness. He can feel the night around him, pressing down upon him, screaming in his ears. Behind him strangers who are kin to him make night noises asleep, and Millard Post cries because of them, not for them. He hates them, hates this place, everything in it. Everything about it.

He tastes his own tears with wonder; how long since he's cried? When his mother died? Naw, not even then; wanted to then, but didn't; wouldn't. Damn near cried once when a Diamond cornered him in a lot on 111th and flogged him with a Sam Browne belt; came close that time, but didn't; summoned up his guts instead and caught the Diamond by his knees, dragged him down and wrestled him, caught a rock on the ground in the skirmish and gave it to the Diamond on the head. How long since he's cried? Naw, maybe he never did till now. Can't remember. Jesus!

He is on a pallet, on a friggin pallet like a dog, and the whole place stinks—just stinks—real nigger smell—say there's no such thing- Shit! Millard's smelled it before—not as bad as here, but smelled it just the same, back home around the dirty ones of his people—and he used to think; that's that piss-poor smell a Negro's got that the school books say he hasn't got! Real nigger smell with sweat and stale grease and the stench the slight breeze of the night carried in from the outhouse . . . The friggin outhouse! Millard's never taken a leak in a goddam shit shack before; out behind the house like

134

*some dog. And here, inside, the stink of nigger poorness.
How long since he's cried, and now why? Not because of
that—naw—not the strangeness, not the poorness; the shabby
shadows of make-do furniture crowded around him; and
sleeping bodies of half-clothed strangers who are his blood—
not just for that—for everything here and before here:*

*For the pillow kicked back at him; the front seat in the
plane when he'd had to change airlines; the necktie he'd had
to take off for some dog-faced square who called him a nigger;
for the way his guts ran watery the whole time, knees shook,
heart had a drum in it; for the way, f'Chrissake, he'd even
found himself saying some chicken prayers for God or anybody around to help him; and for the baby-weak way he
wanted out, and still wants it, wants it worse now, out and
back home. He wants to hear his old man giving him hell for
some crazy thing he'd said that Cousin Al had taught him—
Jesus what a lily Al would think he was to see him blubbering
on a piece of stick on the goddam floor—lookit the big man
now! and wants to hear Pearl laughing, and to stroll out into
the street wearing his Panther jacket and just hear somebody
—anybody, f'Chrissake, even a Diamond with a sprung switch-
blade in his hand—say, "Hi, man, how's it hanging?" Weeping J.H.C.!*

*Lying crying, Millard Post thinks that he has no name for
this enemy that has attacked him, no single name he can say
in his teeth and taste and hate, say and damn in his mind. No
one single name, like other times. Other times there was kike,
spic, wop, mick—times when he felt this frustrated hate, fear,
worry and anger curl through him like a slimy snake coiling
its body tightly around his insides—times when he did not
cry as now he cries, but when he knew some iota of the
emotion enveloping him now—he had a name to say and
hate. . . .*

*In the darkness he tests names. White? Goddam lousy white
man? Naw, no—because he cannot hate white people; he
cannot suddenly learn to hate them, remembering those back
in New York City—Miss Foder, his English teacher—classy-
ass he calls her; and he likes her; last term she gave him B,
said he should have had C, but he tried; things like that—
and Mr. Josetti, the fruit man up at the public market place
under the tracks—he always gave Millard something extra—
an orange, an apple; once a goddam coconut no one in hell*

could get open anyway; but he was okay. Naw, Millard couldn't hate him; not the white kids at school either—Paul Posner, Cliff Heath, Ginny Holt. He can't hate white; not white he knows. What does he know about this white—these white: the man on the plane, the ticket man, the agent in Manteo? What white is that?

Besides—Millard wipes his nose with the back of his hand, thinking, Not just white anyway; more. F'Chrissake, lots more. Here—this place, this room, this fugging piece of wood supposed to be a bed, the smell, the big boy, his cousin, with the creepy name—Major. What the hell war was he ever in? What the hell is he Major of?

South. How about South?

South.

Don't sound like nothing; south . . . Can't hate South like he can hate jew, spic, mick, wop; they all got guts in their names. South. Just a fuggin direction.

One thing, Millard thinks; whatever your name is, whatever the hell they call you that's got me bawling on way past goddam midnight, you won't kick me. Naw, hell! Didn't grow up knocking the hell out of all kinds of trouble for nothing, didn't get tough reading books, didn't get guts just to sit on my hands with. Not going to lick me cause you got me bawling a half-inch from the floor, whatever your fugging name is! One thing for sure!

And another thing, f'Chrissake, Millard thinks; sniffling the goddam tears back up his nose; this don't mean I'm scared. Naw, this don't mean I'm chicken; I've got news.

Still—God, the night! And this place that isn't home! And everything that happened; and nigger, someone called him; nigger, and he didn't fight.

Whatever your name is; whatever the hell they call you—

20

THE MORNING AIR is muggy in the bedroom; the beginning of this day, hot. Still asleep, Thad Hooper kicks back the sheet, pulls his leg up to his stomach as he turns on his side, and clutches the pillow in his hands, dreaming.

Lying again on the green boyhood bank by that river that day; lying and letting his toes dip in the cool dark eddies over the bank; hot, hot day when he is twelve again in August, tangled curls falling on her face beside him. "Aw, let's Thad! Let's go in the water!"

"Huh? We got no suits."

"I don't care if you don't care."

"We'd catch it, boy. *Would* we!"

"Who's going to ever know? We'll swear on our eyesights not to tell."

"I just as soon."

"C'mon! First one in's going to win a trip to Paris, France!"

Tearing off the shirt, dropping the pants, kicking the shoes and ripping the socks off his feet, diving into the eddies of that river; and coming up with water in his mouth to see the white and gleaming new young body on the bank's edge. "Is it cold? I'm coming!"

Swimming together, laughing and spitting out water, racing from the rock out and back, swimming in the cool blue liquid on the hot day, and climb back then to stretch their bodies on the earth, out of breath laughing, kidding, teasing: "You got your birthday suit on, Thad."

"So have you."

"Boy, would we catch it!"

"Boy, *would* we!"

"You look funny naked."

"Me? Lookit you!"

"You look funnier than me. Boys look awful funny," she said, giggling, "I like to died laughing."

"Who you think you're laughing at?" He poked her back, catching her arm. "I'll make you say uncle."

"I'll never say it."

"Yes, you will." He pushes himself over on her; holding her down.

"Say uncle!"

"Never! Never! Never!"

"I'll make you!"

"Never, never!"

"Who looks funny?"

"*You* do."

"I'll make you say it!" He holds her while she wiggles under him, wrestling with her on the bank, wrestling and rolling and rolling, laughing with their bodies wet.

"Never make *me* say it!"

"Oh, yes I will, Thel, I will! I did before!" He's growing now, growing right there on the boyhood bank into a man, arms and legs growing taller and longer; and then the funny sound that people murmuring together in a crowd make: people behind him, watching him wrestling naked on the river bank, angry now at her, yelling now, "Vivie, stop your wiggling! What are you wiggling for!"

"Make me say uncle like you did that day, Thad."

"Shut up! Shut up!" He holds his hand on her mouth. People are gasping now behind him on the river bank; he's turning to them, crying desperately, "Can't you see I'm only trying to make her hold still? Can't you see she won't hold still?" Crying that and thinking why am I naked? How did I get naked here like this? And the bell is ringing, the river boat coming, people standing on the deck watching, seeing them. "Vivie, stop, God, stop! Hear that bell! You want them to see us?"

"Uncle!" she says, and people behind him murmur: "Did you hear *that?*"

God, God, the bell is louder, louder; God, the bell!

"Are you going to answer it, Thad?" she says from the other bed.

"What?"

"The telephone."

"Oh!" He sits up dazedly, reaching for the phone's black neck. "Hello?"

"Hello, Thad? This is Doc Sell. Sorry to bother you so early but—"

"God, man, what time is it? I was just in the middle of some kind of dream. Can't even remember what the hell it was about, but what time *is* it?"

"It's seven o'clock, Thad . . . I thought you'd want to know that Ada Pirkle passed. Had a stroke last night."

"Huh? Say that again."

"Ada passed. Ada Pirkle's dead."

And from the other bed, leaning up with her elbows propping her flimsy-gown-clad, lady body, "What's the matter?" Vivian Hooper asks. "Is there something wrong, Thad?" At the beginning of this day, hot.

"Hot!" He hears his Uncle Bryan's voice from the kitchen of the Post shack in The Toe; lying on the pallet in the other room; waking with the stranger's early-morning start in some new place on the floor; missing home with the sudden breath-aching shock of nostaglia; lying looking at walls peeling their paint; smelling the grease-strange odor of grits cooking; and listening.

"Never mind hot, you Bryan! Mind trouble! We gone catch hell now."

"Aw, Biss, law, don't study it s'mornin. Hot. Gonna be like the devil's front room over in that spinning room, s'morning."

"Yeah, and gone be like the devil's house all over when Mr. Thad catch his hands on you."

"Aw, Biss, what you want? I 'spose to slunk around here like a suck-egg hound cause I had myself a little accident in that pickup that ain't got brakes for stopping ten miles 'fore it's time?"

"*Corn* ain't got breaks, is all. Pickup stop, but *corn* don't, and you had a bellyful."

"Aw, Biss, aw, Bissy—"

Millard sighs, turns on his side on the hard pallet, and looks into Claus Post's wide-open eyes.

"You wake, Cousin Miller?"

"Yes."

139

"I'm Claus. I'm your cousin. My brother gone to work, but I'm gone stay wid you t'day, cause you come all the way from up North. Hus said you got three shirts in your suitcase, an' a jacket wid your name on it an' a black panther on it!"

"Umm-hmm. What's your name—*Claude?*"

"Claus. Cause I was born Christmas day. . . . Hus said your daddy is de boss of six elevators up in New York City."

Millard sits up gradually, scratching himself under his pajama top. "Yeah; Dad's a starter of the elevators."

"Hus said them elevators can't go no place lessen your daddy say dey can. Can't move an inch at all lessen he say dey can."

"Umm-hmm." He looks around him at the old poor furnishings, the orange crate table, oil paper thumbtacked to it, smelling in the stickiness of the room; and the grease of the grits frying. Claus is his name, Jesus! Santa Claus Post, Christ! Yesterday's traveling gnaws at his loneliness—*"but our niggers are niggers and our niggers know it";* and a ticket to go back home not until Friday. Three days in Paradise, God!

"I gone stay wid you t'day, Cousin Miller." The colored boy's brown round eyes are wide watching Millard Post; wide with wonder and awe and admiration. "All I got to do is take de rubbage out an' burn it. Don't got to pick or study books, cause you come from up North!"

"Ummm-hmmm."

"Boy, wait I sashay round dis town wid you. We sho gonna strut Miz Lucy, Cousin Miller!"

Millard Post smiles wanly at the beginning of this hot day, the fingers of his hands touching the flesh of his cheeks where last night's tears dried. He's done with crying now.

Waking alone in their bed, hearing from down in the bowels of their house the piano and her singing, Storey Bailey knows there is something wrong, but in the sleep-dulled distance of his mind in the early morning, he does not yet recall for those first seconds; just lies on his stomach with his face in the pillow, listening to the symptoms—the sound of the piano and Kate's voice singing at seven-thirty A.M.

140

No-oh lov-li-er place in the dale
No-oh spot is so dear to my child-hood
As the lit-tle brown church in the—

When he remembers, he groans, socks the soft mussed pillow with his fist, fights the unlikely suspicion that she could have seen him last night before she called to him, came, maybe, and seen him kissing Viv. No! Only guilt fabricating punishment! And he believes more in her complaint coming home in the car after the barbecue. *Storey, you were certainly gone a long time. I felt a little abandoned.*

He had said, *"Me abandon you, Katie?"* meaning too, in the inference of his tone, that he could never exist apart from Kate, but hiding at the same time the remembered thrill, coupled with the shame he realized when his arms held Thad's wife. He had said, "Viv was sure in a swivet 'bout something, though, Katie. Took forever to convince her wasn't bad as all that." He felt as he said it the sharp, sensual pulse to his groin; glad for Kate whom he loved, but not sorry for the surprise inconsistencies of life; regretting the deed, while nurturing the secret and tremulous body-memory that was its consequence.

He had said to Kate coming home in the car, "Why, land!" exaggerating his tone, chuckling, "I think you're jealous, Kate Bailey," as though she would be out of her mind to be in any way envious of Vivian Hooper; and Kate had not accepted this remark as all the atonement he need give for leaving her so long alone, but hummed the rest of the way back to the house, as she always did when everything was "not quite settled."

So this morning, Storey Bailey thinks into his pillow, she persists in sulking, and expects more; and for a horrified half-second he wonders what she would be doing now if she were to know the whole truth about the interval he spent away from her with Thad's wife. But by no stretch of his imagination can he conjure up any vision of his wife under such a circumstance.

He must get up, fetch his robe, and go to her; talk with her, make it all right, before breakfast and the day's work. Yet not until he can momentarily relish once more the memory of Viv; enlarge and improve upon it, in the way of the accomplished daydreamer and the impotent aggressor; for it is not likely that such a moment will occur again—he was very high;

141

too high, he decides—though it would spoil Storey Bailey's fantasies this morning to allow that reality to take precedence over the more delicious unreality of himself and his best friend's wife's hungry-trembling body.

Rising afterward, he slips into his robe, pushes his feet into the slippers and goes dutifully down to the sunporch-music room.

"Good morning, Kate," he says. "How are you, honey?"

"Good morning, Storey." She keeps on with the piano. "I didn't sleep well."

"Now, honey, what's the trouble?" He walks over to her, placing his arm on her shoulder. "Bad dreams?"

"One doesn't *dream* bad things when they're awake, Storey."

"Why don't you stop playing and tell me, Kate?"

"I can play and talk. I prefer to."

"All right. What is it, now, hmmm?"

"Last night."

"That old thing! Katie! You still mad at that old thing?" He walks around to the front of the piano, grinning. "I think you're jealous, Kate. I think my girl's jealous." With his finger he reaches down and tilts her chin up. "Huh, Katie? You jealous cause I talk to my best friend's wife for a bit?"

Kate Bailey lifts her hands from the keys for a brief moment and looks at Storey unsmiling. She says, "I saw you kissing Vivie, Storey. I was on the veranda." Then, while Storey stands gaping, wordlessly, Kate continues to play; singing along with the melody now.

That Tuesday morning, like any other, Barbara James joins the slow parade of the colored bound for work, streaming up from The Toe to Brockton Road, before they pass on to the luxury-lawn-carpeted green streets of the whites, on their way in the muggy sun, still new from sleep to become a part of the waking world of scrubbing, toting, picking, and cooking.

Under her arm that morning, like any other, are the blue composition books, corrected, graded, ready to be passed back. Theme for Tuesday: What do you want to be when you grow old? *"I want to be a boss." "I am going to be a railroad man so I can make plenty of money." "I want to be rich and white but I'm going to be poor and black." "I want to be a baseball player like Willie Mays and drive a big car."*

Coming to Church Street, to cut over to the hill road, Barbara James worries, not like other mornings, remembering her father's cold and angry-in-grief eyes across the table at breakfast as they ate in screaming silence, neither able to help the other with talking. The problem is understood between them now; there is a white man; she was with him.

"Barbara!"

Startled, she turns; then sees the car parked by the curb.

"Dixon! What are you doing here?" She runs over to the car, looking around her first; yes, people see; colored see, ignore, go on. "Dixon!"

"My mother's dead, Barbara."

"Aw, naw, baby!"

"We'll have to cancel our plans for this afternoon. I'll be tied up most of the day."

"Sure, baby, sure. Aw, I'm sorry."

"I don't know whether I am or not, but listen . . . Can you meet me tonight? Late! Midnight, out at the Hag."

"Dixon, I don't know. My dad's angry. He knows . . . Not who it is, of course—but he knows what it is. Midnight's late, and—"

"Please, honey. I can't make it earlier. People will be at the house. I got to stay by my dad."

"Dixon, I don't know, honestly."

"Please. You got to, darling. If I can't see you tonight I'll go out of my mind."

"Dixon, we shouldn't be here like this."

"Will you?"

"Lord, let me think—how will I—"

"Barbara, say you will."

She hesitates; then, "All right, baby. I'll be there. *Somehow.*"

"At midnight!"

"At the Hag."

IF YOU'RE not special, *act* special! That's all special is." Al had told Millard that; had said *just make it so, boy, and suddenly you know you are special. You're somebody and you feel that you are special, and that's all special is.*

Like Millard Post is now, knows it, feels it, coming up from The Toe with Claus, his cousin.

It feels good to Millard. He has made it something big; created it that morning at breakfast as he sat at the kitchen table while his Aunt Bissy gave him grits—god-awful mush in a cracked pink bowl—and told him he'd be pretty much on his own; told him he'd come at a bad time—like f'Chrissake he'd *wanted* to come—and his grandmother sat in a chair rocking and smoking a pipe like some kind of back-woods hillbilly and made some tart remark about his clothes: *All dress up like you had a purpose.* Then and there he'd remembered what Al had said, and in his mind he'd started to make it happen, to feel it, until now he does. It feels nearly real.

It is a gift, this feeling he has made; a reward, maybe— maybe a kind of reward for yesterday; for last night's gutless agony, the child-lost loneliness that visited those hours when others slept and gave no name to Millard he could curse; and the morning that began to ignore him, until he could counter and sass it back.

It is a gift and Millard basks in it; walks straight and tall and cool because of it; sets his face in the sullen and sure expression of the special, that same expression all the Panthers acquire when they "fall in" at a dance. They make their entrance en masse, all of them glancing around at the surroundings with stony indifference, cool style, fine and clean. He holds his shoulders back and lets his eyes meet the sun directly. Over his arm he carries his leather gang jacket, and his left hand, sunk into the pocket of his sweet-tapered slacks, plays with change, making a jingle . . . A little behind him, at his heels, his cousin follows him; wide-eyed, idolizing, servile, like a punk pushing after a big man, hoping some of it will rub off.

It is nearly noon; they are on their way to the Black Patch across from the county courthouse. There they will meet Major Post and eat lunch with him out of the brown paper sack Millard's aunt made up for the three of them. . . .

Back home, the kids would be heading for the cafeteria . . .

Back home, it'd be cool, jacket-wearing weather . . .

Back home—but what the Christ! This is Paradise, and Millard Post is special. Say it, act it, that's all special is— even a million miles from nowhere. Like Al said, just make it so!

It's lunch hour out behind the Paradise Feed Company. Jack Rowan wads up the wax paper his sandwiches were wrapped in, and leans his head back against the wooden beam by the loading platform. He says to Pit Raleigh, "Boy, he's working us today, nigger."

Raleigh swigs from the neck of a Coke bottle. "Ain't *that* the truth!" He spits and wipes his mouth off on the back of his strong dark wrist, scratches his head under his cap, and sighs. Staring out at the dust-dry road behind Main Street, leading out of The Toe, he moans, "Yeah, yeah," while he squints ahead of him. Then he leans forward. "Hey, lookit, Jack."

"Huh?"

"Lookit what's paradin' our way wid Major Post's brother."

Rowan moves his head to see, studies the tall, neatly dressed light-colored Negro boy walking with Claus; Claus jumping up and down beside him like a yo-yo as they come along; the boy placid-looking, his countenance keen-eyed, confident. He's wearing a white shirt, navy blue pants, a gold watch chain by Gawd, loafers and good-looking store-bought red socks. "Shh-eet! Who de hell's dat?"

"I don't know, Jack, but he certainly do recommen' hisself mos' high!"

"I know who dat is, nigger, S'that up-North cousin they was spectin. Sheet, yeah; dat's who!"

"Oh yeah?"

"Sure, sheet. Dat's who."

"Comin' our way."

145

"Uh-huh."

Rowan and Raleigh sit up and watch, wearing their wash-worn, faded blue denim coveralls, their shoulders and arms naked where the coveralls end, dust from the sacks they've wielded on their backs through the morning clinging to the sweat of their bodies, their ankle-high shoes stuck on their naked feet and laced loosely to let in air. They watch, waiting for the pair to get closer.

Claus says, "Hi, fellers. We on our way to meet Major."

"Hi."

"Hi."

Claus grins widely, tugging on Millard Post's sleeve. "This is my cousin Miller." Millard jerks his sleeve free and looks calmly at the two boys sitting on the ground, while Claus adds brightly, "From up North in New York City."

Millard says, "How's it hanging?"

"Heavy," Rowan says.

Raleigh says, "Could be lighter."

Millard stands there, one hand sunk into his trousers pocket tinkling the change there. Rowan and Raleigh regard him head to toe. Millard feels their eyes on him; let 'em look!

"He sleeps in pajamas," Claus says. "Top and bottom."

Millard growls, "What else is new?" turning his head non-chalantly, pretending to regard the back of the stores along the street; an eyebrow raised for effect.

"Now, *do* tell!" Jack Rowan cackles, "You hear dat, Pit?"

"Sho! I hear up North dey don't even take dem off to fug; jest fug right through dem."

Millard looks down at them coolly, takes his hand out of his pocket, folds his arms across his chest, smoothing out his jacket, and stands spread-legged looking down at them.

"Is dat de truth, Yankee boy?" Rowan says.

"They only ribbin' you, Miller." Claus grins.

"I got eyes," Millard answers. He says to Rowan: "Sometimes they screw with 'em on, sometimes with 'em off."

"They only ribbin' you, Miller."

"Can it, Claude!"

"He call me Claude and not Claus." Claus Post giggles. "He says Claus ain't no name at all."

"You gonna be around long?" Rowan asks.

Millard shrugs. "Couple days."

"Up North where he come from his daddy bosses the

yelevators!" Claus Post announces. "Dey cain't go up and dey cain't go down, lessen his daddy say it."

"Aw, Claude, can it!"

"Yeah, Claus," Rowan says. "Let him talk his own self . . . Yeah, tell us more about up North, nigger. So dey hump wid 'em on sometimes, and sometimes wid 'em off, hah?"

"A piece of ass is a piece of ass," Millard says.

Claus Post puts in, "Some are oven-belly bitches, I'm sure to tell you."

"G'wan, Santa Claus," Raleigh laughs. "Whata *you* know, you little inch."

Rowan doesn't take his eyes off Millard Post. "Tell me, Yankee," he says. "You ever humped with a white girl?"

"If the mood hit me, yeah."

"You kiddin'? You had white meat?" Raleigh asks.

Millard Post puts a hand to his mouth, feigning a yawn. "That news?"

"He belong to a club," Claus Post says. "He's got a black panther on the back of dat jacket he carryin', wid his name on it in solid gold."

"Let's see," Rowan says.

Millard takes his time unfolding the jacket and showing them the back. He says, "We all got jackets like this. What the hell!" He folds it back and shifts his weight to his other foot.

"We don't got no jackets wid our names in gold, have we, nigger?"

"Ain't *that* the truth!"

"He come down here by air-o-plane," Claus says. "An he's got stickers to prove it too."

"Yeah? That right, Yankee?"

"Sure."

"Sheet, I didn't believe him. Do you, Pit?"

"Not a word, Jack; not a word."

"I don't believe he knocked up any white gal neither, do you, Pit?"

"Naw, Jack. Uh-uh. He be scared."

Millard smirks. "You guys flipping your lids? White girls dime a dozen up home."

Rowan nudges Raleigh and says to Millard, "Down here's the same way. White women come to The Toe hot and begging. You better not sit out on de Post porch after dark. Dem white women come in droves just pantin' for some jog-jog."

147

"They just ribbin' you, Miller."

"I'm hip!" Millard Post says.

"We got to go meet Major," Claus announces.

"We ain't ribbin'," Rowan says. "Oh, we got good times in Paradise. You jest don't know. Haven't we, Pit?"

"Sure, Jack. Big ole high times we got!"

"We ought to show you around later, Yankee. Huh?"

"I don't mind," Millard says, pleased now, glad they want to impress him.

"Sho, Jack, we oughtta," Raleigh agrees.

"Course," Jack Rowan says, "I still of not believin' his story about humping white tail, but that don't have to spoil me from showing him our sights. An' after all, you *is* Major Post's from-up-North cousin!"

"You show me some white tail, I'll show *you* what to do," Millard Post answers curtly.

Pit Raleigh guffaws: "Yeah, boy, we jest might do that too!"

Rowan glances up behind him at the company clock, stretches, and pulls himself to his feet. "How 'bout me and Pit meet you later on in the day, 'round six o'clock, when we finish up."

"Sure," Millard says.

Claus Post beams. "My cousin sho am poplar."

"Oh, we're doin' it for Major mostly, ain't we, Pit?"

"Sure, Jack," Raleigh answers. "We jest crazy 'bout Major."

Coming out of the small red brick clinic that afternoon, carrying his black physician's bag and rushing so that he does not see where he is going, Doctor Edward James collides with the Reverend Joh Greene on the winding cement sidewalk.

"I beg you pardon, Reverend."

"Hello, Doc. How are you?"

"Fine, but very rushed. Old Mrs. Downs out on the highway's got a stroke."

"Wait just a minute, Doc." The reverend catches the small man's coat sleeve. "Could you kindly take just a minute, Doc? I came out here especially to see you."

"Me, Reverend?"

"I'll be brief and to the point, Doc."

"Yes sir?"

"You know, Doc. I never have made a practice of butting my nose in on matters that pertain to The Toe. You got your

148

own minister for that, and I think he does a right good job, on the whole. Why, I have the highest respect for Reverend Fisher!"

"Yes, Reverend?"

"What I mean, Doc, is if I thought he could talk to you about this matter, I would not hesitate to let him. I never have made a practice of selling in another man's territory, particularly when we're selling—basically—pretty near the same product."

"Is something wrong, Reverend?"

"Wrong, Doc? Well, I don't know about *wrong*. Something's just a bit off kilter, I'd say. I mean, I'm going to come right to the point because I know you're in a hurry . . . Something is going on that isn't *right*. It isn't right in the eyes of the community, and it isn't a very good advertisement for the Lord Jesus either in the Toe or in the rest of Paradise."

Doctor James looks carefully at the reverend. "I *may* know about it already," he says.

"About your daughter, Doc? You know about it?"

"Yes, Reverend. I do."

"Now, Hollis Jordan may not be a very reliable sort of—"

Doctor James straightens himself and snaps angrily, "He certainly is not! Don't gloss over it for me, Reverend. I quite agree that it is not right; I'm thoroughly disheartened at Barbara's behavior."

Reverend Joh smiles benignly. "You know, Doc James, that's the word I've been searching for since I first learned of this matter. That's the word that most truly expresses my own reaction. I was disheartened too. Sorely disheartened."

"I'm searching my soul, Reverend, to find some course of action to stop this immediately, and I think this morning at breakfast I found it. It's worth a try."

"Doc, I knew you'd be a man I could approach directly. We both know things like this have happened before in Paradise, but—"

"Not in *my* family, Reverend."

"Exactly! You've always lived like a decent colored man, Doc. You don't want anything that isn't rightly yours, and you don't want your family to step outa bounds either. Now I *know* that."

The doctor stands silently for a moment, then says more quietly, "Thank you, Reverend, for confirming my suspicions.

149

It makes me more sure my course of action is the right one."

"Not at all, Doc. I'm glad we could hash this thing out."

"Good day, Reverend," Doctor James says.

Joh smiles. "Bye, boy. And give my highest regards to Reverend Fisher."

Kate Bailey rocks, darning socks, the afternoon sun streaming in on the glass shelf with its motley antique pitcher collection. Her mind wanders from the symphony on the radio back to the morning and her conversation with Storey about last night, and about Vivian Hooper. It had embarrassed her to a point of near tears at the time, to a point where Storey had to shout at her: "Well, if you want to hear my explanation, stop pounding the piano, Kate!"

And she had wanted to say, "If I stop, I'll cry," but she would have cried if she had tried to say it; and so summoning up all the self-control she possessed, she had taken her hands from the keys, folded them in her lap; looked hard at them; and let him continue.

"Now, Kate, you *know* there are women like that. There's a name for them. A scientific name even. I mean I'm not just making it up. There's a scientific name for them!"

"But not Vivie," she had murmured; yet she had thought to herself, Yes, maybe; remembering Thad's eagle-eye way of watching her, his possessiveness, and his reluctance to let her too long out of his sight, a characteristic of Thad's that Kate had always pitied Vivian for. She had thought often what a shame it was Vivie could not take up an instrument and meet afternoons with the Bigger Band, and felt vaguely uncomfortable at those times when Thad would flare up at Vivie over some little thing like that day at the Legion picnic when he criticized her for letting her skirt fly up while she was swinging; and Kate had imagined simply that it was a price Vivian Hooper paid for being so beautiful, so very beautiful that a man who had won her, even a strong man like Thad, must always be wary of losing her even in Paradise where almost nothing like *that* ever went on. . . .

Once, on television, Kate had seen a play about a beautiful woman whose husband forbade her to do any of the shopping in town, for fear she would meet another man. He forced her to spend all her time with him, and wherever she went, he went, always walking close beside her, with his hand touching some part of her, and his eyes never off her. While everyone in the community gossiped about it, and pitied the woman because of it, her husband never relented in this manner of treating his wife. Then one day, when a close friend came for tea with her, and managed while he was out of the room, to ask her how she stood it, the beautiful woman said: "Oh, I know that it does *seem* confining. But I stand it much easier, perhaps, than my husband. For I love him very much, and I *know* he loves me. But he, poor darling, is never quite sure . . . So it keeps us together a good deal of the time, and in the long run—I wouldn't have it any other way." The picture faded out on her smiling face as she added, "He's quite charming, you know—but of course, you *don't* know. How could you?"

Kate had sat puzzling after; trying to decide whether it made any sense; and glancing over at Storey, she had said:

"I don't know why I think of Vivie and Thad, but it reminded me of them."

Storey had said, "Heck, Viv is a lot better-looking than that skinny toothpick."

"No, I mean—they're sort of together all the time."

"Thad don't have to worry about Vivs," Storey had yawned. "A guy like *Thad* worry about his wife!"

Mulling it all over in her mind, Kate decides probably Storey was telling the truth about last night—about his sudden discovery that Vivian Hooper was one of *those* women—but it had pained her to hear him say:

". . . and I suppose she just couldn't stand it any longer or something. She and Thad were having that spat and she just had to have some loving. Didn't have to be me—could have been anyone."

"Then why was it you, Storey?" Kate had come close to bursting right into tears, because a thing like this had never threatened their marriage before, and because they had never once actually sat face to face and discussed the fact of sex. In bed, in the hushed darkness, they had often whispered about it; they were well aware that their sex together was good; and Kate often fancied it was more imaginative, too, than most of the couples she and Storey knew; that it was perhaps somehow unique.

In Paradise it was not common practice among the women to confide their feelings about the intimacies of marriage; but

151

things were dropped now and then, and Kate Bailey had gradually begun to learn that there was a surprising lack of actual passion among those of her friends to whom she was closest. Marianne Ficklin, for instance, had spoken once of how she sometimes dreaded "those fifteen minutes every third night, like clockwork, when the urge comes over Fick just as we get into bed." She had added: "Sometimes I just wish it'd take seventeen minutes, it'd happen in the middle of the night, or we'd do it on the living room rug—anything to stop the monotony of routine. But I'm just a rebel, I guess; always have been."

Hearing her say that, Kate's mind had wandered back to all the nights and days, and *ways*, which she and Storey had had; and she had felt suddenly gratified to realize that they were— she had heard the expression somewhere—*good in bed* together, not dull victims of routine, not tired old married folk.

So it had stunned Kate to know that Storey was vulnerable to Vivian Hooper. Even though it was little more than an embrace between them, it had stunned her and disappointed her that he could be tempted by the kind of woman he said she was.

"Because," he had said, "I happened along, and Kate, I'm only *human.*"

"Human?"

"A man is a man. Even when he's happily married."

"But, Storey, she wanted just *anybody*. Not just you. You said that yourself. That makes it seem so—common. Why you had to go ahead and—" Her voice had trailed off.

"Kate, you've always agreed she was attractive."

"Yes, I've always admitted that."

"Well, Kate, don't you see? It was just one of those things. I had a lot to drink and she—well, she seduced me, damn it!"

"All right," she had said. "I guess it's just silly to carry on about a little thing like that . . . but it seemed—maybe it still seems—like a big thing, Storey." And she had left it at that, thinking that it had dulled some of the shine of her sense of security with Storey, even though Vivian Hooper was a vamp. Kate had always been so sure that despite her physical plainness, she was the only woman who could arouse in Storey the lust their marriage reveled in as love.

Storey had sworn—she hadn't asked him to—that it would

never happen again. "Gawd, how *could* it, Kate?" he had said. "Don't you think I feel pretty tacky for even touching her?"

And when he had left the house after breakfast and started toward his car, she had watched him without his knowing it from the dining room window, hoping that what did happen would—that he would turn and come back, despite the fact it was payday at the mill and the time lost would make the day even more harassed than usual.

Letting it all fade now from her consciousness, Kate Bailey rocks and darns, until eventually she is concerned half with reminding herself to send a spray to the Pirkles for the funeral, and half with concentrating on Mozart's *Jupiter*.

"What do you study?" Major Post asks, ripping the wax paper off the sandwich, propping himself against a tree in Black Patch, gulping a bite from the bread hungrily.

"Save that paper," Claus tells him. "Ma say to save it," he says, reaching for the frail wrapping Major has absently tossed to the ground. He folds it carefully.

"Books," Millard answers, squatting but not touching the ground; keeping his sweet-tapered pants clean.

"Naw, I mean, *what*? History? English? Arithmetic?"

"All that stuff."

"What're you going to be?"

"You going to get the stomach cramps, you gulp like that, brother," Claus says.

"Can't help it, got to get back to Ficklins'. She sure has the bug today. Moving things around. Move this, move that. That's why I was late. Got to get back." He swallows another huge piece of the sandwich and asks Millard Post again, "You know what you're going to be?"

"I got contacts," Millard answers.

"What you mean?"

"Big men!" Millard says. "I know plenty."

"Lawyers?"

"Lawyers? What for? I mean big money men."

"I don't follow you."

"Big shots. *You* know."

"What's their line?"

Claus Post says, "Miller had him white tail. Lotsa times!"

Major Post glares at his brother. "You shut up!" he says.

153

"You little clown! Where the hell you get so big you got to talk smart?"

"I'm sorry," Claus murmurs.

"I have," Millard Post says, "but that's not news."

"I'll tell you different." Major stops eating and looks at him carefully. "You want trouble down here you keep thinking that isn't news, boy. Hear?"

Millard turns his eyes from his cousin and shrugs.

"I mean it!" Major Post says.

"Okay! Okay! Don't blow your top!"

"I don't care how you talk up North, you just put on the brake pedal down here."

"I know. I been all through it."

"All through what?"

"Traveling. I know." Millard claps his hands together and cracks his knuckles. "Came down in a goddam DC-Six."

"Yeah?"

"You ever fly?"

"Naw."

"Big deal!" Millard shrugs. "Once you get off the ground it's not like anything. Nowhere. Everybody always talking about what a big deal it is to fly. Haw."

Major continues to eat, watching his cousin thoughtfully, listening to him talk. Millard talks in an idle, compulsive way, finding it difficult to think of things to say to this big Negro with the somber eyes and great, strong build, feeling himself scrutinized by him and peeved, even resentful of the quick way Major Post had reprimanded him for talking about white women. Who the hell was *he* Major of; what the hell proof did he want? It was true—nearly true—that Millard had had a white girl in a gang line-up once, some little spic had spread for the Panthers, but Millard had not been able to do anything, and the other boys had pulled him off her. But it was nearly true; if he'd wanted it, he could have had it. And Major Post made out like he was just so much blow; well fug him, with his: *What do you study?* Why the hell didn't Major Post ask him where he got his sweet clothes? Bet Major never saw them sweeter, but he doesn't mention them; just a lot of polite crap about whadda you study. Didn't even notice the jacket: oh, *noticed* it all right. Just didn't say.

What're you going to be when you grow up? Pansy birthday-party talk for four-year-olds.

154

Put on the brakes. Afraid I'll show you up, boy?

"The Panthers are the toughest gang up in the *barrio*," Millard continues, "they can beat any—"

"What's that mean, *barrio?*"

"It's a region. A section. I don't know what the word means. It's spic."

"Oh." Major Post wipes his mouth on the back of his hand and stretches.

"We have wars and everything. Rumbles."

"Yeah?" Major looks at him coolly.

"People get killed. Man, like, they're *real* wars!"

"Yeah?" Claus Post says, his eyes saucer-wide. But Major Post acts like he doesn't hear; he pulls a weed from the lawn and sticks it in his teeth.

"I got to get back," he says. "Have to hear about your wars some other time, Cousin Millard," he says sort of sarcastically. Millard takes a burn at it—cocky square! What the hell's he know about wars with a fuggin Major for a name; why the hell can't he act like a cousin; show a little goddam interest; well, fug him and his mask for a face.

Major Post gets up. "Wanna remember something, Cousin," he says, standing with his hands slipped into his rear pockets. "Don't know much about wars down here. Don't know much about big men, 'cept big in *size*, see. That kinda big man totes easier than the rest. That's a big man down here. It's sorta different."

Major and Millard eye one another momentarily; Millard thinking he'd like to *show* this guy, like to *show* him; Major thinking he should have let him blow his steam off, comes all the hell the way down for nothing. Should have let him strut, dumb kid's probably scared, strange place, kin carrying on like he's the Fuller Brush man staying overnight or something. Ought to do more for your own kin, but Lawd it don't work out that way, with the chores and the aches and the worlds apart kin from up North is. Lookit his clothes; dressed up like a band-box, playing tough and all. Should have given him more room to roll in, but we can study that tonight. Tonight he can play the colonel. What the hell—all the way from up North.

Major's face relaxes suddenly into a grin. He slaps Millard on the back. "Well, see you later," he says. He smiles, meaning

155

well. "Don't get the burying clothes dirty." Must have bought them special for the funeral.

"These are just everyday," Millard answers.

"Yeah?" Major patronizes him. "If you say so. Look right peart."

And Millard senses that he is being patronized, senses it and resents it; how come that big boy thinks he's so special? What's the matter with everyone around here? Cripes, it's like another world. Man, it's like Mars.

22

FROM inside the large, two-storied, white-colonnaded house, Marianne Ficklin watches Major Post as he comes up the front lawn from burning the trash, lugging the empty, dusty big aluminum can. As she watches him, she removes her black cotton gloves and black-veiled hat in an abstract fashion, setting them on the round redwood lamp table by her suede pocketbook, and on top the note from Fick announcing that he will be at a board of trustees meeting probably until after eight.

She is a small, Roux-flaxen-haired woman with a good shape, slightly too prominent bust-wise, so that she appears a trifle top-heavy; but slim, with fine thin legs; pretty-faced, with jade almond-shaped eyes; and a rather startlingly sensual-looking mouth for one with small, narrow lips.

It is just after six, still light outdoors but growing dark, and in the living room it's dim and shadowy. Restlessly she fumbles for a cigarette, scratches a match to light it, and lets the smoke out from her lungs in short, quick clouds. She waits until Major comes as far up the lawn as the cellar steps, where he is taking the trash can; then she raises the window and calls out to him.

"Yes, ma'am?" he says. "Oh, hello, ma'am. I didn't know you were back."

"When you get down in the cellar, stay there, Major," she

156

tells him. "I want to go over my jams in the fruit cellar. I'll need help."

"Yes, ma'am."

She stays at the window until he disappears down the steps, the aluminum clanking against the concrete walls as he goes into the cellar. Then she reaches into her pocketbook, digging for her lipstick and compact. Turning the lamp on, she studies her face as she repairs the makeup, then takes the little miniature atomizer from her change purse, and squirts some Arpege on her wrists. . . .

The cellar is divided into three parts; the washroom, Fick's carpenter shop, and her canning closet. Major is standing by the door of the latter when she comes down the steps, and he moves back slightly as she approaches him, her hand reaching out for the doorknob. She turns around suddenly without opening the door and looks up at him.

"Did you get the bedroom furniture moved all right, Major?"

"Yes, ma'am."

"You don't mind working a little late, do you, Major?"

"No, ma'am. I guess not."

"If I hadn't had to go to the Pirkles we could have done all this earlier today."

"Yes, ma'am."

"Poor Colonel Pirkle . . . It was quite a shock to him," she says, looking up at his eyes, which are lowered.

"Yes, ma'am."

"Cindy is working her fingers to the bone trying to get the house all in order for the funeral . . . Do you know Cindy, Major?"

"Cindy Bennett? Yes, ma'am. She lives near me."

"Do you ever take her—dancing, Major?"

"I don't dance much, ma'am."

She gives a little laugh. "Oh, no? I thought you all danced. The colored have such a good sense of rhythm. I just thought you'd probably be a dancer too."

"I guess we better get those jams taken care of, ma'am. My cousin from up North is visiting me, and I'd like to get home for supper."

"Oh?" She's slightly peeved. "Very well, Major. Come along."

He follows her inside, where it is dark, and she says, "You want to reach up for that light, Major? I can't reach it."

157

He turns it on, but it gives only a slight illumination.

"Down there are the peach jams," she says. "We'll start down there. I'll check them, and hand those up to you which I want to take to the kitchen with me."

She is wearing a black cotton sheath dress; high spike heels, and fine-gauge nylon stockings. As she squats to reach for the jams, her skirt slips up past her knees, an inch of the black lace of her petticoat shows.

"Let's see, this was January, last year . . . I didn't know we had any of that left. Here, Major, take this." She hands it to him. "Well, do you ever take her *anywhere*, Major?"

"Pardon me, ma'am?"

"I said, do you ever take Cindy anywhere?"

"No, ma'am."

"Don't you have a girl friend, Major?"

"Yes, ma'am."

"I thought you would. A big boy like you . . . Umm-hm, this is last year's, too. We've got a lot more of it left than I thought. Here, Major, take this too . . . What do you and your girl friend do?"

"Same as anybody, I guess. Go on walks. To the pictures. Same as anybody." Major sighs.

"Oh? What's the sigh for, Major?"

"I don't know, ma'am."

"You nervous about something?"

"No, ma'am, I haven't got anything to be nervous about."

"Uh-huh, here's more . . . Major, why don't you kneel down here by me and help me look for them. Then we can just stack them, and take them out all at once."

"Yes, ma'am."

In the crowded area of the canning closet, Major stoops down beside her, straining his eyes to read the labels on the small Mason jars.

"Your cousin from New York arrived last night, Major?"

"Yes, ma'am."

"What do you think of him?"

"I don't know him too well."

"Oh? . . . Here's a plum. What's that doing with the peach? Here, Major, take it." She hands it to him, turning her body a little toward his, her legs parting at the knees, so that she squats in an open, spread-legged way. Major takes the jar from her,

158

notices her position, and looks quickly back down at the bottles in front of him.

"I suppose your cousin will tell you all about life in the big city."

"Yes, ma'am."

"Would you like to go to New York, Major?"

"I don't know, ma'am."

"You'd probably like New York, Major . . . You know I'm a New Yorker."

"Yes, ma'am."

"Up there things are different. More lenient, you know. Up there the colored can do just about as they please. I even went to school with colored."

"Yes, ma'am."

"Of course they're trying to get that rule passed down here, but I wonder if they ever will. Don't you?"

"Yes, ma'am."

"Would you like to go to school with white girls, Major?"

"I don't know, Miz Pirkle. I guess I don't care either way."

"You can talk to me about it, Major. I'm not a Southerner. I went to school with colored, so you don't have to watch yourself around me."

"Yes, ma'am."

"Is that all you'll say?"

"*What,* ma'am?" Major picks up a bottle, sets it aside, not looking at her.

"Stop a minute, Major."

He stops. "Ma'am?"

"Look at me."

Major looks once, sees the open legs—open so that he can see to her thighs—and looking up to her eyes, they meet his directly.

"I'm not like the others down here. You can trust me, Major."

"Ma'am?" he asks, turning his glance away from her; feeling the heat climb in him. He's suddenly scared.

"No matter what you did, Major, you could trust me."

"I didn't do anything, ma'am," Major mumbles.

"No, but if you *wanted* to . . . Lots of times when I was young I wanted to do things I wouldn't do because I was afraid grown-ups would find out and punish me. It's like the colored

159

down here. They're afraid to do things for what the whites will do to them . . . You can trust me, Major."

"Yes, ma'am . . . There's nothing I want to do, but—"

"But what, Major? Hmmm?" Her hand brushes his knee.

"But get my work done, ma'am."

"Major, you can trust me. I'm telling you! Major, look at me!"

Major turns his head slowly, and does not dare to look below her eyes. She is staring hard at him, and he is aware of her legs spread as she squats, of her hand then, pulling her dress (down or up? No, Gawd, boy, you *know* up; you're not imagining this time, no, Gawd, boy!).

Suddenly, Major Post jerks himself to his feet, knocking over two jam jars as he does, bolting out of that room as she begins to scream at him, "Where are you going? You're not through! Come back here!" But Major is already halfway up the stairs and out of that house, shaking all over, and swearing inside of him at everything. Shaking and sweating and swearing—running.

Outside the Post shack in The Toe, sitting in the car waiting for Thad, Vivian Hooper reviews the day's incidents, and feels an immense shame for last night. The fact of Ada's death contributes to her depression, and the quarrel she had had with Thad at the barbecue which evoked such self-pity in her, and ultimately caused her to confess her thoughts to Storey, is no longer even clear in her mind.

Her mind is dominated now by one emotion—guilt. She is guilty at the fact she built the quarrel—what was it about? Simply that Thad wanted her to change her dress and she was stubborn—to such preposterous proportions, then exhibited her infantile anger by sulking, leaving her guests and sulking until Storey came along. How could she have ever reached such a nadir? Crying out to him like an alley cat in heat, offering herself to him like a lust-hungry bitch! How had she let that happen?

She muses that perhaps Thad is right about her "wiggling," her clothes, her character—that part of her which she had always felt was simply a natural side to any woman, and which she had imagined Thad was just too damnably prudish about. Maybe Thad had been right all along. Storey never would have acted as he had last night if she hadn't provoked it (*What do*

you think I want to do, hearing you talk this way? he had said);
and afterward, when they had broken away from each other
suddenly at the sound of Kate's voice, Vivian Hooper had seen
the sick look on Storey's face and known he would never forgive her for the shame he felt. Storey, who always spoke of
Kate's goodness, was probably just as shocked as Thad at any
sign in a female that she could *enjoy* the physical . . . God,
maybe women really weren't supposed to enjoy that.

Then this morning had begun particularly badly. First with
Vivian's awakening very early to realize her memory of all
this; lying in her bed feeling the numb disbelief at what happened last night, followed by the agonized mumblings Thad had
made in his sleep—the "No, please, Vivie! No, please!" which
he had groaned out in such pitifully pained tones—and then
the phone call from Doc Sell saying Ada had died—and the
way Thad had responded with the strength and properness and
appropriateness that characterized Thad Hooper.

He had said, "Whatever happened yesterday, honey, is pretty
much outshadowed by this, isn't it? We've got to do what we
can for Colonel and young Dix . . . I guess we never realize
how fortunate we are until something like this shows us . . .
Do you want to go over there for the evening to help out?"

There had been nothing more said about the barbecue, and
she and Thad were their old selves again save for how *she*
felt. As they drive to The Toe tonight—typically, Thad had
not forgotten his responsibility to the Posts regarding the
accident; and typically, too, he *had* forgotten his anger at Bryan
—their palaver had been easy and warm and friendly. They had
even seemed somehow closer than they had been in a long time.

Vivian Hooper wishes she could forget the guilt stealing all
through her; and shut out the suspicion that Thad has been
right all along about that side of her which she had always
adamantly insisted was a natural part of being a woman.

Well, thank God for Thad, Vivian Hooper thinks.

Thinks: From now on I'll be what he wants me to be—all
the way down the line.

The four boys wander down toward The Toe in an aim-
less, careless fashion; handing sass back and forth with
studied nonchalance—Millard Post, Claus, Jack Rowan and
Raleigh. They had met as they had arranged, at six, up in
front of the feed store; and now they are scuffing their shoes

161

along the dusty path, laughing and quarreling and teasing one another.

"Naw, I'm not lying either," Millard Post snaps, more indignant now. "Why don't you dig me, man? I got news about white girls."

They had been dwelling on this subject more than on any other, Rowan and Raleigh riding Millard about it, and Millard responding vehemently, slightly put out at their incredulousness but finding a rather easy camaraderie with them now knowing that they admire him, even envy him, despite the ribbing and the quibbling.

"What you think, Pit? He a liar?"

"Jack, I don't know, now. I don't know. 'Member, he Major Post's cousin from up North."

Claus squeaks, "He mine too."

"You squares ought to come up North and know what living is," Millard says. "Up North you get a job, you get a real job, man. Not a cotton-picking job. I never even saw cotton before I got down here."

"You saw white tail though," Raleigh says, not letting Millard change the subject.

"I *told* you that! Man, you got a one-track mind!"

"And you ain't?"

"I got more on my mind than that, man. I'm gonna *go* in this life. Go!" Millard socks the air with his fist and chuckles.

Rowan giggles, pulling his old battered hat down over his eyes. "Hear dat, Pit? Nothin' but nothin' faze this boy, *he* say."

"Yeah, Jack. He most non-cha-lunt for a nigger."

"I bet he scared to do anything," Rowan says. "Bet he scared like a chicken."

"You crazy?" Millard gives a debonair chortle. "I never chickened in my life. Beat up spics twice my size."

"He not scared of nothin'," Claus put in. "He flew all de way here in an air-o-plane."

"Hey!" Jack Rowan comes to a halt in the road. "Lookit down in front of your house, Clausy. Dere's dat Linoleum Hill quail sittin' dere proud as *you* please in dat car. All by herself, hah?"

"Dat's Miz Hooper," Claus says.

"Yeah, we know who dat is. Prettiest piece around. Huh, Jack?"

"Sure." Jack laughs. "Just like we tole you, Yankee. Dey come down to The Toe beggin' us. See dat?"

"Dat's Miz Hooper," Claus repeats.

"Hey," Jack Rowan says, "you, Yankee! I bet I know something you'd chicken out on."

"Naw, you don't."

"Well, if up North dey just don't bow and scrape around like you say, maybe you *won't* chicken, but I bet you will."

"Put your money where your mouth is."

"Bet you don't dare go up to dat car an poke yo head in de window and cluck yo tongue at her."

"Huh? Cluck my tongue? Man, I'd dare go up to that car and do more than that."

"Like what more?" Rowan looks at Millard. "Huh?"

Millard shrugs. "Ask her for a date."

"You'd dare do that?" Raleigh says.

"Sure I'd dare."

"Miz Hooper, she nice," Claus says. "Don't scare her."

"He ain't gonna scare her. He just gonna ask her for a date. Oh, dat wouldn't scare her," Raleigh says.

"Uh-uh," Rowan says. "She be thrilled to her white bones."

"Sure," Raleigh says. "Dat happens all de time round here."

Millard Post says, "Now who's a chicken?"

"I ain't saying *I'd* ask her for a date; *you* saying it, boy. Not me!" Rowan answers. "You making the big talk; not me."

"I would, too."

"I got a quarter says you wouldn't," Raleigh says.

Millard looks at him, looks down at the car, figures he could do it and run like hell. What the hell? Show these damn squares something. Woman wouldn't know him anyhow. He says: "You want to pay me now or after?"

"Hey, don't scare Miz Hooper, Miller. She nice."

"I'm not going to scare her, f'Chrissake!"

"I'll pay you *after*," Raleigh says, his eyes waiting for Post's to relent.

Rowan nudges him. Rowan says: "We don't want no trouble, Pit."

163

"He ain't gonna do nothin'," Raleigh tells Rowan. "He just talk!"

"You watch talk," Millard Post says. "You just watch talk." He looks again at the car, at the fields to the left, where he could run. He calculates and says again, "You just watch talk," and then starts to move.

"You damn fool nigger!" Rowan barks curtly. "You damn nervy nigger. You want to hang?" But Millard doesn't listen; Millard feels big now, bigger than anyone. He feels them watching him; he'll show them. Christ, he can run like hell after.

"Hey, I ain't giving you no quarter!" Raleigh blurts out. "Hey, nigger, bet's off, you hear?"

"Cousin Miller!" Claus squeals. "He ain't givin' you a quarter."

"Gawd, Pit, he gonna do it!"

"Bet's off!" Raleigh yells, watching Millard Post's back, watching him amble down slowly in the direction of the car.

"I'm going after my cousin," Claus cries, starting to run; but Jack Rowan grabs the boy by the collar. "No you ain't either, nigger," he says. "You going the opposite way, same as us. C'mon! C'mon. Let's get outa here!"

"He my cousin," Claus protests.

"C'mon," Pit Raleigh yells, helping Rowan drag Claus. "Fly, legs! Gawd, fly!"

Millard Post doesn't look back, doesn't see them run; he just keeps going toward the car; thinking, I'll show them; you just watch talk; then afterward, I can run like hell. How she going to know who did it?

Inside the Posts' shack, Thad Hooper stands with his coat and hat on, ready now to leave. Bissy and Bryan stand by him near the door. Old Hussie sits in the corner in the rocker, smoking her pipe wordlessly.

". . . so now that it's all settled," Hooper concludes the matter, "you stay off that corn, boy. You hear?"

"Yes, sir, Mr. Thad. I certainly do most 'preciate all this, Mr. Thad."

"Well, I figured there was no sense deducting that money from your family's share of the crops, or from Hus's wages. No sense them paying because of you. And God knows you'd never save it from your mill check, so we'll

drop it. And you can do those extra chores I mentioned . . .
But I'm warning you, boy. No corn on my place!"

Bissy says, "Don't you worry, Mr. Thad. I'm gone keep
tight rein on dis no-good nigger."

Bryan, looking and sounding sheepish, scratches his head
and drawls, "Don't worry 'bout me, Mr. Thad. I got my
lesson studied by now."

"Okay." Hooper starts to reach for the doorknob, but
glances back at Hussie before he does. "Nice to have a day
off, hah, Hus? We sure appreciate your taking the trouble
with the barbecue last night."

The old lady rocks and nods.

"Well," Hooper says, his hand going to the door, "I'll
be—"

When suddenly from outside there is the sound of a
woman screaming.

Jerking the door open, Thad Hooper sees his wife running up the path, the car door left open behind her as she
comes stumbling toward him. In the dusky lige off toward
the fields he sees a Negro running, sees his dark pants
and his white shirt; sees a jacket drop in the road; then
he feels Vivie's arm cling to him, her body trembling.

"Thad, he—" She is sobbing now so that she can hardly
speak the words. "He—tried to—"

"Who, honey? *Who!*" Thad Hooper demands. "Who tried
to do what?"

23

THE sharp sound of a knocking on his front door jolts Hollis Jordan awake. He had fallen asleep on the old stuffed divan beside the fireplace in his front room, where he had been since noon, when he came back from town, dazed by the news of Ada Pirkle's death. For hours he had lain there smoking and tossing, getting up now and then to pace from the fireplace to the window and back. The bag of groceries he had bought still leaned against the chair on the floor where he had let it fall when he had come home. His thoughts had been as restless and desultory as his movements, thinking from Kathryn to Ada, and from Juddville to Paradise; from the boisterous boy—heir to half the wealth of Criss County, cocky and arrogant and aggressive—to the shell of a man living off the land, listless, lonely and unwanted. . . .

Shaking himself as the rapping continues and grows more and more impatient, Hollis Jordan sees the hands at midnight, on his clock. He frowns and forces himself up to his feet, mumbling, "Who the hell at this hour?" He shuffles sleepily toward the door and opens it.

"Where is she, Jordan?"

Jordan blinks back at the little Negro man.

"Don't pretend," Doctor James says. "She left my house half an hour ago." He stretches to try to see behind Hollis Jordan's large figure into the front room, standing on tiptoe, his dark face sullen and angry.

"I don't know who you mean!" Jordan says, stepping back, allowing the doctor to enter.

He pushes past Jordan.

"I don't know who the hell you're looking for," Jordan says, "but there's no one here."

The doctor leans around the corner of the front room, glancing over it; then glaring at Jordan. "Reverend Greene told me about it, Jordan."

"Huh?"

"Don't act dumb. I'm going to have it out with you *and* Barbara. She may as well come on out!"

Hollis Jordan begins to understand. "Well, my God, you don't think she'd be *here*, do you?"

"I'm asking you where she is."

"I don't know . . . I'm not her keeper."

"She's not here?"

Hollis Jordan shakes his head. "Did you think she would be?"

"All right," the doctor says, "I don't know whether you're telling the truth or not, but you're going to listen to some truth, Hollis Jordan. I'd planned to call on you tomorrow to straighten this whole matter out, but when Barbara left suddenly tonight, I decided it couldn't wait."

"Look, it isn't my fault," Jordan protests, "I don't know why you're placing the blame on me because your daughter—"

"Just hear what I have to say." The doctor stands peering up at Jordan angrily. "Then we'll see . . . I vowed I'd never say this to you, but I'm forced to."

"I think you're mistaken somewhere along the line."

"No, listen. You're the one that's mistaken. You've been mistaken since you left Criss County . . . about a lot of things . . . Did you know that Kathryn is dead?"

Jordan stares at the man. "Kathryn? You *know* her?"

"Kathryn was my sister-in-law . . . But how would you know that, Jordan? You were never much for coming around and meeting the family, were you?"

Jordan stands stunned. He murmurs, "When did she die?"

"About two months after the baby died."

"I'm—sorry to hear that."

"*Are* you?" The doctor glares at Jordan. "I thought you'd be relieved."

"My father should have written. Things would have been different."

"Your father never got over what you did to Kathryn. No, Jordan, I'm not talking about the fact that you married her. That was the only decent thing you did do, even if it wasn't legal between white and Negro—"

"Kathryn wasn't all Negro!"

"She was Negro, Jordan. You never wanted to believe it. She was a light Negro, but Negro—or nigger, as you put it that night. The same way Barbara's a Negro."

Jordan leans against the wall, rubbing his eyes. "Christ!"

"Your father loved Kathryn as if she was his own. He was a good man. After you left he helped Kathryn as much as he could; did everything he could to save her. He never got over how you treated her."

"I loved her," Jordan says almost in a whisper.

"You didn't love anyone. You just took what you wanted."

"No. No, I was just—just very young—and a coward," Jordan answers, his mind a web of confusion spiraling dizzily back through the years.

Seeing the scene of their childhood—his and Kathryn's—the same long, green, luxurious lands enveloping them, drawing a circle around them. Inside was the plantation —for him the manor house, for her the colored quarters; but for both, a life inside the same circle.

And growing up together in the glad-easy game of boy and girl, leaping through the same wind-stirred fields together, and running down the same sprawling hills to the same secret meeting spot by the glen . . .

Until Kathryn to him became not the little Negro girl who lived on his place, but a feeling—an easy sound of soft laughter, husky voice inflections, funny-sweet way she said his name—*Haw-lis*. She had brushed-up hair above her temple, a vein that throbbed there when she was tired. He knew the sudden way she would lean forward when excited, though her voice stayed always low.

Kathryn, the girl he loved; soft body and the look of her lithe limbs wearied from loving. Kathryn, the girl his life was bound to, swelling her female flesh with the blossom of their passion. Kathryn, whom he married, stealing off with her on the wild-crazy night he swore nothing would keep them apart again; and whom he brought back as his bride, arrogantly, rebelliously; until the secret of his rebellion broke open, baring the unconscious time-worried white man's scorn: *I married a nigger!*

168

And letting whisky feed the fire, he kicked her with his coward's love-and-hate crazed hardness, shouting, "I don't want a nigger kid!"

"Yes, you're a coward." The doctor's solemn voice slices through the dizzy recollecting. "And you wear it like a medal."

"I could never bring myself to act the way I believed," Jordan says quietly. "When I married Kathryn, my father gave us his blessing. He actually did . . . He had guts— I never had. I couldn't forget she was a nig—Negro. Always—" Jordan grimaces—"always I put a match to something and then when I get it burning, I'm scared. Can't follow through; never could . . . even during the war. Used to read the papers and just cuss the goddam Germans; just cuss them and cry, and I couldn't—"

Doctor James cuts in tersely, "Jordan, I didn't come out here to soul-scratch with you. I came out here to tell you I want you to stay away from Barbara."

"Me?" Jordan stares at the Negro doctor. "But you must be crazy!"

"Joh Greene confirmed my suspicions, Jordan."

"*Joh* did! Hell, part of the reason—no, no—the whole reason I went to Joh was because I saw myself somehow in Dix Pirkle. Saw him about to do what I did, and got angry; angry at *him* for what *I* did a long time ago. I'd see them meeting night after night up here around my place, and I'd get reminded—and in some funny way, I felt a loyalty toward Ada. I might have married Ada, and Dix might have been my son. Might have been me."

Doctor James says, "Wait a minute. *Dix Pirkle?*"

Standing in her nightgown at the top of the stairs, Kate Bailey calls down to her husband, "What is it, Storey?"

She sees him in his robe and pajamas at the doorway to their house, hears the gruff voices of men who are angry and excited, and calls again, "Storey, what is it?"

Then he shuts the door and bounds up the stairs toward her, taking the steps by twos. "Trouble," he says. "I have to get dressed."

He starts into the bedroom, but she catches his bathrobe sleeve. "Storey, it's midnight! What kind of trouble?"

"That smart nigger from up North. He made a pass at Vivs!"

"He *what?*"

"Thad was down in The Toe tonight and Vivs waited out front of the Posts' for him. That smart nigger came along and made a pass at her. Put his hands on her! Smart, goddam Yankee nigger! Thad's got him out in the car with Doc Sell. We going to learn him a lesson," Storey says.

He pulls away from his wife and rushes into their bedroom, slipping out of his robe, and the jacket of his pajamas. He grabs his pants from the back of the chair and pulls them over his pajama pants. "That smart nigger! We'll show him what for!"

Kate Bailey stands in the entrance to the doorway, watching her husband carefully.

Then she says, "Storey, what are you going to do to the boy?"

"What do you think we're going to do? Give him a good whupping!"

"I don't like it, Storey. I don't like it at all!"

"Listen, Kate, when a smart nigger comes down here after our women, what the hell *can* a man do! Stand by and let him maul whoever he takes a fancy to? Let our niggers see him get away with it so they think *they* can get away with it too?" He pushes his feet into his shoes, not bothering with socks. "Smart nigger!"

"Well, what exactly did he do?"

"He made a pass at her! He mauled her! I can't give you a blow-by-blow description now, but he made a pass at her!" He pulls a shirt from a hook in the closet, getting it on his back frantically.

"I don't want you to go, Storey."

"Kate, Thad's my best friend! If some smart nigger had tried it on you, you think he wouldn't go along with me?"

"Are you sure it could have happened to me?"

"What's that mean, for the love of Pete?" He grabs his belt and shoves it through the loops.

"You know what you told me about Vivie this morning."

Storey Bailey stops what he is doing and stares at her. "Kate!"

"Well?"

"Oh, Kate, look—after all! This is a nigger!"

170

"You said this morning it could be *anyone.*"

"Kate, you and me and Thad and Vivs have been friends for years." Storey looks uncertainly into his wife's steady gaze. "Look, you don't actually think that Vivs—"

"I don't want you to go. I'm not saying any more than that. I just don't want you to go."

"Kate, I think the world and all of Thad!"

"That may be. I don't deny that. I feel very sorry for Thad."

"Oh, no, Kate! Not a nigger . . . She wouldn't."

"Storey, I didn't say she would, or she did. I simply say that I don't want you to go along with them. I've never liked Doc Sell's ways anyhow. I don't want you to be a party to this. It's after midnight."

Storey Bailey stands limply, holding the unfastened belt buckle in his hand, frowning. "Kate, Thad would never understand if I—if I didn't go along. Kate, he's beside himself with rage. I'm afraid if I don't go, Doc Sell will work him up all the more."

"I'm sorry for what Thad can't understand . . . I suppose some day an understanding will be forced on him, if it's gone this far."

"Kate, I think you're jumping to conclusions. What I mean is—about last night, Kate. About last night . . . Now, sure, Vivs was upset, but maybe I made it too strong when I said she was—well—*that* kind of woman. I was drinking a lot."

"It's natural to want to protect her, Storey, but I'm only going to say two more things on this whole subject. One, I don't approve of this kind of midnight justice, particularly when Doc Sell is involved. We have courts of law, Storey, and it isn't right to take the law in your own hands. Two, let Thad Hooper set his own house in order. It's not your job to do that."

"Kate, listen! It isn't Thad's house only! It's mine, and it's every white man's in this country. Kate, you know yourself there's five niggers to every white man. We got to keep them in line! If that smart nigger gets away with what he does—"

"It isn't likely he will, Storey, if he's in Doc Sell's hands."

"Thad's my best friend, Kate. He's in an awful rage!"

"I'm sorry for Thad, *and* for Vivian Hooper."

"You don't believe she had anything to do with it, Kate? I wouldn't want you believing that! About last night—I exaggerated, Kate. I exaggerated, hear?"

"I know your loyalty to Thad. I hope I know your loyalty to me, Storey. I don't want you to go. I don't *want* you to!"

"Kate, what'll I tell Thad?"

"Tell him you're not going."

"He'll never forgive me, Kate, if I don't go."

Kate Bailey answers flatly, "And I'll never forgive you if you *do* go. Make your choice, Storey."

There is no wind, only light from a shadow-striped moon, and the leftover heat from the day. A few feet behind them the Naked Hag stands like a shabby shack long since deserted, left for the night to hide. In the distance, the midnight freight squeals at the crossing off in the cypress swamps, and down on Route 109 the sparse traffic of trucks and cars seem like minute dots occasionally lighting the blue-colored blackness.

They have found an open space on the hill which is free of cinder dirt and bears some grass; they have spread the auto robe on it and are sitting beside one another. Below them lays Paradise, dark and sleepy, but inescapably there.

"Look at it," he says. "It's like some bitch asleep. Looks almost vulnerable. Tricks you."

She puts her hand on his knee.

He says, "Dad's taking it hard. Poor Dad. My God, he really loved her, I think." He laughs harshly. "I think it's the only way we're different. I mean, Colonel loves what belongs to him. He loves his own, no matter. Sort of my country right or wrong, only applied to family, and to people in Paradise. He told me tonight that some day I'd realize that my roots are me, and if one of my roots is pulled up, part of me goes with it. In a way it's like saying you never escape the world you're born into, because it's you, both good and bad. Somehow I don't believe that."

She lets him talk, knowing his need to think himself out, watching his profile as he stares out beyond them, where the night's light sharply defines the palmetto clumps, pine and oak trees. His cigarette dangles loosely from his mouth, the blue smoke drifting off lazily in the still air.

He says, "She was a drunk, and I don't believe she ever

172

loved him. He would have stuck by her no matter what. That's his flaw."

Only a pressure of her hand.

"That's where I'm different, Barbara. If a thing's wrong, I won't stand by it. I think that's phony loyalty. What do you think?"

He turns to her, looking down at her hand, a light smudge against his black trousers.

"Yes, Dixon," she says. "Yes, baby."

"God, I'm tired, Barbara!" He sighs suddenly.

She draws his head down to her lap; letting him settle against her body. His eyes close. Softly her fingers press his temples and move along the nerve back of his ears, down into his neck.

"That feels good . . . Everything you do; everything about you feels good to me. Sometimes, particularly after I've had you, sometimes I'd look at Colonel and wonder to myself, how does he live without this tenderness? How does he keep going? I couldn't, I swear. I thought today I'd never last the day if the night didn't promise us what we have now . . . God, Barbara, I can't do without you. I have to find a way we can——"

"Hush, baby. Just relax, Dixon." She leans over and kisses him; as she moves her breast touches his throat; he moves closer to its warm softness.

"We're going to have each other a long, long, time, aren't we?" he says softly. "Hmm?"

"Yes, we are Dixon. We are."

"I love you so much. I love *you.*"

"Oh, baby. Dixon."

She holds his head to her breast, cradling him gently there like that, and they do not try to talk. He tamps out the smoked-down cigarette he clutches in his fingers, lets his lips rub against the silk of her blouse at her breast, and they stay quiet.

After a while he says, "What's that?" leaning up on his elbows slightly.

"I don't know, baby. I was trying to make it out."

"Looks like a car pulling up down there. No lights."

"It is."

"More lovers, maybe."

"Uh-huh," she laughs lightly; her fingers following the

173

path along his temples. "It's nice to be here with you, Dixon. I want to tell you that. It's so nice, baby."

"They getting out of the car?" he asks, hearing the slight sound of a car door slamming down at the bottom of the hill. He sits up abruptly. "They are! Who are they?"

"Can't make out. Looks like two men and a kid."

"They coming up here?"

"Can't tell, Dixon."

"My God, they *are*, Barbara. They're heading up." Dixon Pirkle jumps to his feet. "Hey, honey, we got to get. C'mon!"

Quickly they scramble to their feet, grabbing the auto robe, then running back near the Naked Hag, where Dix has parked his car.

"Wish there was a back road out of here," he says. "Jesus!"

He tosses the robe through the open window into the back seat and climbs in the front beside her. He says, "We'll just gun it and pass them fast."

"Wonder who it is. Oh, Gawd, Dix, I hope it's not—"

"Not who?" he says, turning the ignition on; lights, throwing the gear in reverse.

"Not my dad."

"Who'd be with him?"

"I don't know. No, it isn't."

"You sure? Couldn't you tell the car if it was."

"I can't be positive."

"Well, duck down. I'll go as fast as I can by them, honey. Hold on."

After he ha˙ turned the automobile around, Dix steps on the gas pedal, and the car tears down the winding dirt road, its headlights glaring ahead, momentarily illuminating the three figures trudging up the hill they're rushing down.

"Wonder what the hell all that is?" Dix murmurs. "Okay, baby."

She draws herself back up; glances over her shoulder.

"Did you see who it was, Dixon?"

"Yeah. It was Thad Hooper and Doc Sell with some colored boy."

"Huh? You kidding?"

"No. Hooper and Sell, and some Negro."

"What Negro?"

"I couldn't make out. He had his head down. They had him by the arms."

"Dixon, that don't sound good at all."

"Oh, hell, they didn't see us. They might have made me out, but they didn't see you. You were out of sight."

"No, I don't mean that. I mean—what would they be doing with a colored boy? You know Doc Sell."

"Yeah, yeah—but Hooper's not like him."

"It don't sound good at all, Dixon. Not at all."

"Naw, I don't think they're up to much."

"Much?"

"Or anything."

"Aw, baby, look—you know something's in the air."

Dixon stares at the road ahead of him, as he swings off the dirt and onto the pavement.

"I'm worried, Dixon."

"Barbara, for Christ's sake, what can *we* do!"

"We could go to the sheriff! Something!"

"You and me go?"

"You could go, Dixon."

"We don't know what it's all about. Hell, honey, we got our own troubles. What do we know about it?"

"It's trouble, Dixon. Don't need to know much to know that."

"You're building it up, honey. I'm not even sure they had him by the arms." He glances over at her. "We just had a narrow escape, is all, honey. It's made us tense."

"I hope so, baby—but still, we ought to—"

"Aw, look, darling." Dixon smiles at her, taking his eyes from the road momentarily, putting a hand in her lap. "We haven't had any trouble like that in years around here. We're just tense."

"Maybe you're right, Dixon."

"Sure. Sure, I am."

"Pray God," Barbara James says, placing her hand over his.

24

INSIDE the Naked Hag they tie him to the chair, the big man and the runty one.

"Know where you are, nigger?" the runty one asks him.

"Please, mister, let me go. Please!"

"You're in a school, nigger. You're gonna git educated, nigger. Ain't that what you city niggers like?"

"I'll do anything, mister. Please!"

The big man says, "You done enough already, you black ape! What'd you do to her?" He kicks his shins Jesus-hard! "I want to know all you did to her."

"Nothing, sir. Please. I didn't do anything. I didn't!"

"You *tell* me!" the big man says. "You put your black hands on her, didn't you?"

"Naw, aw, naw. I told you! Naw."

"Tell me again!"

"Mister, sir, I just—just clucked my tongue. I didn't even say anything, I—" He gets a knee in his belly. "Ow!"

"You felt her, you nigger! Say it! Say it!" The big man grabs his collar. "Say what I say to say! Say it!"

"I—I—f-felt her."

Hands slap his jaw like a rock crushing it. "You black bastard! You feel up a white woman, you black ugly-skinned ape!"

"Naw, aw—please! I didn't!"

"You heard him say he did," the big man says to the runty one.

"You're goddam right," says the runty one. "We'll learn you a lesson, nigger. You're in school, nigger! We'll learn your nigger brain to think like a nigger."

"You heard him say he did!"

176

"You're goddam right."

"Felt her body!"

"Filthy nigger with your goddam dirty black brain," yells the runty one.

"You heard him say he did!"

"Aw, naw, mis—" He gets a kick in the stomach.

"I heard him plain as anything," says the runty one.

"Trash. Black trash!" the big man mutters.

"Ought to burn him like trash," the runty one says.

"Please, please, please, please—"

"Shut up!" The runty man puts his fist in his groin.

"Yeah, burn him for it! Nervy black ape! Doing his dirty things to a pure, pure white woman."

"Burn him and all the schools that give him and his black monkey brothers thoughts. Monkeys ought to stay in trees and outa schools."

The big man says, "What'd you do to her? Felt her, didn't you?" He pulls him up by the collar, still tied to the chair; pulling him up and the chair under him. "Put your black ape hands on her till she said uncle, huh? Vile, vile!" He socks him back down. "Vile!"

"Burn him and burn this nigger school," the runty one says.

"That's right," says the big one. "Get the matches out."

"Burn everything nigger in sight. Smelly nigger books smell from niggers reading them!"

The big one grabs him, his big hands on his neck, blood oozing from his nose onto the big man's hands. The big one says, "You felt her up, didn't you, nigger? Nigger felt up a white woman. Vile black ape put his hands on a pure white body. Didn't you? You felt her?"

"I got matches. I got them," says the runty one.

"Say it. You felt her," the big man says. "Say it."

"Pl-pl—please, God—n-naw—" He gets a punch in the groin.

"Say it! You felt her."

"N-naw, n—" He gets a second punch there.

"Say it! Say it!"

"I—f-felt—" He slumps limply, held by the rope around his boy's body.

"You heard him say he did," the big man says.

177

"You're goddam right," says the runty one, scratching a match.

* * * *

THE NEW YORK BULLETIN
CLUCK-TONGUE CASE GOES TO JURY

Paradise, Georgia: Emotions are running high in this little county seat town in the heart of the red hill region of Georgia, as an all-white jury sits down to deliberate the fate of Thad Hooper, 38, whose wife was involved in the cluck-tongue case, and Doctor Warren Sell, county coroner—both on trial for the lynching of Millard Post, 15.

The New York schoolboy, who was spending a three-day vacation at the home of an uncle, was "taken for a ride" by the two white men, after he clucked his tongue at Hooper's wife. Hooper and Sell claim they drove him only as far as Hooper's Place, a gas and pop stand on Route 109, just to scare him, then let him out of the car to go on back to his uncle's home by himself.

That same evening the Negro school was burned to the ground, and a charred body, discovered amid the debris, was identified as that of young Post.

Witness for the defense, Tink Twiddy, 17, testified that shortly after midnight that evening, as he was hunting bait for fishing, he saw a boy answering Millard Post's description, walking up the hill toward the school, unaccompanied. The defense maintained that Millard Post, too ashamed to return to his uncle's after his impudence to Vivian Hooper, 28, went up to the school to stay there overnight and ran into foul play. It was suggested further that many of the local colored boys were displeased with the Naked Hag because it was old and run down, and had perhaps planned to burn it to the ground on the same night young Post had supposedly gone up there to spend the night.

The most dramatic witness for the prosecution was a light-skinned Negro teacher, Barbara James, 28, daughter of Doctor Edward James, who claimed she had seen two men and a boy approach the Negro school shortly after midnight. Miss James testified that she was on top of the hill, in the company of Dixon Pirkle, 19, son of Paradise's newspaper editor, when

178

both of them saw a car without headlights stop at the bottom of the hill. She testified they saw two men and a boy emerge from the car, and as they hurriedly drove down the hill past them, Dixon Pirkle identified the men as Hooper and Sell.

Young Pirkle subsequently declared under oath that he was not with Miss James, nor anywhere near the Negro school that evening. While he was on the stand, an uproar broke out in the courtroom when Hollis Jordan, a citizen of Paradise, began shouting "Liar!" Jordan was rushed out of the courtroom and order was restored while Pirkle continued. Pirkle stated that he was at home mourning the death of his mother, Mrs. Ada Pirkle, who had died only that day.

Sobbing as she spoke to reporters, Miss James refused to comment on her relationship with Pirkle, but insisted that: "I have told the truth. It was the only thing I could do and still live with myself."

Miss James said that since giving her testimony before the grand jury, she has been threatened numerous times by anonymous people, as has her father been. A job has been offered her in Cincinnati, but she declined to say whether or not she would accept this teaching position.

While ostensibly the citizens of Paradise are carrying on as calmly as can be expected under the circumstances, there is a considerable undercurrent of violent feeling. Rumors have gone so far as to suggest that Mrs. Hooper was actually molested by the Post boy, and an unidentified woman, wife of a professor, told this reporter there nas "no doubt in anyone's mind that it was rape."

Mr. Hollis Jordan has been accused by many as "being linked to the N.A.A.C.P. and Russia," and the evening of the day of his outburst in the courtroom, his house was stones. Jordan has left Paradise for an undisclosed place.

The following is a reprint, in part, from an editorial appearing in the Paradise Herald, *yesterday's edition, written by Dixon Pirkle's father, the editor:*

> . . . *The fact remains that Thad Hooper and Doc Sell have been two of our leading citizens, family men who have broken bread at our family tables, men who have knelt with us to pray, fought for us and with us in war and in peace for the ideals we hold to be godly; men whose children play and laugh and learn and grow along-*

179

*side our own children, men whose hands we have gripped
countless times in the clasp of brotherhood, and men
wtih whom we have become men under one sky and upon
a common ground. They are our own. They have stood
before us, and before God, and given us their testimony,
and we will, under God, humbly judge them with all the
wisdom human beings possess . . ."*

25

Now THAT it is over, dark comes gently again in Paradise.
Dark comes without strangers. The streets are quiet and sleepy
at nine o'clock near Thanksgiving time. The courthouse under the harvest moon is stately and still; its green laws cleared
of the debris of camera wires and the big gleaming machinery
of television mobile units. Faces along Main are familiar ones;
and talk at the drugstore centers once more about the new
moonshine drive; crops, and the livestock show over in
Manteo.

The early night freight chuffs south toward Galverton,
clanking its short-lived signal of commerce as it passes; and
in the East the line of pinelands casts its shadows on the spent
fields, picked clean of cotton. North on the hill red lanterns
warn that the hole is dug for the basement of the new Negro
school, now under construction. West in The Toe, blue supper
smoke curls up from the shacks of the colored.

At the Ficklin's, Marianne glances across the living room as
her husband drops the evening paper on the pile beside his
chair and yawns, stretching. "Want to watch T.V. honey?"
he says.

"Ummm. Guess so." She balances a small white pad on
her lap, licking the tip of a pencil. "Fick, just don't let the
papers stack up like that. We've got enough to start a dump
already."

180

"I told you, honey. Get a boy in." He walks across to snap on the TV. "How about getting Cindy Bennett's brother?"

"I just can't imagine it," she says.

"Why not? Cindy's been with the Pirkles for years. Colonel says she's right reliable, and the boy is too."

"Naw, I mean——Major Post going up North like that with his Northern uncle."

"Oh, that again . . . Well, I suppose he'll sort of be like a son to the fellow, now that he lost his own . . . Picture's kind of blurry tonight," he says, fooling with the set's knobs, frowning. "Major deserves the chance he'll get up North. He's a smart boy."

"Too smart. If he'd hung around long, I'd probably get the same thing Vivian Hooper got."

"Look, Marianne," her husband says emphatically, "I don't know what you and some of the others *think* Vivian Hooper got; it doesn't excuse murder!"

"*Rape* doesn't?"

"Oh, cut it out! It makes me sick!"

"A lot you know! I can tell you, Fick, I had to watch myself every minute even with Major. The way he'd look at me sometimes—"

"It's the first I've heard of it . . . If you're still trying to get me to change my mind about Saturday, you may as well forget it. They're not coming!"

She slaps the pad down on the table beside her. "We can't just ostracize them! We can't! Besides, we owe them for the barbecue."

"Just forget it!"

"You're the only one around here feels Thad and Doc Sell didn't do right."

"No, I'm not the only one. Not by a damn sight!"

"Oh, if you mean Hollis Jordan . . ."

"I don't mean Hollis. I mean men and women in this county who abhor the killing of that child! Men and women who live here, and are going to continue to live here——not just blow up at what happened and skip town. Men and women who are going to wear this murder like an albatross around their necks."

"Fick, don't be so dramatic. Honestly."

"And Thad himself isn't going to find it easy. We respected Thad, thought a lot of him, had him to our homes. Well, we

181

never respected Doc Sell one whit, and he never got asked around either. Now Thad's in the same category."

"As far as we're concerned—not as far as others are. Not as far as I am, Fick, we got to forgive and forget. I saw him today on Main. Looked pale as a ghost."

"Oh, he knows how we feel. Town stood by him, but *he* knows what we think of him."

"You keep saying we. Who's *we?*"

"Time'll tell that . . . One thing's sure, he's not coming to this house. No more."

"I'm not going to be able to face Vivie."

"Yes, well, I admit. It's too bad for Vivie and the kids. Best thing they could do would be to move on out of Paradise." Ficklin walks away from the set. "Thad ought to move away . . . There, picture's fine now."

His wife reaches for the lamp chain and pulls it, darkening the room. "Law," Marianne Ficklin murmurs, "Poor Vivie . . .

At the Bailey's, Kate looks up from the checker board set out on the card table in the sun parlor, and says, "It's your move."

"Hmmm? Oh, sure."

"You're not concentrating, dear. I jumped you three times in a row."

"I just can't seem to get my mind fixed on the game, Kate."

"Storey, you're not still thinking about Thad?"

Storey Bailey sighs, rubbing his forehead. "I don't know. I saw him today, stopped out for gas. Some folks around here aren't even buying their gas from him now. It's awful. I don't know. And Thad was kinda different acting with me. Sorta snappy."

"Oh, he'd have *liked* to have had *you* mixed up in it all."

"I keep thinking if I'd gone along, Kate, it never would have happened. But there was just Thad and Doc Sell—Thad, all worked up in a rage, and Doc Sell heaping coals on the fire. If I'da been along—"

"Thank God you weren't!"

"Then I keep thinking about what you said about Vivs walking into band rehearsal today . . . I don't know."

"Storey, *everyone* was very nice to her."

"Well, why shouldn't they be! She didn't have anything to do with it!" he snaps.

She looks across the table at him with a fixed stare.

"Aw, heck." He pushes the checker board back, getting up, beginning to pace. "I feel sorry for her. I can't help it. I don't know, it's crazy. I just feel—well, like *I'd* done something."

Kate Bailey begins to place the checkers back in the box.

He says, "I wish I'd never told you anything about that night."

"You owed me some explanation, Storey," she answered quietly.

"Well, maybe I exaggerated . . . I *did* exaggerate." He digs his hands down into his trousers. "And now people are saying she went and enticed that nigger. Do you know people are actually saying that? I wonder how come. Wonder who's been telling things."

Kate puts the top of the box on and folds the checker board over. "If you're trying to say that *I* am, Storey, you're mistaken."

"Then who is?"

"I heard it from Marianne Ficklin."

"And you believe it, I suppose?"

"I don't have any opinion; just that I don't condone what Thad did with Doc Sell . . . I'll never feel the same about Thad."

"I think the world and all of Thad," Storey says. "We were best friends. I think if I'd been with them—hell! Hell!"

"Please, Storey, there's no need to shout!"

"Well, hell—heck, I just can't help thinking of Vivs walking into band rehearsal and starting to play the saxophone."

"She didn't just walk in and play the saxophone. She'll have to learn it first. A musical instrument isn't an easy accomplishment. Not as easy as other things."

"Kate, I wish you'd stop talking like that."

She gets up and crosses the room, saying, "Well, I can't see that a musical instrument will do anything but improve Vivian."

"Maybe she doesn't need to be improved."

"What do you mean by that?" She stops, staring at him.

Storey shrugs. "Oh. I just mean I can't imagine Vivs playing in a band."

"Well, *thank* you." Kate Bailey stands and walks over to the piano.

"And I just wish you'd stop making dirty insinuations about Vivs," Storey says. "After all, they're our best friends. I think the world and all of Thad, and they're our best friends!"

Kate Bailey begins to play, lightly, at first, softly; then gradually more loudly, until all the other noise is drowned out, save for the resolute strains of "Old Hundredth."

It is quiet in the rectory. Joh Greene hardly looks up as his wife opens the door quietly, slipping into the room with a tray of hot chocolate and crackers.

Then he says, "Oh, thank you, Guessie."

"Working hard, darling?"

"I don't know why next Sunday's sermon is giving me so much trouble. But it seems important to me."

"Of course it is."

"I've got my basic selling points, but I can't seem to write the copy."

"Want me to try and help?"

"Well, if you'd sit down and discuss this, it might do me a lot of good. Somehow I've got to get the idea of almighty Christ's great gift of forgiveness across. Do you understand that?"

"Because of Thad and Doc Sell?"

"Not just them. Dix, too."

"Yes, Dix . . . I'd almost forgotten."

"Most everybody did. Nobody put any credence in the James girl's testimony, but you and me know what Dix musta gone through up there. Somehow we got to help Dix forgive himself."

"He's young, Joh. He'll have to grow out of it. Then he'll see he did right. For Colonel's sake, he did."

"That's just it. It's between loyalty to his own blood and loyalty to the law, and Dix chose his own. But it wasn't easy for him."

"It hasn't been easy for anyone—none of it has."

"That's why I got to give people peace of mind again. I just don't seem to know how to do it. I got my selling point —the almighty Christ's great gift of forgiveness," he says, sinking back into the leather swivel chair, "but I can't seem to write my copy so that it has any punch. I got my product, Guessie, but I can't seem to hit on a way to present it."

"Maybe you ought to wait, Joh. Give your apple one this Sunday. You haven't given that one in a long time."

Joh Greene shakes his head wearily. "Nope, Guessie, this hasn't got anything to do with apples. This is a real hard one ot figure out."

Through the darkness she makes her way down to The Toe, passing the tall empty field off Brockton Road, when the figure lurches out and grabs her wrist.

"Barbara," he moans, pulling her into the field with him, back near the clump of bushes. "Oh, my God, Barbara."

Her voice breaks as she says softly, "Hello, Dixon." She looks down at his hand on her arm. "Do you have to do that?" she asks.

"I have to talk to you, Barbara."

"You're drunk, Dixon. Very drunk."

"I've been drunk a long time. Ever since—they say you're going away. You're not going away and leave me, are you?"

"You don't have to hold on to me, Dixon," she says quietly.

He sways, looking at her, then lets his grip on her loosen.

"You're going away. You're going to wherever Hollis Jordan went. That's what they say."

"That's what they *would* say."

"Is it the truth?"

"No, of course it isn't. I don't even know him."

"He took up for you. He acted like he—Why'd he take up for you?"

She looks away from him, off at the fields. "I don't know. Maybe he just cared about the truth."

"I couldn't help it, Barbara. I *couldn't!* My dad was—he was like a ghost around the house. It coming on top of my mother's death. You shoulda seen my dad's face, Barbara."

"I saw *my* dad's when he came back from looking at that boy's burned body."

"You think I'm a coward? You don't know. It took courage. I love you, Barbara. God, when I sat across from you— It took—" he sways, steadies himself, placing his hand on her shoulder—"courage."

"Good-by, Dixon. We don't have anything to talk about." She shakes his head off her shoulder, and he grabs her wrist again.

"We don't have anything to talk about? I love you. I love you, Barbara." His voice is a half-sob. "I couldn't be any

185

other way in that courtroom. I couldn't! Barbara, listen—"
He pulls her toward him, lurching. "You're so white. I always
thought of you as white. I loved you. I still do."

"I used to love you too, Dixon. I always thought of you
as colored," she says.

He laughs, his shoulders shaking, his black hair tossing over
his forehead. "Me a nigger! You thought that, thought of me
as colored, God!" he exclaims, laughing, and then drawing
his breath in and giving a dry sob, he says, "Barbara! Barbara! Help me! Put your hands on my head. I'm hot, honey.
Your hands are cool. Let's forget all of it. I need you, Barbara. Barbara."

"You're very drunk, Dixon," she says. "I wish you'd let me
go."

"I take after my mother. Don't you know? I'm going to
be a lush like her. Drink and drink and drink."

"Let me go, Dixon."

"Where? Where are you going?"

"Just down to see the Posts to say good-by."

"When are you going to leave Paradise?"

"Tomorrow."

"Going up North, huh?"

"Yes."

"No!" he pulls her to him again, trying to kiss her, while
she struggles out of his reach.

He says, "You love me."

"No, I don't, Dixon. I don't love you."

"I love you!" he says angrily. "If I love you, you love me.
You're a—nigger. That's right. If I love you, you love me."

"You're hurting me, Dixon."

"I want you to love me."

"I can't. I can't love you again, Dixon."

"You're not going away if you don't love me. You're like a
disease." He begins to talk in a husky, panting way. "You
got into me like a disease. Now you want to walk out on me.
Well, you're not going to!"

"Dixon, you're hurting me."

"Love me! Kiss me, Barbara."

"No."

"You're not up North yet."

"Please, Dixon, you're hurting me."

"Then love me. Then kiss me."

186

"No! No, Dixon!"

He stares at her, swaying as he holds her, his eyes narrowing. "Barbara, you're not yourself."

"I am myself."

"You never refused me. Never! You been with that N.A.A.C.P. crowd! That Hollis Jordan."

"Stop it, Dixon. Leave me alone!"

"Listen to me, you nigger," he snaps. "Don't talk that way to me. Lower your voice. You lower your goddam voice. You nigger! Don't tell me you won't love me, because you will love me, because I love you. Now c'mon!" He pulls her along the path.

"Dixon, stop it!"

His hand whips out suddenly, striking her. He says, "There!" while she holds the stinging part of her cheek with her fingers. Tears fill her eyes. "Don't do this to yourself, Dixon. Don't," she says softly.

"Don't tell me what to do. Kiss me, Barbara."

"No."

He slaps her again. "You kiss me, nigger, you kiss me!"

"No."

He says, "You're in the South! I'm white and you're a nigger, and I need you. I love you. I'm going to have you. I'm going to have you, and you're going to take it, because you're a nigger," he says. He shoves her down; she kneels in the dust.

A tear rolls down her cheek, but she says nothing; she stays still on her knees.

"Get on your back!" he says. "Spread out flat."

Then stumbling, he falls on top of her. . . .

When it is done, Barbara James gets up, leaving him lying face flat in the clump of woods, his agonized sobbing sounding bleak in the night air as she walks away from him.

He cries, "Barbara!" into the dirt.

"Kids tucked in?" Thad Hooper asks Vivian as she joins him on the veranda. She wears the black dress with the white Peter Pan collar; her face is white and drawn; devoid of make-up. She sits down beside him in the glider.

"Yes, they're all tucked in."

"Why do you sound so tired?"

"I don't know. It's chilly—I ought to go in and get my sweater," she answers, not moving.

"I wish Hus would shut up! Can't she do dishes without singing like some revivalist?"

"Singing 'Never Said A Mumbin' Word again." Vivian Hooper sighs.

"It gets on my nerves! Damn nigger!"

Vivian Hooper reaches over to touch him, then draws her hand back and places it in the other. "Oh, Thad, Thad," she says. "When will everything be back to normal again?"

"It's not easy! I been through a lot, that's sure!"

"Yes a lot. A lot."

"You sound like you're sorry or something."

"There's not much to be glad about, Thad."

"Most any other woman would be goddam glad her man thinks enough of her to defend her honor!"

"Oh, I'm—grateful, Thad. It's just—just too bad."

"And now I got that damn nigger Tink Twiddy stealing me blind to top it! Never shoulda promised him work here. Damn nigger upstart! Hate having him around here all the time!"

"He's a help, with Major gone, though."

"Major never helped. Got so Major spent all his time down to the Ficklins. Got like a house pet down there. The way Bill Ficklin's carrying on, think he was soft on him or something."

"Major used to help."

"Sometimes I actually think you miss that goddam nigger."

"Thad, no . . . let's not start. No tonight. I want to go on in and get my sweater . . . Can I bring you something? A drink?" she asks, starting to move.

"Wait a second."

"Hmmm?"

"I said, wait a second. Don't walk away from the subject any more. I'm getting tired of the way you walk out whenever it comes up."

"Thad, it's chilly."

"There's always an excuse. You just want to avoid the subject."

"I don't like to think about it, if that's what you mean."

"Why not?"

188

"Well, it isn't very—pleasant. Dwelling on it." She knots her hands together, looking down at them as his eyes study her.

"After what I did for you?" he says. "I did it for *you*, you know! I did it for you, and the things happening as a result are because I did it for you! My best friend backs down on me, but that doesn't stop me, because you're my wife, and I did it for *you*, Vivie!"

"I didn't ask you to, Thad. I never even knew about it until it was—over."

"You came screaming to me, didn't you? You came screaming to me that that that nigger molested you, didn't you? Screaming to me to protect you, didn't you?"

"I didn't say he molested me. No, Thad, I didn't say that."

"You don't know what you said! You were screaming. You were scared outa your head. You came screaming to me for protection, didn't you?"

She answers quietly, "Yes, I was frightened. I was very frightened. Shocked, really. I'd been sitting there in the car thinking and when he looked in the window and did that— a stranger to me—it shocked me."

"Did what?" Thad Hooper asks. "That's what I want to know. And I want to know the truth!"

"Clucked his tongue, Thad. We've been all over it . . . Do we have to—"

"Look," Thad Hooper interrupts her. "We haven't been all over it! Not by a long shot! After what I did for you! All them Northern communist newspapers writing insinuations about me in their yellow rags like some slimy snake crawling across my good name. Them—and people right here in Paradise; my own people, never mind the Northerners, *my own people,* talking behind my back, avoiding me on the street, acting sheepish around me. My own people!"

"People have tried to be nice, Thad. It's very hard. But people stood by us, Thad. They stood by us—all through the trial."

"Us! Don't say us! It's been me who's had to fight this, single-handed. It's like Doc Sell didn't have a dongedy-dang part in the thing. Just *me*. Not you. Not anybody else. Me!"

"People don't expect much from Doc Sell. He was always a troublemaker for the Nigraw . . . Thad, oh, honey—let's forget—"

"We're not going to forget! I have to pay for what I done,

189

don't I? Have to *pay* for it! For keeping a nigger from molesting my wife. Isn't that the truth?"

"All right . . . Yes, Thad."

"And what's the rest of the truth, Vivie? Hah? I want the rest of it, do you hear? The whole truth, if I have to pay! Come on, Vivie, talk!"

"What, Thad?" She looks up from her hands into his eyes. "What is it you want to hear?"

"What I want to hear," Thad Hooper says slowly, emphatically, bitterly, "is who spoke to who first?"

"What?" Vivian Hooper stares incredulously at her husband.

"That's what I want to know," he says, "who spoke to who first? Did the nigger speak to you first, or did you speak to the nigger first? That's what I want to know," Thad Hooper says, "and I won't rest until I hear you say it!"

Dark closes in on Paradise and settles down to stay.

Printed in the United States
By Bookmasters